WHIRLIGIG

WHIRLIGIG

A Novel

Russell Jack Smith

Bartleby Press
Silver Spring, Maryland

Printed in the United States of America

Published and Distributed by:

Bartleby Press
11141 Georgia Avenue
Silver Spring, Maryland 20902

Library of Congress Cataloging-in-Publication Data

Smith, Russell Jack
    Whirligig : a novel / Russell Jack Smith.
       p.   cm.
    ISBN 0-910155-29-1 : $9.95
    I. Title
PS3569.M537974W48   1995
813'.54—dc20   94-40034
                                               CIP

For Rosemary

And thus the whirligig of time brings in his revenges.
—William Shakespeare

The changes of this trumpery whirligig world.
—Sir Walter Scott

Life is a whirligig, and who knows what next?
—Rose Macaulay

Prelude: Spring 1994

Unexpectedly, the green car ahead braked hard, tires screeching. Microseconds later, the rear end bucked up from an impact and glass splattered on the pavement. I stopped easily, being a conservative twenty feet behind, and watched, amazed, as a man leaped out of the green car, ran to the car ahead, and fired three or four pistol shots through the side window. He then ran back, a chunky, red-faced man in his twenties, slammed his car in reverse, backing almost into mine, and then pulled out and around, engine and tires screaming. I sat stunned for a moment and then walked up to the car ahead. Two people, a middle-aged man and a young woman, arrived just as I did. "My God," said the woman as we gazed at the slumping figure with its face half shot away. "My God!"

In time, the police arrived and I distinguished myself with the downy-cheeked cop by being able only to identify the car as "rat poison green" and either an Izubishi or Nissatoya. In my time, cars were readily identifiable as GMs, Chryslers, or Fords and were easily told apart. But now—The fuzz-cheeked officer responded to this information, such as it was, by asking, "Were you observing the alleged incident and the subject from inside your own vehicle, sir?" This I could answer with a simple "yes."

"Thank heaven you called from the police station," said my wife as I walked in the front door three hours later, her eyes speaking relief. "I would have been out of my mind with worry."

1

"It was incredible," I said. "Barbarous and incredible."

"There were three shootings like that in South Boston last week," she said. "It's becoming trite."

"Commonplace perhaps, my dear. Never trite."

"I'll stick with 'trite,' professor. How was your monthly meeting with the nature sanctuary committee?"

"Fine. Ben Coffin asked about you."

"Good. Nice man. By the way, I had a frantic call from my sister this morning. She's in quite a dither. Kimberly thinks she may be pregnant."

"Our little grandniece, Kim, pregnant?"

"Think so."

"By the man she's been living with this past year?"

"Presumably. The unemployed graphic artist."

"Is he going to marry her?"

"Probably not. Kimberly's not sure she likes him well enough to marry him."

I pondered over this for a moment. "Likes him well enough to share his toothpaste for a year, and go to bed and spread her legs for him but not well enough to marry him." I shook my head. "God, the screwed up moral values of kids these days!"

She smiled at me reprovingly. "Am I hearing a holier-than-thou suggestion that our generation indulged in sex only within the marriage sanction? Don't I seem to remember—"

"That was different, my love. Quite different. Besides, you were a married woman and took advantage of my innocence."

"Ha!" She shook her head slowly, her eyes smiling knowingly.

I leaned over and gave her a husbandly kiss. "Any other tragic news to top off this shocking day?"

"Yes. Kevin has been suspended from Harvard for drug possession, probably LSD."

"Kevin, the golden boy; the favorite grandson! Sweet Jesus! What next?"

"Don't I remember you had a drug case or two while you were teaching?"

I nodded, grudgingly. "Well, yes. But those were problem kids.

Kids from broken homes. Not wholesome kids like Kimberly and Kevin."

"We live in a different world, my dear. Stories like this come every day. I suppose you might say they were commonplace."

"This time I prefer trite. No, banal." I gazed at my wife appreciatively for a moment. "Just to round this off, any bad news about any of our brood?"

She shook her head. "Not that I've heard. All seems to be serene."

"It can't last," I said. "Can't last. Not in these sick and ugly times."

"Oh, now Stephen. Don't be an Eeyore. The sun still comes up every morning and flowers still bloom in the spring. The world is not coming to an end just yet."

"Might be a good thing if it did," I said morosely. "You know, when I think back to the simplicity and sunny innocence of our early days, the 40s and 50s, I am simply appalled—heartsick and appalled—by the tawdry, degraded popular culture of our time, the hullabaloo over ethnic slights and slurs, the clamor for homosexual and minority rights, and the mindless violence on American streets." I paused for breath. "I know that men of my advanced years have always felt that things had gone to hell since their youth. Old men have always felt that way. But the difference now, my dear wife, the difference now is that, by God, it is true!"

"Stephen, my love," she said. "Come sit down and have a scotch on the rocks. You'll feel better."

"Numbed, probably," I said. "But not better."

One

Somewhere between the seventh and ninth pulls on the starter cord I knew the British Seagull had not the slightest intention of starting. It sat sullenly on the transom of the skiff, its flywheel still and mute as a stone. With the cord in my hand, I pondered what to do next. The skiff was tied to the Brixton town dock. In the little harbor, really just a wide place in the Yare River, an ancient catboat and three fishing boats tugged gently at their moorings. The rippling water of the Yare tickled and chuckled along the flanks of the skiff. Three herring gulls (*Larus argentatus*), perched on pilings in the slanting sunlight of a New England September morning in 1951 looked down at me, observing my failure with their customary laconic indifference. At least, they were not laughing gulls (*Larus atricilla*).

Striding down the dock toward me was Clinton Avery, the man from whom I had rented the skiff. "Is that ornery little cuss giving you trouble?" he asked.

"Doesn't want to start. But I'm not surprised. Outboards just plain don't like me, for some reason."

"Let me give you a hand." He jumped into the skiff a wiry, sharp-faced man of forty-odd. "You know these British Seagulls are like redheaded women. You either love 'em or ya hate 'em."

"Is your wife redheaded?" I asked innocently.

He chuckled. "Yeah. Sort of." He moved past me to examine the stubborn machine. "Four things you gotta do to make her start. You don't do all four she'll sit there and laugh at you all day long. First, open the fuel line valve. Second, open the choke. Third, flood the carburetor by jiggling this little plunger. Fourth, open the throttle half way." He straightened and wound the starter cord around the flywheel. "Now, pull like hell!" He pulled sharply and the little engine fired up, the flywheel spinning and the propeller thrashing the water below. "There you go, you're all set." Avery looked down under the seat. "I see you got your can of fuel mix. How far you goin'?"

"Just down to Tingree Island."

"Oh, you'll be okay. But don't forget those four things when you start back or I'll be comin' down lookin' for you after dark."

He put his hands on the dock and vaulted up on it. He loosened the lines fore and aft, tossed them in the boat, and waved his hand. "Off you go!" As I opened the throttle and pulled away from the dock, he yelled, "Watch the tide in those creeks down in the marsh. They drop real fast and you'll find yourself sitting on the mud."

"Okay."

I pointed the skiff downriver as the sun climbed the eastern sky and cast sheets of diamonds on the incoming tide. Tides and tidal creeks were new to me. I had grown up in southern Michigan where the clear waters of Clark's Lake, Brown's Lake, and Devil's Lake were tideless. Intellectually, I had known about tides but I was not prepared for the startling transformation a ten foot rise and fall of the sea twice each day creates, the river brimming high along its banks at one time and laying bare a hundred yards of mud flat at another. Tides, I began to appreciate, were an inevitable, irrevocable fact and needed to be respected by anyone using the waterways of seacoast New England.

I had arrived in Brixton three days earlier after cruising

between Boston and Buryport looking for a place that offered easy access to the salt marsh where I could do my research. The village of Brixton, founded in 1652, bordered the Yare River and provided just what I wanted. I had parked my twelve year old 1939 Plymouth coupe in front of the general store and had inquired of a grey-haired, neatly aproned woman inside about a place to stay, perhaps a room to rent.

"Well, now, I think they is one." She looked toward the back of the store and raised her voice, "Henry! Didn't you say the other day that Meg Satterlee's got her spare room up for rent?"

"That's right. Lady teacher she had moved to New Hampshire."

The woman turned to me. "Meg Satterlee's the town librarian." She looked up at a Seth Thomas schoolroom clock ticking solemnly above the counter. "Four o'clock, she's at the library now. Just four doors down there on the left."

As I walked along the sidewalk of the classic New England village, the maple trees overhead were marked here and there with splashes of autumn red. Across the street a white throated sparrow (*Zonotrichria albicollis*) piped his single note song, faltering slightly at the start as though uncertain he was in the right key. I turned in the entrance to the small, white-framed building bearing a gilt-lettered sign, "Brixton Library." Meg Satterlee looked up with a gentle smile as I approached her desk. She looked to be a little older than me, perhaps mid-twenties, and she wore her ash blonde hair pulled tightly back around her head. Her eyes were brightly blue; her face wore a sweet but somewhat resigned expression. "May I help you?"

"Yes. I think so. I was told at the general store you might have a room to rent."

"Well, I do." She hesitated. "But we've usually rented to a lady."

I grinned in my best boyish manner. "Well, as you can see, I'm not a lady. But I'm a graduate student, and I'm here in Massachusetts to do research for my thesis."

"I see." Her blue eyes measured me speculatively. "Well, how long would you want the room?"

"I'm not sure. Several months. Maybe till spring."

She nodded. Then she stood up, her doubts apparently resolved. "Let me show you the room. It's just two doors down the street. I'll close up here for a few minutes."

As we walked down the sidewalk under the great spreading maple trees Meg Satterlee asked, "You spoke of research. What kind of research will you be doing?"

"I'm a biologist, an ornithologist"—I quashed an inner rebuke that I was still a mere student of ornithology—"and I am studying the behavior of certain ducks in the salt marshes."

"Interesting."

The room Meg showed me was a snug, second floor bedroom under a slanting ceiling on the front side of a lovely old Cape Cod house, white-shingled and green-shuttered. There was a maple-armed easy chair, a graceful kneehole desk, and a single bed covered with a hobnail white spread. The front window looked out through the branches of an ancient maple tree toward the salt marshes glimmering in the distance.

"Perfect," I said, and the room was mine.

On the way out Meg Satterlee introduced me to a white-haired woman sitting in the corner of the living room. In her lap was a ball of grey yarn, and she seemed to be knitting a wool sock. "Mother," Meg said, "this is Mr. Aspen. Stephen Aspen. He studies birds and he's our new roomer."

"How nice," the old lady said and beamed a vague smile in my general direction.

Now, three days after my arrival in Brixton, with the Seagull chugging in its plucky way down the Yare River, I was beginning my first day of field work for a thesis on interaction among various species of ducks. Some ducks, like mallards (*Anas platyrhynchos*) and pintails (*Anas acuta*) raft freely together with one another while feeding or at rest. Other ducks, like blue winged teal (*Anas discors*) and canvasbacks (*Aythya vakisineria*) tend to keep to themselves in tight groups. I hoped by daily observation to get a better understanding of this behavior, at least enough of an understanding to make a passable thesis for my master's degree at Cornell.

A broken-winged great horned owl (*Bubo virginianus*) that I found by the side of the road ignited my interest in birds when I was a ten-year old boy in Grass Lake, Michigan. I threw an old towel over the agitated bird, managed to get it into a box, and took it to the town veterinarian, Tom Bailey, a curly-haired, thick-armed man, and watched with sympathy and fascination as he sedated the big raptor and set its wing. Over the next two weeks I visited my patient daily, and during my talks with Tom I decided to be an ornithologist. Later, it was with Tom's help and guidance that I won a scholarship at Cornell, and there my faculty advisor counselled me to make biology my major with a minor in ornithology. Still, birds, especially big birds like ducks and cranes and hawks, were my main interest.

Now, chugging down the river, I savored the rich smells suffusing the salt marsh. They were unlike any I had ever known—a conglomeration of fermenting mud, decaying marine vegetation, and stranded seaweed. Pungent and penetrating, and to me exciting, they promised exploration and discovery. More important, they spoke of the outdoors. After four years of university study I was delighted to be outside the classroom and the library.

When I found a small creek draining from the marsh I pulled over to the left shore and tied the skiff to a scrubby bush. According to the tide table I had bought at the general store high tide was still an hour away so I had no fear of stranding the skiff. Binoculars strapped around my neck and field notebook in my pocket, I jumped out of the boat and walked along the edge of the creek. The coarse grass under my feet was a mixture of beige and tawny, reminding me of the pelt of an African lion. I hoped to come onto a flock of bottom-feeding ducks somewhere in the creek but all I saw in the first hour were a pair of high flying black duck (*Anas rubripes*) and a single common merganser (*Mergus merganser*) flying low and fast over the surface of the creek. When I came to a wide, pond-like place I sat down and scanned the horizon for flying ducks.

Several minutes later, I was startled by the brusque voice of a man standing some fifty feet behind me. "I don't know who the hell you are but you are on private land. Trespassing."

I jumped to my feet. I stammered out an apology and offered the explanation that I was a Cornell graduate student doing research on duck behavior.

The man stood silent for a moment. He was broad and square with a finely carved nose, small mouth, strong jaw. He looked to be in his late 40s. "You don't have a weapon? You're not poaching?"

"No, sir. Just observing. So far without luck."

"Wrong place for ducks," he said. "You need to be over there." He pointed to the east. "On the shore of Beach Plum Island Sound." He stood studying me for a moment. "Well, I don't suppose I can object to a fella doing research." He walked toward me, hand outstretched. "Cornell, you say? Well, I'm damned. I'm an architect. I graduated from Cornell School of Architecture about a quarter of a century or so ago. I'm Stuart Price."

We shook hands as I said, "I'm Stephen Aspen."

He nodded as a slight smile spread across his strong-featured New Englander's face. "Come along, Aspen. I'll put you in a good place to observe ducks." I followed him then as he led me about a quarter of mile to a low mound about fifty feet wide overlooking the Sound. Beach Plum Island lay against the horizon about a half mile to the east.

So began my first day in the field and thanks to Stuart Price it was a good one. Several rafts of ducks lay before me—redheads (*Aythya Americana*), goldeneyes (*Bucephala clangula*), oldsquaw (*Clangula hyemalis*), buffleheads (*Bucephelala albeola*), and other species I could only dimly make out—all intermingled and gabbling loudly, alternately diving and rising just above the water with flapping wings, and in general behaving in that goofy, endearingly peculiar manner of ducks. I spent several happy hours, lying on my belly, elbows propped on the ground to hold my binoculars, and taking innumerable notes in my field notebook.

Mindful, then, of Clinton Avery's warning about the swift dropping tide, I walked back to the skiff, untied her from the scrub bush, shoved off, and then went meticulously through the four ritualistic steps necessary to appease the British Seagull's pride before starting. I planted my feet firmly and gave a sharp yank on the cord and behold! the Seagull answered with a series of staccato explosions. I made my way triumphantly back up river to the Brixton town dock. Later, after a hearty supper of cheese omelet, parker house rolls, and apple pie a la mode at Zeke's Diner, I went back to my snug room at Meg Satterlee's and read myself to sleep with Henry Thoreau's *Walden*.

One day about six weeks later I was back at Stuart Price's mound at the edge of the Sound. I was intently watching a fascinating performance by several widgeons (*Anas americanus*) and a group of redheads when a sudden, sharp blast of icy wind driving slashing rain struck my back like a heavy blow. I knew at once I had stayed too long. The radio weather forecasts that morning had warned of an approaching violent front, and even as I lay elbows propped and watching the ducks I had been dimly aware of an oncoming roar. Low at first and then louder as it swept eastward across the salt marsh. But I had been very intent on observing the widgeons as they quickly approached the redheads as they broke the surface after a dive and snatched from the redhead's bill a piece of dangling vegetation. I had seen anecdotal references to this behavior before but I was intent in making precise scientific observations for my thesis.

Now I was in trouble. And I discovered as I stumbled along leaning against the buffeting wind and trying to see through the sheets of gale-driven rain that I was in greater trouble than I first realized. I had lost track of time and tide, and the skiff was not only carrying several inches of water but she was stranded, her flat bottom firmly planted on the mud a good fifty feet from the receding water. The tide was running and every minute lost would add to the distance I had to drag the boat. I plunged into the mud, my boots sinking deeper with each step, and the heavy viscous ooze holding my foot more and more firmly each time. I wiggled my heels, as I had learned to do, in order to free the boot as I lifted my leg. Once my foot came free, leaving the boot upright in the mud, but I was able to keep my balance and insert my foot back in. After two or three minutes of staggering forward while the wind and the rain belted and pelted me, I reached the skiff. Inside a small rubber bucket floated on its side. Decision: should I bail the boat out first—she might be holding forty or more pounds of water—or should I start at once dragging her toward the outgoing tide?

I decided to try to move her first. Holding on to the port gunwale I was able to walk more easily. I got to the bow of the skiff, grabbed hold of the bow stem and pulled. The boat came forward four inches. I pulled again. Same result. Maybe it would be better to bail her out first. I moved back and began scooping water with the bucket and flinging it out into the wind. It took three or four minutes to get the boat as dry as I could with the bucket. Once or twice I had to stop and hang onto the gunwale as a vicious gust struck at me and tried to knock me down.

Back at the bow I planted my feet and yanked. The boat came to me at least six inches. Encouraged, I began a series of hard pulls, again and again and again until my chest was heaving. As I rested, hanging on to the bow stem for support, I looked back at the distance left. About ten feet to the water and then maybe another ten before she would float free. No time to waste. I grabbed again and made a mighty heave but this time my hands, weakened by fatigue, broke loose and I fell sprawling on my back into the black, soft mud. Trying to get up, I slipped and fell on my left side. When I finally got to my feet I realized my boots were half full of marsh mud and my feet made a sucking sound as I stepped.

But now I was fired with anger, and I attacked the boat in a frenzy. In several more minutes I was standing in water and shortly I had her floating. I climbed over the gunwale and without resting turned to starting the Seagull. I carefully enacted the four operations, peering hard through the driving rain to see the fuel line valve and the carburetor flooder, wound the cord and pulled. The engine went through three or four quiet revolutions but did not fire. I carefully checked through the four steps again, naming each one aloud, and then pulled. Same result. Three or four more tries with no success. When I looked up I saw the wind had driven the boat a hundred yards offshore and the running tide was carrying me out the mouth of the Yare into Beach Plum Island Sound.

I dropped the starter cord and got the oars out from under the thwarts. I wanted to get in the lee of the left bank of the river for shelter from the wind. Rowing against the blustery gale and the running tide was almost as hard as dragging the boat over the mud. After several minutes I felt the bow ground in the mud as the water shoaled. To hold the skiff in place, I drove one of the oars down into the mud and tied the bowline to it. Then back to the outboard, the four step routine, and the hard pull. The stoic Seagull refused even to cough. Three times. Four times. I looked forward, exasperated, and saw the skiff had pulled the oar free, and we were once again moving before the wind on the running tide toward the Sound.

Dusk was gathering rapidly over the river while the storm raged on without pause. I knew I needed to get out of the weather, and my choices were either to walk over the marsh, crossing its many little creeks in the growing darkness or to row the waterlogged skiff up the river against wind and tide.

I chose to row. And for the next two hours I rowed, dig-
ging deep with the oars and pulling hard with long full
strokes. My shoulders and back ached as I strained to move
the heavy skiff. Several times I ran aground on the waning
tide and had to stand up and push the boat free with an oar.

At last I could make out the looming shape of the town
dock ahead, and I pulled the skiff hard until we bumped a
piling. I scrambled forward, half falling, and got a line
through one of the mooring rings. I shipped the oars and
crawled onto the dock. I lay flat with my face down on the
rough, sodden planks for several minutes, gathering strength.
Then I slowly rose and walked ashore.

The limbs and leaves of the maple trees overhead
thrashed and writhed in the wind as I walked slowly down
the walk to Meg Satterlee's house. Through the white-cur-
tained windows the lights shone yellow and warm as I came
up the steps and walked inside. I stood hesitantly, a sopping, mud-soaked mess of a man, too beaten to think
straight.

Meg came running toward me. "Oh, Mr. Aspen! You
poor man! You must get into a hot tub straight away and
then go to bed. You look half dead."

"I am," I said.

"Well, go! Go! Drop your wet clothes outside the bathroom door. I'll pick them up. Meanwhile, I'll dish up some
fish chowder and make some hot tea."

Too tired to respond I slowly climbed the stairs and went
into the bathroom. Soon I was up to my chin in hot water,
and I could feel the chill running up my legs and arms and
out the top of my head. In another ten minutes I was in the
soft bed with the covers up to my chin. Meg came in carrying a tray, her blue eyes anxious and maternal. "The fish
chowder is piping hot. I made it myself. And I put rum in
the tea." She pronounced chowder "Chowdah" and the "p's"
in "piping" and the "t" in "tea" had that incisive clip of
New England, both exotic and piquant to my Michigan-
tuned ears.

"You're very kind," I said.

"I was worried about you, Mr. Aspen. Being down river in this bad storm."

I looked up over my soup bowl. "I thought we'd agreed you would call me Stephen. Or Steve."

She smiled softly, her sweet face as shy as a little girl's. "Well, then, Stephen." She shook her head to dismiss the shyness. "Anyway, I was worried. What happened?"

In between sips and spoonfuls of tea and chowder, I told her about my adventures down in the salt marsh. "Gracious!" Meg said, "what a time you had!" She looked thoughtfully at me. "Shouldn't you have some kind of a shelter down there where you watch? I'm certain Mr. Price would let you put one up."

"Yes, he said I could. Trouble is, I'm no builder. I got D's in 8th grade manual training."

Meg smiled gently at me and said nothing.

Two

Sometime later, maybe a week, Meg met me as I came in after another soggy day on the marshes. "I have something for you, Stephen," she said with her quiet sweet smile, and handed me a tan booklet. "Maybe this will help you overcome those D's you got in manual training and you can build some kind of shelter for yourself. It's a book on carpentry I got from the Government Printing Office."

I opened the booklet with "Technical Manual on Carpentry, U.S. Army" on its cover and inside I found sketches, diagrams and photographs picturing details of wood frame construction. I was intrigued at once but what made it love at first sight was this passage I ran across: *"To drive a nail—* (a) Hold the nail in place with the thumb and first two fingers of one hand. (b) Grasp hammer handle as shown in figure 71 [photograph of hand grasping hammer]. (c) Tap the head of the nail lightly to start it into the wood and remove the guiding hand. (d) Drive the nail." Who could fail with a book like this? Not only were there precise instructions about the most basic procedure in carpentry but there was inspiration and lift, even poetry, in that terse, rhythmic command: *"Drive* the *nail!"*

But even with the help of this admirable guide that reduced all operations to their basic essentials—citing each step in driving a nail except for telling you which end to apply to the wood, the point or the head—when I began real work I encountered a series of baffling problems. It began with the question of how deep to dig the holes for the foundation piers. Around me the sun was casting sparkling October sunshine, and the air was winey and brisk with urgency. Out in the Sound a great raft of ducks performed and clamored for my attention, while I was concentrating on problems as baffling to me as the courses of the planets were to ancient man. The holes needed to be twenty-four inches deep to get the base below the frost line, but the ground was not level where the shed was to stand and if the holes were all the same depth then the floor of the shed would be as uneven as the ground! What to do?

Looking back, I find it astonishing that I was baffled by so simple a problem. But at that stage I was a neolithic man in the realms of carpentry. Each problem presented itself raw and unformed and had to be hand-hewn into solution. Eventually I realized that the solution was to dig the hole deeper where the ground was higher, enough deeper to make the tops of the piers level with one another.

The next task, laying down a four-inch pad of cement for each pier, was not quite as intellectually challenging but my virginity in the act of preparing cement mix made me as nervous as a new bride making her first cake. Would I use too much water and get the mix too runny? Would the salt water interfere with the hardening? In the considered judgment of Mrs. Avery at the general store "it wouldn't make no difference," so I pressed on, nervous as a witch, and finally got pads of slightly erratic thickness in each of the holes. That completed construction for the day so I went down to the skiff lying on the shore with tiny wavelets licking along her sides and headed back upriver. With the bow of the skiff pointed toward a round red sun lowering in the west, I mused dreamily about the structure I was building. It was to be 10 by 15 feet, dimensions I had found in Thoreau's *Walden*: "I have a . . . house ten feet wide by fifteen feet long . . ." he had said in modest triumph. Ten by fifteen was bigger than necessary, but I had to have some vague plan in mind, and Henry Thoreau's guidance seemed as appropriate as any. Besides, I told myself, with that much space I could put in a cot and perhaps a tiny stove and thus save myself from an exhausting trip up river in bad weather.

The next day I laid cinder block to form foundation piers. Again, I was in a fury of frustration most of the time—much mixing of cement, running back and forth from the shore with buckets of water, sighting along a carpenter's level, and tapping on the blocks to get them aligned—but when the day came to an end and the fury subsided I had seven sturdy piers whose tops were within a half inch or so of being level with one another. I did not know it at the time but the worst was over.

That afternoon, having had a bath and plucked bits of mortar out of my hair and eyebrows, I met Meg as I came down the stairway on my way to supper at Zeke's Diner. "How did it go today?" she asked, her head tilted slightly to one side and her face wearing its usual sweet smile.

"Pretty fair. I got the foundation piers up, but now I've got to buy lumber for the framing."

Meg pursued her small mouth and narrowed her eyes. "You know, on my way back from the dentist yesterday I passed a place this side of Plympton Center where they're tearing down old houses. There was a sign there saying 'Used Lumber for Sale.' Might be cheaper there."

I grinned at Meg's pronunciation, "cheapah," and said, "Good, I'll run up there tomorrow."

The wrecking site was on the southern outskirts of Plympton Center. Beside it was a junk yard with the materials from the old houses. I eased the Plymouth up beside a small shack near the curb where a fat man with a three-day growth of beard, his pants held at about half mast on his melon belly by sagging suspenders, stood in the door-way. "Do anythin' fer ya?"

"I guess so. Do you have any two by sixes?"

"Yep. How much you need?"

I consulted my slip of paper. "One hundred and ninety feet. That's lineal feet," I added with professional accuracy.

"Huh?"

"Lineal feet. Not board feet." This distinction was a bit of erudition I had gleaned from the Army manual, and I hoped the fat salesman would gather that he was not deal-ing with a novice.

The fat man, his blue eyes pale and blurry above the stubble, grunted. "You mean runnin' feet. C'mon back here." He led me through the cluttered yard, rusty nails and bits of glass underfoot and lengths of pipe and derelict plumb-ing fixtures lying around. As we rounded the first corner, out of sight of the shack, he stopped and took a pint whis-key bottle from his pocket and took a long pull. "Lumbago's so goddammed bad this mornin' I tole the wife I doubted I could get through the day." He trudged on a little farther. "There's your two-by-sixes," he said pointing. "Good dry stuff. Ten cents a runnin' foot."

I lifted one of the top boards in the pile in a casual, expert sort of way. "They look okay."

"You gonna haul 'em yourself or you want 'em delivered?"

"I guess I can't carry them in my coupe, so we better have them delivered."

"Where to?"

"The Brixton town dock."

He belched a sour whiskey burp in my direction. "We can manage that." He turned and hailed a short, skinny man stacking wood nearby. "Hey, Charley. Come help this fella pick some stuff and load it on the pickup."

I picked out some two dozen sound pieces of timber with Charley's help and loaded them on the battered Chevy truck. The fat man came out and surveyed the load. "Call that a hundred eighty-six feet. At ten cents a foot that's just eighteen dollars and sixty cents, so we'll round her off to eighteen and fifty."

I took a twenty out of my billfold and got a dollar and two quarters back, thereby depleting by $18.50 the research grant funds the University had provided. Thoreau had kept a meticulous account of the money he had expended, and I, following in his footsteps, determined to do the same.

I followed Charley in the pickup down the highway the three miles to Brixton, and got in the skiff as he handed me the two-by-sixes one by one. Then I climbed back on the dock and fished the dollar bill I had got in change out of my pocket and handed it to Charley. I made a mental note to charge it, as Thoreau had done, to "transportation."

It was three o'clock and dead low tide, so I decided to wait until morning to take the lumber down river. It was what New Englanders call an "in-and-out" day with the sun briefly shining full and gold in the western sky and then blotted out by fat, plodding clouds. The air had that tang of the sea and shore I had grown to love, and I realized as I walked slowly down the stone block sidewalk under the crimson maple trees that everything about my surroundings delighted me. As a mid-Westerner, I had a special reverence for New England. The whole region seemed somehow suffused with a romantic glow, springing both from its history and tradition and its physical structure: its compact terrain, the craggy coastline, the grassy hills with their stone outcrops sheltering secluded valleys, the neatly defined villages—all so unlike the sprawling expanses and wide horizons of the Middle West. To me, it was as though some mystery, some secret born of time and tradition dwelt unseen among the old white houses in the narrow village streets, a mystery known and understood by native New Englanders but only dimly felt by outsiders like me. While New England seemed polished and refined by the hand of man, my native region seemed raw and still forming. In New England I lived with a constant sense of enhanced well-being, a little like the glow of early love.

As I came in the front door Meg met me, eyes serious and her manner earnest. "Oh, Stephen, I want to have a word with you. Come sit down for a moment."

"Something wrong, Meg?"

"No, not really." She turned back and looked at me. "Well, yes. Sit here for a minute and I'll tell you about it."

We sat on the maple-armed settee and Meg said, "My sister, Molly, is coming to stay with us for a while. She has left her husband in Boston."

"Oh, I'm sorry."

"So are we, Mother and I." She shook her head. "I don't know what it's about, but Molly has always been sort of— well, flighty."

I was gazing sympathetically at Meg's concerned expression when it struck me: the house had only three bedrooms. Was I being asked to leave? "Oh, Meg," I said, "you're going to need my room for Molly, aren't you?"

She looked up quickly. "No, Stephen, no. That's what I wanted to tell you. Mother and I have talked it over, and we want you to stay. We don't know how long Molly will be here, and besides we like having a man in the house. There's a trundle bed in Mother's room where I'll sleep, and Molly can have my room. You stay right where you are."

"Are you sure that's what you want?"

"Absolutely. We'll be fine. I'm only concerned that you might not be comfortable with three women around. The bathroom and all, I mean."

I grinned at her. "I grew up with two sisters and a mother. I can manage."

"It's settled then. Molly's being here won't change things a bit."

Three

A northeaster had moved in over New England next day and a raw wind off the North Atlantic drove thick mist and drizzle over the salt marshes. But the passion of building was upon me, so in defiance of the weather I put on my rain gear and hurried under the dripping maple trees to the town dock clutching the thermos of hot tea Meg had pressed on me as I left the house. True to its customary caprice, the Seagull started on the first pull despite the wet and I chugged down river through the driving mist with the lumber-laden skiff's gunwales only ten inches above the water.

Like a college student preparing for semester exams I had studied the Army manual exhaustively the night before. The task at hand was to saw and nail my two-by-sixes into sills and joists, the understructure which supports the walls and floor. After I had beached the skiff I hauled the two-by-sixes one or two at a time across the sandy verge and up through the sodden salt meadow grass, the tawny blades sparkling with droplets of mist. Then, remembering poignantly my carpentry failures of the past, I measured for the saw cuts with extreme care—usually checking each measurement two or three times—and then sawed with great deliberation. By noontime I had formed a wooden outline with the sills, and as I sat down on the edge and took a ham sandwich and a banana out of my backpack, I could not help thinking it was already beginning to look like a shed, my observation shelter.

The wind and mist continued to bear steadily out of the northeast and the handles of my hammer and saw grew wet and slippery. Out on the Sound a raft of ducks bobbed silently on the grey sea. My rain jacket held the wet at bay over my chest and arms but mist had seeped through the collar onto my shoulders and my dungarees were sodden. Ordinarily, I would have been stiff with cold but the exertion of lifting, sawing, and hammering kept me warm, almost sweating.

That afternoon while fastening the nine feet four inch long joists to the sills I began to appreciate for the first time the disadvantages of working alone. Holding a joist in place while nailing it fast calls for three hands, one for the hammer, one for the nail, plus the one for the joist. Having only the standard issue of two, I tried a variety of tricks with limited success. But at last, I found a solution—tapping the nail far enough through the sill to support the joist before nailing it home. This discovery gave my spirits a mighty lift. Despite the raw weather and the gloom of the salt marshes, I sang and whistled and the bang of the hammer on the nails rang out in the damp air.

Dusk was not far off when I nailed the last joist in place, and began to gather my tools. Just then I heard the sloshing of footsteps, and when I looked up I saw Stuart Price striding toward me, rubber-booted and wearing a yellow slicker and sou'wester hat. "Heard your hammer and thought I'd check on how you're coming." He stopped about ten feet away and studied my construction. Then he grinned and shook his head. "Man, that's some foundation you've got there! What are you going to put on it, an apartment house?"

I peered at him closely, uncertain whether I was being praised or blamed. "What's the matter with it? It's the first thing I ever built. Something wrong?"

"No, no, not a thing. Question is whether it's not too good. It looks strong enough for a railroad bridge."

"Well, that's what it calls for in the book. Doubled two-by-sixes for sills and two-by-six joists."

Stuart Price grinned at me. "It's fine," he said. "You're doing great, but I still maintain it's strong enough to hold up a freight train."

We chatted for a few minutes, and he invited me to stop by his place for a drink before going back up river. But I was concerned about making it back on a dropping tide in the settling darkness, so I begged off for this time. I gathered my things and dumped them in the skiff and shoved off. Happily, the mercurial Seagull came to life on the third pull. As I rounded the end of Tingree Island into the Yare River, it came to me that I had just drawn my first compliment on my building skills.

Molly Satterlee was a more exuberant version of Meg. It was as though her creator had decided after crafting the demure and sweetly quiet Meg to let out the stops. Meg's figure was slim and economically molded, like "the hull of a racing yacht," as Hemingway describes Brett Ashley in *The Sun Also Rises*. Taller than Meg's five feet four, Molly was luxuriantly rounder in every direction. Her face had a sister's likeness to Meg's but in all dimensions it was more lavish. Her nose was broader, her eyes larger, her mouth bigger. Especially her mouth. It was a voluptuous, sensuous mouth—a seeking, questing mouth. In all, there was a current of attraction, almost like the scent of musk, flowing from Molly.

I found it difficult to keep my eyes off her as I sat drinking tea in the living room with her sister and her mother. Meg had met me at the door as I had come in after supper at Zeke's Diner and invited me to have a cup of tea and meet Molly. Old Mrs. Satterlee sat in her rocking chair, a dim and vague figure seemingly only partially present. Meg sat straight-backed on the sofa, legs crossed at the ankles, smiling gently at me.

"How did the building go today, Stephen?" she asked. "You must have got very wet."

"What are you building, Mr. Aspen?" asked Molly.

"A small shed," I said. Then looking at Meg, "It went fine, but you're right, I did get wet." There was a pause and then seeking for something to say I described how I had finally solved the problem of nailing the joists. "Working alone causes problems sometimes," I finished.

There was another pause. Then Molly smiled winningly at me and said, "I would be glad to give you a hand any time while I'm here." She looked at Meg, "I used to be Daddy's little helper doing odd jobs when we were little girls, wasn't I, Meg? You read your books and I helped Daddy."

Meg pursed her mouth. "That's true," she said, while I gazed at Molly and mused over the changes time had wrought in "Daddy's little helper."

I set out early next morning to buy flooring. I was on hand at the used lumber place at Plympton Center at eight o'clock. The fat man with the half-mast pants looked even blearier than the last time. "Good morning," I said cheerily, "how's that lumbago?"

He looked at me dispassionately. "What'll you have?"

"I need material for flooring. Got any used one-by-sixes?"

"Nope. Got plenty a regular tongue-and-groove flooring though. Seven cents a square foot. Whyn't you use that?"

"How is it? Pretty clean stuff?"

He leaned over and emitted a long, dark stream of tobacco juice. "C'mon back and see for y'self." I followed as he trudged, heavy and silent, through the mud and debris of the yard. "Wife's sick," he said suddenly, still walking along and not looking back. "Real sick. Damned worrisome."

"Sorry to hear that. What seems to be the matter?"

"Stomick. Can't keep nothin' down. Hasn't had a square meal in three weeks."

"That's bad," I offered. "You had a doctor for her?"

"Naw." He spat another dollop of tobacco juice. "If she ain't better next week we'll get a doctor around." He stopped and pointed to a misshapen pile fifteen feet high. "There's your floorin'. Some's pretty good and some ain't. Pick out what you want and Charley'll help you load it."

I mounted the small hill of lumber and began picking at the pieces and soon discovered I had to make difficult choices. Some pieces had broken tongues, others were cracked or partially rotten. Also some were oak and some pine, and some were three and three-quarter inches wide and others five. I soon found that any single criterion only caused me to find more pieces I could not use than those I could, so I decided that it was important only that the piece be sound. Even so, it was very slow work. I needed approximately two hundred square feet and two hundred square feet divided into widths of three and three-quarter inches results in an unbelievable number of pieces.

Charley and I labored for nearly an hour, turning pieces over and putting them back, searching deeper and deeper into the pile, hoping to find a vein of sound, splendid flooring. Finally, we had a pile Charley reckoned "might just do her." I called the fat man who gazed for a moment at the stack and then announced with extraordinary precision, "Call that one hundred and ninety-eight feet. Stop by the office when you and Charley get the pickup loaded."

As Charley and I shoved the pieces over the tailgate of the Chevy pickup I was struck by their variety, both in length and in color. Some were bright red, some mottled green, others a sort of disgusting brown. Some natural wood. Also, along the upper edge of each tongue was caked the filth of decades of human detritus, the precise chemical content determined, no doubt, by its location in the house, whether bedroom, kitchen, hallway, or bathroom. One section, as I later found while nailing it down, had been saturated with a pungent, musky perfume, a discovery which sent my imagination scampering off in fascinating pursuits. But no matter, whether the history of that used flooring had been romantic or sordid or commonplace, it was dry, sound, and wonderfully cheap. It would serve admirably as a floor.

The fat man met me at the door of his shanty carrying a grubby notebook. "That'll be $13.86," he said. I fished fourteen dollars out of my pocket, and he rang it up on the brass ornamented cash register. "Ya got some real good stuff there," he said as he handed me my change. "Make you a good floor." There was a moment's silence while I groped for some kind of an exit line.

"God damn!" he said suddenly. "I sure hope my ole lady gets better." His unshaven face with the red capillary streaks showing through the stubble wore a deep scowl. "That ole woman's been awful good ta me. Do anything' for me—*any*-thin'," he said with fierce emphasis. "Never no complainin' 'bout my drinkin' or anything. I'd sure as hell miss her if anythin' happened."

"She'll get better," I said reassuringly, fatuously. "But you better get her to a doctor and see what's wrong."

"Guess I will," he said morosely. "Guess I will." He turned suddenly and went back into his tiny office. "Be seein' ya," he said as his shapeless form moved through the doorway.

I watched as Molly Satterlee stepped down from the dock into the skiff. She giggled as she straightened up. "Meg's blue jeans are so tight I can scarcely move," she said. "Tight" was hardly adequate to describe the molded fit over Molly's thighs and haunches. "I hope I can sit down without busting out somewhere." She lowered herself gingerly on the thwart facing me and smiled a broad, open smile. "Made it," she said.

I had met Molly in the hallway as I was leaving the house. "Mind if I come along?" she asked. "Meg's gone to the library and Mother's sleeping. I'm bored to death with the quiet."

"No, come ahead. Glad to have company."

"Can I be helpful?"

I looked at her grey flannel skirt and angora sweater. "Not in those clothes."

"Give me a sec. I'll find something of Meg's." And she had bounded up the steps.

I waited on the porch, listening to the October wind rustling the crimson leaves on the maple trees, until I heard Molly's quick step behind me. She had giggled and said, "Meg's jeans are so tight on me I practically needed a shoehorn to get inside them." I had gone down the three steps, and as I looked back she pirouetted on the porch above me, her lovingly molded hips and precisely delineated pelvis revolving before my eyes. "See?" she asked, grinning.

"Yes," I said, "I see."

"C'mon," she said as she galloped down the steps and grabbed my hand.

With Molly seated without mishap, I turned my attention to the Seagull, hoping it would not embarrass me before her. But in its usual fickle fashion it fired off on the third pull, and we headed off down river with a load of flooring. It was my second trip of the day transporting the material. I had made the first on the falling tide at 7:30 and now, after lunch, I was meeting the incoming tide flooding up the Yare River.

Now, with Molly's help I was ready to begin laying the first pieces of flooring over the supporting joists.

Four

"Tell me something, Stephen," asked Molly. "Do you have a girl at home and if not why not?"

We were lying side by side on the just-completed floor of the shed, a task that had taken us three full days, and the afternoon sunshine of mid-October lay bright and warm on our outstretched bodies. The crisp air of the salt marsh was laced with the tang of rich creek mud and beached seaweed.

"No. But why do you ask?"

"Wel-l-l, curiosity mostly. You're a good looking guy, dark hair, sleepy eyes, strong shoulders. Besides, I've practically told you my life story over the past three days. You know all about my mixed up situation with Charles and Doug, and I know nothing about *your* personal life. You might not even like girls for all I know."

I lifted my head and grinned at her. True, I had learned about her unsatisfactory marriage with Charles, the Boston Symphony double bass player, and her flaming affair with Doug, the married graduate student of anthropology—the tangled situation that had caused her to leave her husband and come to Brixton—but to suggest that I might not like girls! Me of all people! Do small boys like milk chocolate?

"How in the world could you imagine I might not like girls?"

Her eyes locked into mine and her red lower lip thrust forward teasingly. "Well, you and I have been alone together, side by side, now for three full days, and you haven't touched me, haven't patted my bottom even once."

"Did you expect me to?"

"Judging by my considerable experience with healthy young males, yes."

I grinned at her again. "Is that an invitation, or perhaps a request?"

She smiled a lazy smile. "If you like. Sure." Then she rolled over invitingly onto her back. I leaned across to kiss her slightly open mouth. It was like grabbing hold of a flaming rocket rushing skyward. Molly's instant response, her lips and tongue caressing mine and her fingertips stroking my head and neck, lifted me off the sunlit deck toward euphoria. I had never known such love-making, and I had no thought except to soar higher and higher. But after several moments Molly put a hand on my chest and pushed me away. "Not here, sweet. Not here."

I cocked my head questioningly. "Not here?" I asked somewhat thickly.

She smiled and kissed me on the nose. "It's too exposed, too open."

"Who could see us?"

"God," she said. "And the ducks." She sat up then and looked out toward the Sound and pointed at the raft of ducks riding the spangles of slanting sunshine. "Besides, you've settled my doubts about you and girls."

Feeling slightly sulky, I said, "Happy to oblige."

She turned quickly and squeezed my hand. "Look there, Stephen, what are those ducks doing? One of them keeps taking something out of the other one's bill. What's going on?"

I sat up and saw again what I had seen many times before. In the midst of a raft of ducks, a cinnamon brown widgeon with black-tipped wings swam quickly up to a redhead just as it broke the surface and snatched a piece of vegetation from its bill. "That's a widgeon," I said, "and that's how he gets to eat weeds that grow on the bottom. The redhead has just pulled some up."

"Lazy fellow. Why doesn't he go down and get his own weeds?"

"He's not a very good diver and the redhead is."

"Fine excuse. Why does the redhead put up with it?"

"I'm not sure. It's a question I'm working on for my thesis. One theory I've got is that the widgeon is a wary, nervous duck and being on the surface because he doesn't dive he can sense danger and sound the alarm for the diving ducks. Maybe in some queer ducky way the redhead perceives that and surrenders some weed in payment." I thought for a moment. "Sounds pretty anthropomorphic, I admit. Maybe it's just a case of the widgeons being aggressive fellows and the redheads passive. Anyway, it's a behavior pattern that enhances survival for both breeds."

"Fascinating." She gazed a while longer at the birds diving and flapping on the shimmering sea. "Tide's falling," she said. "We'd better start back."

That night, during the small hours of the morning, I was wakened by a soft hand over my mouth and Molly's whisper in my ear, "Stephen, slide over. It's me. Molly."

Several moments later in the warm, soft bed, she whispered in my ear again, "Careful, darling. Don't make the bed creak."

The mission for my next foray to the used lumber yard was to get two-by-fours for framing. I found my unkempt friend standing in the doorway of his office. Time had not improved his personal grooming. He stood before me, unshaven, with a driblet of tobacco juice marking the corner of his mouth. "Haven't seen you for a while," I said cheerily.

"Guess not," he said. "What'll ya have?"

"Two-by-fours for framing. Got any?"

"Hell, yes. All you can use. Back here." He sloshed his way through the mud, rusted nails, and bits of glass.

"How's your wife?" I asked while picking my way around a particularly large and, for all I knew, bottomless puddle.

"What's that?" he said, obviously surprised and made suspicious by this personal question. Apparently he did not remember our previous conversation.

"Is she all right again?" As I asked it, I suddenly realized I was venturing onto dangerous ground. After all, the woman might be dead, or dying.

"*Her!*" His tone was bitter. "Hell, yes, she's all right. You couldn't kill that old woman with a ball bat. Tougher'n a goddammed mule." He spat a glop of tobacco juice in cold exasperation. "Drivin' me crazy now, pickin' at me to go visit her sister out in Vermont. Cost too much money." He spat again. "Her sister's no goddammed good, anyways. She'll just fill her full of ideas 'bout how to spend *more* money." He shook his head, filled with the angry sorrow of a plain man trying to understand the foibles of womankind. He stopped by a stack of two-by-fours. "Here you are. Take your pick."

"Okay," I said. "Anyway, I'm glad she's better."

"Shee-it!" he said morosely.

Molly and I had got the framing for the north wall of the shed up and braced in place when the east wind picked up and swept across the Sound, flinging a stinging mist at us. "Better pack up and start back," I told her.

"Darn!" Molly said. "I was hoping we could get one of the side walls up so we could see how it will look."

"Tomorrow, maybe." I started gathering tools and stowing them in the canvas duffle bag. Molly stowed the nails under the floor and covered them with a scrap of tarp. Then together we pushed the skiff off and headed for home.

It was our second day of putting up framing, and it had been fun. Framing *is* fun. All it takes is accurate measurements, square cuts, two ten-penny nails top and bottom of each stud, and there you have it. Of course, I encountered the usual muck-ups because of my basic ineptitude. After determining that the studs should be just six feet, eight inches long I measured the first two-by-four with a precision that would have been admirable in a watchmaker, while Molly stood silently beside me, and then I sawed gingerly along the line. I repeated this exactly with the second piece and then, gaining in confidence, I attacked the third piece with greater abandon, flopping the six-foot rule onto the board, making a mark at the end, sliding the rule forward and making a second mark eight inches beyond. Molly handed me the saw and I made a neat and precise cut at the six foot mark, making the stud exactly eight inches too short.

"Bad luck," said Molly.

"Bad luck, hell," I said. "Terminal stupidity."

Molly did not dispute this analysis.

Our relationship after her post-midnight visit to my bed had reverted to mere companionship. For a complex of reasons, including the fact that Molly was already entangled in a three-way affair, I did not want to get further involved, and Molly seemed content to leave it be. For me there was still another angle, surprising and hard to define. It had to do with Meg. Somehow, after that romp with Molly, I felt awkward around Meg. Not exactly ill at ease, but not at ease either. It had become harder to gaze directly into those blue eyes, calm and kind.

On this day, after docking and tieing up the skiff, Molly and I walked briskly through the driving drizzle toward her house. I was musing, head down, staring at the glistening wet stone sidewalk, when Molly suddenly stopped dead. I turned to look at her. She was staring at the front porch of the Satterlee house. There, sitting on a straight-backed, kitchen chair was a man in a black coat and black hat. "Charles!" Molly murmured.

As we walked up the front walkway, Charles stood up, a short and broad, black-eyed and sharp-nosed man. "*Allo, Molly,*" he said. "*Comment va tu?*"

"*Bien, Charles, bien.*" Molly pronounced her husband's name, "Sharl." She turned to me, "This is Stephen Aspen, Charles."

We shook hands silently, his hand as broad as a blacksmith's and as strong. His face was set, unsmiling. "I've come to talk with you," he said. "Come with me in the car."

She looked questioningly at him for a moment and then said, "Let me change clothes first."

"*No!* Now! I've been waiting here for two hours."

She hesitated briefly and then said, "All right, Charles," and walked with him to the black Oldsmobile parked at the curb. I watched as they drove off, she with her face white and grim.

Meg met me at the door as I came in. "I tried to get him to wait inside but he insisted on waiting on the porch so I got him a kitchen chair."

"Strange," I said.

The clock by my bed said 11:25 as I put *Walden* down and turned off the light. Moments later I heard the front door open and then Molly's tread on the stairs.

I did not see Molly at all the next day, but I put in a full day by myself and got the framing for the two side walls assembled and in place. I saw the three Satterlee women sitting quietly in the sitting room as I came back from supper at Zeke's but I stuck to my rule not to intrude unless invited and went up to my room for an evening of quiet reading.

Next morning Molly was waiting for me as I was leaving. "Mind if I join you?" Her face was set and serious, her eyes grave.

"No. Come along."

The sun was gliding up a mackerel sky as the skiff chugged down the Yare River. High up in the east a great

Vee of Canada geese wavered and undulated across the sky, moving southward. The air was nose-stingingly crisp and my left ear and cheek tingled as a steady northwest wind pressed against my face. Molly said not a word during our voyage down river but she jumped quickly out of the bow as we grounded and pulled the skiff farther up the beach.

I was determined to let Molly be the first to speak, keeping silent as long as she wished. For a while we worked together without speaking, following the routines we had previously established. Molly had handed me the saw and I had cut the final stud for the front wall when she said quietly, "Charles wants me to come back. Says he'll forget what's happened."

Wary, I merely said, "I see."

Molly handed me the hammer and a ten-penny nail. "I've got to give him an answer soon but I'm confused. I don't know what I want to do or what I *should* do."

I muttered a neutral "Mmmm."

Molly was silent again for a time but then she burst out. "Damn it, Stephen, you're an intelligent guy. I need an outsider's point of view. Mother and Meg are no help but you *can* be. Give me a reason, *any* reason, why I should go back to Charles."

I know nothing about personal counseling but I have done a little high school debating, and it seemed to me that any reason I offered Molly would just provide her with a point to argue against. But instead, a question would force her to provide a reason of her own. "Let me ask first, what reason did you have to marry him in the first place?"

She looked up quickly, startled by the question. Then her expression softened. "Oh, I found his French manners charming. And I liked the people around him, the professional musicians and the music."

"And for a while you found that satisfying, fulfilling?"

She smiled as she remembered. "Yes. It was lots of fun. Travelling with the orchestra around the country and even to Scandinavia and Paris. Going to lavish receptions given by rich patrons in their fabulous houses. And Charles was highly regarded by his fellow musicians, sort of a leader among them. We were a popular couple."

"And all that has changed?"

She hesitated. "No, not really. Of course, in five years it's become everyday, commonplace." She paused, looking down at the ground. Then, softly smiling, she said, "And then Doug came along and I found out what I was missing."

I was beginning to feel a little like a trial lawyer, but I asked, "What was that?"

She smiled broadly, girlishly. "Oh, spontaneity and passion. Excitement. My love life with Charles had become a set routine, *never* before a concert, *always* after a concert. And always after we had gone to bed at ten o'clock. But after Doug and I became lovers he would show up in the morning while I was ironing in the kitchen and carry me off to the living room sofa."

"That's spontaneity all right but do you suppose that in five years even that might become everyday, routine?"

She looked up sharply and then glared at me. There was a long, long pause while her eyes glowed with anger. Then she hissed, "You son of a bitch, Stephen Aspen! You dirty son of a bitch!"

I smiled at her. "Seems to me a fair question."

We were silent for several long moments. Molly's face was grim and I could see her mouth working in agitation. Finally, I said, "Just let me ask you one more question. No, make that two. First, will Doug divorce his wife and marry you?"

"No. He's made that very clear. No divorce."

"And that's satisfactory for you?"

"For a while I thought I could live with it, just be content with what he gives me. Now I'm not so sure."

"I see. Well, then, second question. Why does Charles want you back?"

"Oh, well." She looked down at the ground between us.

"He says he *needs* me. Says he's very proud of me, how popular I am among Boston Symphony people. Says I'm a good wife, the only wife he has ever wanted, will ever want. Says he'll try"—here she began to sniffle—"to be more"— she gulped—"understanding of my needs." Then she broke down and fell into my arms. "Oh, God damn you, Stephen! God damn your soul!"

Five

"Caleb Satterlee, Meg's father, was a fine man," Stuart Price was saying, his strong Yankee face—patrician nose, angular jaw, decisive mouth—glowing pink in the light of the oil lamp on the kitchen table. Outside the little cottage sited on a knoll in the midst of the salt marsh—Stuart Price and his fellow New Englanders called it a "camp"—dusk was settling into darkness and a gusty west wind rattled the small-paned windows. "Caleb was a town selectman and village registrar. He held some kind of town office all his adult life."

Price took a sip of bourbon and put the glass down, setting it precisely on a red block in the plaid-pattern of the oilcloth table cover. "But then, so did all his family before him, dating back to Jonathan Satterlee, his ancestor, who signed the articles of incorporation for Brixton in 1652."

I rolled a swallow of Price's fine bourbon around on my tongue and said, "Meg Satterlee is carrying on that tradition, I guess, being the town librarian. I wonder, which generation of Satterlees in public service does she make?"

Price cocked his head and looked fixedly at me. "Let's see. 1652-1951. Three hundred years, isn't it? Figure about five generations a century. That would make Meg the 15th generation of Satterlees in public office."

I sat marvelling over this continuity of family tradition, reflecting that I was not certain of my own grandfather's birthplace and knew nothing about *his* father, not even his first name.

Stuart Price asked, "How's your drink?"

I measured about a quarter of an inch in the bottom of the glass. "Low tide, I'd say."

"Let's do something about that." He reached for the bottle on a shelf beside the iron stove. "I know it's bad form to compliment your own food or drink, but I must say to you, man to man, that S. S. Pierce"—he pronounced it "Purse"—"puts out a mighty fine eight-year old bourbon."

"Lovely stuff," I agreed.

"You know, speaking of Meg Satterlee, I have nothing but admiration for her. She has devoted her adult life to her mother at great sacrifice. After graduation from college in 1948—Mount Holyoke, I believe—she took a job as book editor at Little, Brown in Boston. I'm told by one of my friends that she was rising rapidly in the publishing trade when her father suddenly died, leaving Meg's mother bereft. Mrs. Satterlee had always been a highly dependent woman and after her husband's death she was nearly helpless. So Meg threw up her job and came home to take care of her."

"She's a nice woman," I offered.

"She's a great girl." He shook his head in admiration. "I swear, if she were free from her responsibilities I believe I'd try to get her to marry me despite our difference in age."

Somehow, that remark made me uncomfortable in an ill-defined way, sort of stuck in my throat, so to speak. Was it just the difference between Meg's age and his that made me find it inappropriate? Anyway, I could find no suitable response so I sipped again at my bourbon, thinking that this was the first time Stuart Price had confirmed what Meg had told me: that he was a bachelor, a widower.

"There's a sister, too, you know," he said. "Molly. I've never met her but I'm told she's sort of a wild one. Married, I believe, to some kind of a musical fellow down in Boston."

Again, nothing appropriate came to mind so I took another sip.

After a reflective pause, Price said, "I've been meaning to ask, how's your research coming?"

"I've got a lot of data, counts of the various groupings of ducks and some stuff on behavior. What I need to do now is to come up with some analysis, some theories, and then collect more data to support or refute them. Of course, the work on the shed has slowed me up for the last three weeks."

"Where are you with that?"

"Got it all framed. Need to put on sheathing. Right now, I'm looking for cheap material. My favorite junkyard doesn't have any sheathing. And lumber yard prices are out of sight."

Price said, "Hmmm," and looked reflective. "You know, there's an old fellow runs a sawmill up in the country. Queer old duck, but he has good stuff and cheap. You might try him."

"What's his name?"

"Rose. Old man Rose." He shook his head, grinning. "Lord knows we've got plenty of odd ones in these parts but Mister Rose beats them all. He's an old fella, way past sixty, and he wears a chauffeur's cap. When he talks his bushy red eyebrows move up and down and the cap moves with them." Price chuckled. "He's as honest as a railroader's watch, but he loves to talk. Better plan on half a day, or at least a couple of hours."

Speaking of watches I looked at mine. "Lord, it's getting late. I'd better get back upriver before the tide runs out."

"I'll run you up to where your car is parked," Price said. Out the door, he led me around the cottage and down a narrow path to his little dock beside a weather-beaten boat house. The west wind thrust sharply against my face and the smell of rich marsh mud was strong in my nose. Off to

the west a dark red streak ran across the sky and lucent
Venus winked alluringly through the scudding clouds. On
the dock, Price stopped and raised his head, looking up at
the cloud-cluttered sky. "God, Aspen, isn't this magnificent?
The gutsy smell of marsh mud and sea water and the waving
grass and the twisting creeks. This spot means more to me
than any place on earth. It's the most important thing in my
life. Problem is, I don't know how long I can hold onto it.
Outside pressures keep mounting every year."

"Maybe you could make it a bird and game sanctuary
of some kind," I said, "and still retain resident rights during your lifetime."

Price turned to me and nodded. "You may have an idea
there," he said. "It's a possibility." He stooped and loosened the bowline to his boat. Shortly we were pushing up
a tidal creek against a falling tide in the lap-straked skiff.
"Another half hour, I don't think we could have made it,"
he shouted above the chugging outboard. "We'd have been
sailing on mud."

I was beginning to feel an urgent need to get my little
observation shed finished. Winter was closing in fast, and
each day I sat out in the raw weather was a worse ordeal
than the day before. Besides, I was falling behind on my
research schedule, which I desperately wanted to maintain
in order to complete my Cornell master's degree in June
1952. So I set out for Rose's sawmill first thing the next
morning. Going down the road out of Brixton I counted the
number of side roads Meg had numbered, then turned right
down a muddy lane past an age-worn, unpainted farmhouse.
The lane wound down across a meadow where a lone cow
lifted her head and watched me. Than I crossed a clear-
running stream on a log-paved bridge. As I drew up and
stopped I could hear the high whine of a big saw housed
in an open-sided tar-paper shed which looked ancient
enough to have supplied Henry Thoreau with his lumber.

I got out and stood watching. The screech of the saw sang in the crisp morning air as a young man pushed a big log down the saw bed into the spinning teeth as it sliced off a two-inch plank, then reversed the log and ripped off another plank. A short man wearing a chauffeur's cap stood by giving directions. If he was aware of me he gave no sign so after a moment or two I walked over to look at a stack of new-sawn lumber. Soon he was beside me. "Do something for you?" he asked, his bushy red eyebrows rising as he spoke and the bill of his cap lifting simultaneously just as Stuart Price said it would. "Name's Matthew Rose," he said.

"I need some one-by-sixes for siding."

"Red spruce do you? That's 'bout all I got." He led me over to a nearby stack. "Good stuff, knot's mostly small and tight."

"Is it good for siding?"

"Nothin' bettah."

"How much is it?"

"Ten cents a board foot. That's what I been askin' for fifteen years, and that's all I'm ever goin' ta ask." The vigor with which he said this seemed to make his eyebrows and his cap jump up and down even faster. "How much you need?"

While Mr. Rose and I continued our transaction, I watched with masked amusement the choreography of his eyebrows and cap, the shiny bill on his black cap rising and falling as his thick red eyebrows lifted and dropped. "Nathaniel'll truck your lumber down to the dock tomorry," he said. "Gotta finish up this sawin' job today."

"Fine."

I paid him and started to walk to my car. Mr. Rose stayed right by my side. "Right pretty day," he said.

"Sure is." I glanced sideways at the stumpy figure beside me, trudging along in a sort of rolling stride. "How long you been running the mill here?"

"Been sawmilling since I was nine year old. Took over

from my daddy when I was twenty, nigh onto fifty year ago."

"Long time."

"You ain't just a-mumblin'. Course the mill's been here since seventeen-and-fifty-nine and always with some feller named Rose a-runnin' it."

I shook my head admiringly, thinking again how steady and constant were the strands of family continuity running through the history and traditions of New England.

"'Spect I'm 'bout the last of it though," said Matthew Rose. "Ain't but two or three decent woodlots within truckin' distance now. Not enough logs to keep a fella goin'." He shook his head. "It's not too bad for me. I'm old enough now to start takin' it easy. But these young fellas like Nathaniel'll have to get jobs drivin' a truck or somepun like that."

Nothing lasts forever, not even in New England, I told myself as I headed the venerable Plymouth back toward Brixton. Not even a sawmill that had been owned and run by the same family for nearly 200 years. The long-lived family continuities of the Satterlees and the Roses, not to mention New England families with even longer spans, were mortal too. But still to me, the descendant of Midwestern transients, they were staggeringly impressive.

The tide was out, flat out. As I drove past the town dock I could see my skiff sitting with her flat bottom smack on the mud, and half tide would not come until midafternoon. I decided then to stop by the library and pick up a book to pass the time. Meg had been urging me to read something besides *Walden*, preferably somebody besides Thoreau, but if not that at least Henry's Cape Cod Journals.

As I opened the front door a peaceful library odor greeted me, the smell of books and bindings and printed paper, but then I heard Meg's voice shattering the cloistered library calm, screaming, "Stop that! Put that book down!"

At a table in the middle of the reading area a man was struggling to get up out of his chair while Meg grabbed and snatched at him, trying to get something out of his hands. I ran toward them while Meg tussled furiously with the chunky figure wearing a black overcoat, and suddenly he crashed backward over the chair, sprawling on the floor, his legs thrashing in the air. Meg pounced on him like a panther, still trying to get something away from him. While I stood hesitating for an instant, deciding what to do, the man brought his right arm forward toward Meg in a slashing motion and something shiny flashed in his hand. Meg screamed and fell back while the man scrambled to his feet and started for the door.

"Stop him, Stephen, stop him!" yelled Meg. I have never been much of a fighter but I did play intramural football in college so I threw a hard cut-block at his knees as he passed. He crashed down hard and the book he was carrying went skimming across the floor. I got up and stood over him, hoping he would not come up with fists swinging, but as I waited for his next move he lay on his side, grabbed his right knee, and moaned loudly.

Meg ran to me and I saw blood streaming from the side of her neck and down across her white blouse. "Hold him there, Stephen. Don't let him go. I'll call the sheriff." She was cool as ice and seemingly unaware she was bleeding.

The captive showed no immediate signs of getting to his feet and trying to escape, but I went to the front door anyway and locked it. Then I stood between him and the door, listening to Meg on the phone urging the sheriff to hurry. On the floor beside my feet was the book the man had been carrying. I picked it up and read on the spine, "Harper's Weekly, Vol. IX, 1863."

Meg put down the phone. "He's coming right over. Is the fellow hurt?"

"I think he broke my damned leg," the man grunted.

"Serves you right, you bastard," Meg said, standing over him.

"Meg, I said, "you're bleeding badly."

She looked down at her blood-streaked blouse. "So I am," she said calmly. She reached down on the floor and picked up a small object. "He slashed me with this." She handed me a tool about eight inches long with a razor blade set in its tip. "There are towels in the toilet. They'll stop the flow," she said turning away.

The man started to struggle to his feet, but when he was on one knee I gave him a hard shove and floored him again. "Son of a bitch," he said and grabbed his knee moaning.

"What's this all about?" I asked him.

"Fuck you," he growled.

Meg came back holding a towel to her neck just above the shoulder. "He was cutting pictures out of *Harper's Weekly* for 1863. They were engravings of Civil War battle scenes by Winslow Homer. They're valuable, much in demand by collectors, and we happen to have a complete set of *Harper's Weekly* for that period."

She dabbed at her neck and asked me, "Has it stopped bleeding?"

I could see a thin crimson line about five inches long running diagonally down the white column of her neck. "It's almost stopped but I would keep the towel there until we can get you to a doctor."

By this time the man was struggling once again to get up, but I shoved him down once more. Meg turned and grabbed one of the heavy wooden chairs at a nearby table. "If you make one more move I'll slam this goddamned chair over your stupid head," she said in a low growl, while I stared amazed as sweet, patient Meg became a snarling tigress.

In about ten minutes the sheriff came to the door and Meg told him in crisp detail what had happened. She handed over the book and the cutting tool as evidence. The sheriff handcuffed the man and with my help half carried him out to the patrol car. Then I put Meg in my car to take her down to Dr. Samuel Hathaway's office at the end of the village. "Did you say the guy was cutting out engravings by Winslow Homer? *The* Winslow Homer, the famous marine painter and water colorist?"

"Yes. *Harper's Weekly* had several artists covering the Civil War along with their press correspondents. Winslow Homer was the one who became the most famous later. His pictures of soldiers and battles are marvelously vivid."

Dr. Hathaway looked at Meg's neck and described her wound as deep but not dangerous. "Fix you right up, Meg, my dear," he said as he sterilized and bandaged the cut. As we drove back from the office to her house, Meg reached over and took my right hand from the steering wheel. "You were wonderful, Stephen. Just wonderful!" I squeezed her hand and put mine back on the wheel. Then Meg said, "We won't say anything about this to Mother." And we did not.

The next day I hauled three loads of siding material in the skiff down to the knoll on the edge of the Sound, and then attacked the building in a fury. In three days of intense work I had my observation shed sided, roofed, and finished off with a door and a four-by-six multi-paned window set sideways facing the shore. Now I could concentrate on getting the data for my thesis while sitting dry and out of the blasting seaside winds.

On the next Sunday Meg stopped me as I was going out the door. Our relations had taken on a new, more intimate dimension since the incident with the thief in the library, and she put her hand gently on my arm and smiled sweetly up at me. "Are you leaving now for the shore?"

"Yes, why? Can I do something for you before I go?"

"No, dear. I was wondering whether you would mind if I came along."

"Mind? I'd love it."

"I've never seen your shed, and Mother's sister is coming by so this might be a good time."

"Great." Then a thought struck me. I had been squatting on a cinder block while watching out the window but it was far from comfortable for me and I knew it would not be for Meg.

"You know," she said when I mentioned the difficulty, "there's a folding cot up in the attic that I've been meaning to tell you about. You could take that down and use it as long as you are here."

It was a tight squeeze getting the cot down the ladder steps that dropped down through a trap door into the attic, but together we wiggled it through and down the stairs and into the trunk of the Plymouth. As we drove the short distance to the town dock, Meg said, "Did I tell you I got a letter from Molly yesterday?"

"No."

"Wonderful letter, full of joy. She and Charles are going to spend a month in France this summer visiting his relations. And she said again—she always does—how wonderful you were in helping her think through her marital situation. She's endlessly grateful."

"I'm glad, but actually she did it all. I just asked questions she herself did not want to ask."

"The *right* questions."

"I suppose."

The sky to the east over Beach Plum Island was laden with thick clouds, but *The Boston Transcript* had forecast dry weather so we were not concerned. I beached the skiff, and together we carried the cot into the shed and set it down in front of the window. "This is perfect, Stephen. Now show me the ducks that especially interest you."

Out on the leaden waters of the Sound several rafts of ducks bobbed on the waves, more tightly bunched than usual. "Actually, they all interest me, but perhaps the widgeons most. Do you know the widgeon?"

"Certainly. He's that brownish, black-winged fellow out there."

"That's right. He's got a peculiar habit of snatching

bottom weeds away from the diving ducks, but at the moment no one seems to be feeding."

"No, they all look sort of hunkered down."

As we watched over the next hour the reason for the hunkering down became evident. The thick clouds off to the east thickened more and darkened and suddenly sheets of sleet and frozen rain came sweeping across the water and began pelting the shed with a spattering that sounded like buckshot. We watched a while as gusts flattened the waves into catspaw patterns and shuddered the side of my shed. "It looks like a squall that will pass soon," I said.

"I'm not so sure," said Meg.

After another half hour I was not so sure either. "Maybe we'd better start back," I suggested.

"I think you're right. It's not letting up."

We slogged back to the skiff, heads bent down against the stinging sleet, and shoved off. I performed the preliminary ritual for starting the Seagull and pulled. Nothing. I pulled again. And again. Still nothing. I readjusted the choke, I reset the throttle, and pulled. The flywheel whirled uselessly and the engine made a short of useless sucking noise. I pulled twice more, three times more, five times more—no response. I turned toward Meg sitting in the bow. She sat huddled and pinched, her face sheet white, her arms hugging herself, and her body shivering. "My God, Meg, you look frozen." I of course was almost sweating from pulling that starter cord.

"I am. And soaked."

"I can't start this damned motor for some reason." I looked again at the miserable figure in the bow. "Let's go inside and get warm."

Inside the shed I set Meg down on the cot and put my arms around her. She was shivering uncontrollably, teeth chattering. In a moment I made her lie down and then lay beside her, hugging her to me. Her windbreaker jacket was wet under my hand, and I said, "We ought to get you out of these wet clothes." I sat her up and took off her jacket, and then realized her blue jeans were sodden. "Pants, too," I said.

"I'm wearing long johns," she said miserably.

"So am I. But this is no time for modesty. You're on the edge of hypothermia." I helped her slide her pants down over her ankles, and then stripped off my own wet jacket and pants. We lay down again then and this time I lay on top of her, pressing my warmer body as close to her trim body as I could.

We lay quietly for a while and then she said in a muffled voice, "Would it be all right with you if I took a breath?"

"Oh, sorry." I raised slightly and she inhaled deeply.

"I'm starting to thaw slightly, I think."

"Good." I lay close to her again, and after a while I became aware that her breath beside my ear was coming more rapidly and her pelvis lifted slightly against mine. My own responses were quickening too, and in a moment I raised my head and looked down at her. She was smiling warmly at me, so after several seconds of looking searchingly into each other's eyes I bent my head and kissed her. She moved her hands across my shoulders and then caressed the back of my head. In a little while there seemed to be no turning back. Meg helped me as I pulled her long johns down. Then, as she wriggled out of them, she said, "I want you to know I've never done this before."

I paused. "Shall I stop?"

Smiling, she slowly shook her head. "No, don't stop. I just didn't want you to be disappointed."

Later, warm now and languorously content, I stroked her fine, soft hair, and she murmured something I did not catch. Then I noticed that the sound of buckshot on the roof had ceased. "Rain's stopped," I said.

"Oh, good, Stephen dear, we must get back somehow. Mother will be dreadfully worried and upset."

"I'll go see if I can start that stupid motor. If not, I'll row."

We dressed and stepped outside into near-darkness. I

took a flashlight from my jacket pocket and lighted our way to the skiff. As I was shining the light to set the choke and throttle, I noticed that the wire to the spark plug was loose and dangling. "My God, that's the problem!" I shouted. I connected the wire again and pulled hard on the starter cord. The Seagull coughed, apologetically it seemed to me, and then hit a steady rhythm. In forty minutes we were walking under the bare maple trees toward Meg's house. Just before we went inside, she stopped me and held her face up to be kissed. I kissed her gently and hand in hand we climbed the front steps.

Six

The faculty reception on 10 September 1952, the opening day of Kanaka College in Hochdale, Illinois, nearly caused me to panic and to ask myself, "My God, what have I done!" Outside, through the Georgian style windows September reigned in serene beauty as the late afternoon sun slanted down the sloping lawn and glinted on the broad waters of Kanaka Lake. But inside, in the Faculty Lounge, I seemed to be immersed in thin-shouldered, stringy-haired women, many apparently endangering 40 or some years beyond, and all standing with tea cups or punch glasses in hand, eyeing me narrowly from time to time while chattering nonstop in keening voices. There were just three men in the room, one standing apart and erect with a stern Germanic face—my superior in the biology department, one short and giggly in manner, and one tall man with a sharply narrow face that was like Abraham Lincoln's in that it was either intensely ugly or quite beautiful, depending on your point of view.

In a moment, the tall man approached me. "I'm Roscoe Bilder," he said stiffly. "English Department. Welcome to darkest Illinois. You're the new scientist, aren't you?"

"Instructor in biology."

"Good." He nodded. "Hope you grow to like this appalling place as much as I have learned to."

"Thank you. I plan to try."

He stood before me in shapeless brown jacket and loosely hanging flannel slacks, long legs twined together at the knees, his left hand clutching his right elbow. He sipped his punch and made a face. "Barbarous stuff!" Then he looked intently at me. "Listen, you're a scientist. Tell me, why does hot water *sound* hot? You know what I mean. Out of a boiling tea kettle it makes a flat *splat* while cold water sort of chirps. Why is that?"

"I don't really know. Something to do with its thermodynamic properties."

He smiled wearily. "Good scientific answer. Just give it a term and the question's answered."

"Well," I said a tad defensively, "maybe because it is lighter, being hot. Thinner, while cold water is heavy."

He nodded. "Better. May not be right but it does address the question." He turned and walked away.

Before I could sort out what exactly had happened, I was approached by a five foot ten female whose graying and thinning hair lifted straight off her head and then headed sideways in either direction. "I'm Mattie Pettit," she said in a voice that wobbled between soprano and tenor rather like Eleanor Roosevelt's. "Economics Department." Her mouth shaped a benign smile but I was slow to respond because I could not be certain she was looking at *me*. Her left eye seemed to be aimed southward toward me but her right eye was heading southwest. I decided to look at the middle of her forehead and said, "How do you do. Stephen Aspen."

"I know you have just come from Cornell," she said in her wobbly voice, "where the standards are high but I want you to know that our girls are very bright and *hard* working."

"That last part would be something of a change, at least as far as some of the Cornell men I've tutored," I offered.

A shortish, plump woman approached us, one I seemed

to have missed in my survey of thin-shouldered women. She was nicely rounded across the chest, looked to be in her forties, and still retained signs of striking, though now diminished, good looks. She spoke delicately and cocked her head coyly, "I'm Katharine Harris. Welcome to Kanaka College." She paused and smiled beseechingly. "I hope you like us."

"Thank you. Stephen Aspen."

After some inconsequential chat, while the two women told each other how glad they were that college was resuming, they drifted away.

My superior, chairman of the Biology Department, Helmut Brandenwein, approached me. "Have you met everybody?" he asked.

"Just a few."

"Takes time." He glanced around the room. "Not all of them worth meeting." He sipped his punch. "But that Bilder chap in English is good stuff. A little eccentric but brilliant mind."

"I did have a brief talk with him."

After a pause, Dr. Brandenwein turned abruptly to me. "Have you had a chance to go over that syllabus for Biology I yet? I want to sit down for a conference with you on it tomorrow." He looked sternly at me. "You know, we've never hired an M.A. in our department before, only Ph.D.'s. I want to be certain you can teach the syllabus the way it is written."

"I feel certain I can."

He nodded. "Come to my office at ten tomorrow."

After he stalked away, I stood around a while longer, chatting inconsequentially with my new colleagues, and then slipped out the door and down the stone steps beyond the tall columns fronting the building, McEwen Hall. At the bottom of the sloping lawn, Kanaka Lake twinkled and glinted in the gleam of the setting sun. Though calm and static, not captive of the restless tidal dynamics of the Yare River and Beach Plum Island Sound, the broad expanse of water beckoned reassuringly to me like an old friend. Besides, the area lay on the edge of the Mississippi Flyway, and I knew great flocks of ducks would come barreling down onto Kanaka during the autumnal migration. More old friends. I felt in need of friends.

I walked slowly along Elm Street, parallel to the lake shore, toward my rooming house, struggling against a mounting sense of alienation and depression. I remembered the parting words of sharp-faced, squirrel-mouthed Bill Byer, my professor of ornithology, "You're going to find that Midwestern *fee*-male"—he scorned the word with his nasal rasp—"college quite different from Cornell." He nodded knowingly. "But I don't know what else you can do. Teaching jobs are scarcer than hen's teeth right now with all the old birds hanging on till retirement"—he snickered, "little ornithological joke there—and our Department doesn't have the funds to offer you a fellowship. Besides," he said in his self-appointed role as gadfly and motivator, "that master's thesis of yours, although more than adequate for the requirement, it didn't exactly establish new scientific frontiers. Perhaps a year or two in the sticks will do you good, and you can come back here and do some honest-to-God research for your doctorate." At this moment, after surveying that roomful of my new associates, that "year or two" loomed like an eternity. But as Professor Byer had said, what else was there for me to do?

At the rooming house, a white frame narrow building, I climbed three flights of stairs to my room, one of three on the top floor with a single, antique bathroom for all three. I sat down at the small student desk and gazed out the window at the setting sun, a giant red ball dropping down into the Illinois plain and the vast prairie lands beyond. I picked up the syllabus for Biology I, the subject of my conference next day with Dr. Brandenwein, and found beneath it the latest letter from Meg Satterlee. We had maintained a companionable—I am not certain that word embraces all the emotional nuances involved—correspondence since my departure from Brixton. Her letters told me about daily affairs in the village, her workaday concerns at the library ("that book mutilator got five years for assault with a deadly weapon"), and occasionally ventured into affectionate reminiscence: "I miss hearing your step on the stairway and I miss hearing about your daily progress. Also I confess, I would like to visit your observation shed again, sleet or rain notwithstanding." That last remark was tantalizingly enigmatic to me. After our interlude on that stormy afternoon by the shore, Meg and I had been tenderly circumspect in our relations with each other, warily circling the question, as it were, whether we were now lovers or still just friends who had through circumstance ventured into a once-in-a-lifetime intimacy. For my part, I did not want to give Meg the impression I was taking anything for granted and though I tried to be as sensitive as I could to her feelings toward me, I could not really be certain one way or the other. And so, though the matter remained in limbo remarks like this one by Meg seemed to nibble at the edges of the question.

This letter did, however, touch on a matter of professional interest: "Stuart Price mentioned yesterday when he stopped by—he's been quite attentive to Mother and me since you left—that he is now working on a plan to make his place, along with some neighboring marshland downriver, into a nature sanctuary. He said you gave him the idea, and he wanted me to be sure to let you know." I remembered then the conversation he and I had had that blustery, wintry dusk after drinks at his "camp." I sat then for a while recalling the strange beauty of the salt marshes in winter, their restless creeks with the ceaseless tides always flowing in or out, the ice-sheathed marsh grass along their banks, and the sharp tang of the rich, organic mud on their bottoms. But then, the stern Germanic face of Dr. Brandenwein appeared in my mind's eye, and I set to work reviewing the syllabus.

The conference next day resembled more the oral examination for my master's degree than it did a conference between departmental colleagues, but I seemed to satisfy the strict German at last, and he grunted, "All right. Good enough. Good enough." Then I left the science building, Bradford Hall, with its formaldehyde-scented corridors, and went down the walkway toward the college post office in the basement of the Administration Building. I had no good reason to expect any mail but it was something to do. Part way there I encountered Roscoe Bilder.

"Oh, Mr. Aspen," he said quickly, almost stammering, "I was hoping to run into you." He looked at me fleetingly, then twined his long legs together at the knees and looked sideways, seemingly addressing himself to a nearby tree. "How are you getting along," he asked the tree. "I mean—"

"Fine," I said cheerfully, hoping somehow to ease things. "Good of you to ask."

"Well, I don't suppose—I mean, I know where you are living—I was just wondering—"

"Ye-s-s-s." I drew the word out as long as I could, hoping to give him time to find equilibrium.

"Well, see here," he said briskly. He glared at me, dark-lashed eyes narrowed behind thick lenses, his mouth twisting into odd shapes. "I've got a second floor apartment on the edge of campus. The man living with me last year went back to Yale to finish his degree. I thought maybe—well, I just don't know—" He stopped and turned again toward the tree. "It's not expensive!" he told the tree angrily.

I looked thoughtfully at this gangly, awkward man who seemed to be tortured by involvement in this mundane personal situation. "Well," I offered, "I'm not very comfortable where I am now."

"I should think not." He untwined his legs and then twined them in reverse order. "Well," he exploded, looking directly at me for a moment, "come by this afternoon about five and look the place over. I'll pour you a glass of sherry."

"Fine. I'll be there."

A little after five o'clock I rang the doorbell at the house he had pointed out and heard Bilder shout, "Come up!" He stood at the top of a straight stairway and stepped back into the room at the right as I approached. He gestured toward the large airy room with wide windows looking out toward Lake Kanaka. "Not too bad, would you say?" In contrast to his behavior on the walkway in the morning he now seemed wholly at ease, almost debonair. "Let me show you around."

The apartment consisted of two identical rooms separated by the landing at the top of the stairway. A large, modern bathroom stood between them with its door at the rear of the landing. Compared with my pinched room on the third floor of the narrow house this was luxurious, and it was furnished quietly and comfortably. But two questions concerned me: could I afford it and what would sharing an apartment with Roscoe Bilder be like?

The first question was answered shortly after we had finished our inspection and I had expressed my admiration. "You can have it for the same rent you're paying now," he said. "I've got the place as a steal because the landlady downstairs thinks I'm brilliant." He giggled briefly, putting his hand to his mouth. "Or something."

The second question seemed to answer itself over the next hour as Roscoe Bilder and I drank a fine sherry, chatted about a variety of things, and listened to records. It was clear to me then that living with Bilder would be never dull. Each day would bring a constant flow of revelations and erudition ranging broadly over literature, music, popular culture, and still unexplored matters his questing mind would search out. His conversation seemed to consist only of peaks—no valleys or plains—and it was ever surprising.

"I was teaching 'Romeo and Juliet' today," he said, "and I got that old shiver up the spine Shakespeare always gives me. Do you know, for example, that the first words of conversation Romeo and Juliet exchange form a perfect, fourteen-line, Elizabethan sonnet? A *sonnet*, mind you, the classic vehicle for love poetry! That's remarkable, of course, and great art, but the question really is, why did he bother? Those plays were written to be *heard*, not read—heard by a noisy, raffish audience, many of them standing or walking around eating oranges. Not one person in ten thousand would realize that those lines formed a sonnet. So why did he bother?" He sipped thoughtfully from his sherry. "Obviously because he was a master craftsman and it pleased him, delighted him, to put in those perfect touches. He did it for himself. He did not give a damn whether you noticed or not. He did it for himself, to perfect his craft."

Shortly later, he lifted his lanky form off the low couch across the room from me and went to his phonograph. "Do you like music?"

"Popular music mostly. I don't know much about classical music."

"Singers? Big bands? Who?"

"Benny Goodman. Gene Krupa."

Bilder made a face. "Krupa's a hacker, a tub thumper. Zutty Singleton or Sid Catlett, they're *real* jazz drummers. And Goodman, well, he's good technically but he plays up in an upper register most of the time and makes a clarinet sound like a tin whistle. Now, Barney Bigard with Ellington—there's an elegant jazz clarinetist. Big, broad fat tone you could walk around on. The real truth is," he said with head cocked, "that the black guys do it better. More supple, more taste, more restraint." He fingered a pile of records before him. "How about Fats Waller? Know him?"

"Barely."

"Fats plays a fine jazz piano but he's also a wonderful clown." He placed a record on the turntable and soon Fats Waller's bouncy piano was belting out "The Sheik of Araby." After the first chorus Fats sang and ended with "I'm the Shook, the Shake, the Sheek of Ara-bee!" Bilder on the couch laughed silently, shoulders shaking until he looked ready to fall over. "The Shook, the Shake, the Sheek of Ara-bee!" he chortled. "What a great spoof of that silly song.!"

Seven

"It's the third one over on the rack," Roscoe told me. "The bottle green one." He pointed to the canoe resting on its rack in the Kanaka College boathouse. The dusky light outlined the boats, the oars and paddles, and the spars and furled sails stacked along the walls. The spirited smell of fresh varnish mingled with the musty odor of damp wood in the gloom. We both crouched down below the rack and put a shoulder under the bow and stern, lifted the canoe off, carried her down the wooden-planked ramp to the water's edge, and gently launched her. "Climb aboard first, Stephen," Roscoe said crisply. "Step in the center, hands on both gunwales, and sit down quickly." I did as told and took the seat in the bow. He handed me a paddle and then boarded deftly, an action I found uncharacteristic of this usually gangling, awkward man. "Perhaps I should have asked," he said, "before I was so pedagogical. Do you know canoes?"

"Not really. Skiffs, small sailboats, a little."

"I was canoe instructor for five summers at Camp Hogmakinney in New Hampshire. Canoes are my bag, as the students say." He paddled out from the ramp then with strong, clean strokes, and the arrow-slim, shapely vessel—canoes *are* lovely in shape—skimmed swiftly over the smooth, blue water.

This was the first weekend after I had moved into the apartment, and one week as housemates had gone far to advance our relationship. After our encounter that morning on the walkway when Roscoe had offered to share his apartment with me, he had not again seemed hesitant or uncertain, and I began to think he was one of these people who are pathologically fearful of rejection, a man who would regard personal rejection as a vital attack on the core of his being. As a housemate, he was considerate, entirely respectful of my privacy, closing his door when playing his phonograph, and inviting me to join him once or twice for sherry. On Friday afternoon he had said, "If the weather is fair I plan to take my canoe out tomorrow. Would you like to join me?"

So, today, on a sparkling September morning, we were paddling westward, angling toward the southern shore. "I'm surprised by the size of this lake," I said, "Out here on the Illinois plain."

"Big lake, nearly ten miles long, with two arms that extend sideways from the main body." He chuckled with his characteristic wheezy, "Heh, heh, heh . . . Thank God for it! It's the only thing that saves this female seminary from being a prison."

We paddled silently for a while, and off to my right the red brick Georgian buildings of Kanaka College and the Hochdale town library tower grew steadily smaller. It was a classic September day, the late morning sun warming our backs and prinking the ripples beside the canoe with dancing sparkles. I was reveling in being aboard a boat again with the crisp air washing against my face and the broad blue sky arching overhead. But even while enjoying these surroundings I could not stifle a nagging sense of contrast between this placid Midwestern lake and the creeks and sounds of the New England seacoast. A lake is not like the sea. It is a static thing. It does not surge and fall, at least not perceptibly, and flow powerfully one way or another as commanded by a moon a quarter of a million miles away.

Its water is blue, not a mysterious sea green, and it is like tap water, drinkable, not enriched by the salts and minerals distilled by centuries of evaporation. Compared to the sea, a lake seems new, almost man-made, easily modified and governed, not like the ancient and unruly, willful sea. Oddly, until that morning on Kanaka Lake, I had not realized how much I had become captive to the lure of the seacoast, more particularly the New England coast. Then suddenly, without transition, I thought of Meg Satterlee, Meg with her gentle blue eyes and her blonde hair lying close to her shapely head. Seemingly, the enchantment of New England and thoughts of Meg were inseparable.

"I thought we'd put in at Billings Point," said Roscoe. "There's a funny little hotel there with a bar where we could get a beer and a sandwich."

"Fine with me."

After nearly an hour of paddling we came in sight of Billings Point, a tiny hamlet with a few frame buildings dominated by a Catholic church, identifiable by its bright gold cross flashing in the sunlight. Roscoe suddenly spoke up behind me. "Look at the cross on that church steeple! There's a perfect example of a thing symbolizing something utterly different from what it really is."

"How's that?"

"Well, look, it stands on that steeple as the symbol of Christianity and sanctity. But did you ever consider the original, basic function of crosses, what their purpose was before they became the Christian symbol? The cross was a device the Romans used to execute thieves and social revolutionaries, like Jesus. Think of it, a contrivance for capital punishment has become a revered sacred object like the star and crescent of the Moslems or the yin and yang of Chinese philosophers!" He chuckled, "Heh, heh, heh! What do you suppose would have happened if Jesus had appeared on earth during the French Revolution? Would the guillotine have become a sacred symbol instead of the cross?" He paused for a moment. "Or what if he appeared in 19th century England or here on the western plains. Would the hangman's noose have become the Christian symbol? Well," he chuckled again, "that at least would be better than the guillotine. More shapely." He made a clucking sound. "Well, anyway, you've got to admit it's really strange. One of those familiar things you accept uncritically until one day it hits you between the eyes."

"I admit, it never occurred to me." But then, I thought to myself, Roscoe constantly came up with startling ideas that had never occurred to me.

The barroom of the Billings Point Hotel was small and radiated a strong fragrance of aging spilt beer. Two men sat at the far end of the mahogany bar. Their shirts bore a logo for Jake's Plumbing which connected them with the Jake's Plumbing truck standing outside. As Roscoe and I eased up onto the stools, the bartender swiped the area before us with a greyish rag and asked, "What'll ya have, fellas?"

We ordered draught beers and ham sandwiches. The bartender placed two draught beers before us and walked back to the kitchen to make our sandwiches. 'Skol!" said Roscoe and then after the first sip he said, "I was 18 when I had my first beer at Louie's in New Haven."

"I must have been only 14 when my father invited me to join him after we had spent the morning cutting brush near our cottage at Clark's Lake."

"Yes, well, my father was Headmaster of Gidley's School for Boys in Connecticut. Abstinence and rectitude were our constant guides. You've heard of sheltered lives? Mine, until I got to college was damn near monastic." He sipped his beer and chuckled wheezily and somewhat ruefully. "Not that it has become wildly libertine since then." He turned to me with a knowing smile on his narrow face. "How about you, Stephen? Are you a pretty worldly fellow? Women by the dozen and all that?"

"Far from it."

He nodded at me as he said, "I guess you'd have to say we're a couple of ideal males to be teaching little women in a female seminary." He raised his glass. "Here's to a couple of Abelards with no Heloise in view!"

I raised my glass too but as I did memories of those lovely moments with Molly and Meg Satterlee, and also with Nancy after the high school senior prom, arose in my mind. Perhaps I was slightly misleading Roscoe. But I did not choose to confess.

By the end of the first month I felt I was hitting my stride as a teacher. Miss Pettit, the economics professor I had met at the reception, was right: Kanaka College girls *were* smart and hard-working. Their earnestness was almost intimidating. They hung intently on my every word and immediately wrote it down in their voluminous notebooks. It began to concern me that they were absorbing mere rote knowledge without any genuine understanding of what it meant or how it interrelated.

One day when I was making up a test on the musculature of a frog, I recalled the words of my gadfly Cornell professor, Bill Byer: "Don't recite mere facts; make your knowledge *work!*" His own examinations were models of ingenuity; they challenged you to shape your knowledge into new patterns, to demonstrate you understood how the parts made a whole. Remarkably, I looked forward to taking his exams, tough as they were. I recalled one of his exam questions and modelled my test question after it. I asked, "Suppose you were a frog and wished to sit down. What muscles would you use?" I heard several low chuckles around the room as the young feminine heads bent over their exam books. Afterward, Myra Pickens, an eager, narrow-faced girl, smiled at me as she turned in her blue book, "That was a fun exam, Mr. Aspen. Really fun!" It was my first gratifying moment as a teacher.

That evening, over sherry, I told Roscoe about my small triumph. "Myra Pickens?" he burst out, eyebrows arched high. "Myra Pickens! Why she's my honors student in

English." His tone was stern and proprietary. "Why in the world should she be taking Biology I?"

"To fulfill her science requirement, I suppose."

"That's ridiculous," he snapped and said no more, leaving me thoroughly puzzled and a bit resentful.

One Wednesday I found in my mailbox a small envelope addressed "Stephen Aspen, Esq" in a dainty feminine hand. Inside was an invitation for tea at 4 o'clock the following day with Barbara Harris, the plumpish woman I had met at the reception. I am not much for tea drinking but I saw no reason to affront a colleague by refusing. Besides I was intrigued by the glimpses I had caught of her flirtatious femininity which suggested she still clung to a self-image as a pretty, desirable woman.

She lived in a tiny cottage at the end of the village, and as I stepped up onto the porch she met me at her door, her once quite pretty face now skillfully tinted and creamed to the nearest possible approximation of its former comeliness. She cocked her head a little coyly and said mincingly, "Do come in to my humble abode." She stepped back and gestured me to a straight-backed chair with a round, plump, patterned cushion. She sat nearby on a high-backed sofa, leaning forward toward me. Outside the sun still shone through low clouds in the west but in the room the curtains were drawn and two lamps softly flattered her face and hair.

"Well, Mr. Aspen," she said, head cocked again, "how are you getting on? How do you like us so far?"

"Very much. My students are first rate."

"Wonderful." She smiled prettily, opening her lips slightly to display small, white teeth. "And how do you fancy your tea, my dear sir? With cream or lemon?"

"Neither, please. Just straight."

"My gracious, how very manly!" She looked at me playfully out of the corners of her eyes. Then she poured the tea daintily into a pink-flowered cup and handed it to me. With her own cup of tea in hand she leaned back and said, "I'm not surprised you find our girls capable. Kanaka College has had a tradition of high standards dating way back to its founding in 1905. A long tradition."

A tradition for slightly less than fifty years did not seem remarkably venerable to me after a year in New England, but I merely said, "Yes."

"You know the story of its founding, don't you? A charming little tale." She nodded at me. "Just."

"No, I don't." I sipped my tea which tasted like sweet flower blossoms.

"Mercer Burton, the founder, was a very successful Illinois industrialist who had two daughters. He sent them to the University at Urbana and was so horrified by the stories they told him of carousing there that he removed them immediately and had them privately tutored. Then he decided to establish a college for young women and stipulated that traditions of morality and scholarship must always be maintained."

"I see. And named the college after the lake."

"*Au contraire!*" She said, tossing her head back with a girlish giggle as though savoring an enormous joke. "The lake was *renamed* after the college. Mr. Burton had been fascinated by Indian lore as a boy and knew about the Kanakas, a sub-grouping of the Plains Indians, who lived on the shores of this lake. It was then called Crabtree Lake, but a politician friend of Mr. Burton arranged to have the lake renamed after the College was founded."

"Interesting."

"Really quite charming." Again she nodded and said, "Just."

We sipped our tea quietly for a time, and then Miss Harris asked, "Do I understand you are living in Mr. Bilder's apartment?"

"Yes, I am."

"Well—" she paused and then smiled forbearingly—"I hope you are comfortable there."

"I am indeed. Very."

"I'm pleased to hear that." She paused and then said primly, "But you know, Mr. Bilder is—how shall I say?"— she cocked her head like a bird—"*in-ter-est-ing?*"

"He certainly is that."

"Well—" She put her cup down and looked down as she smoothed her dress over her lap. "I shall say no more." Then after a pause she looked up brightly. "Do you enjoy going to an occasional film, Mr. Aspen? I mean a good drama? The theater over in Herrin—it's just twelve miles away—has quite respectably good films from time to time. I often go myself, and I'm always looking for company. The drive home at night, you know. After dark." She gave me a knowing glance. "So, if I see something good coming along, per-ha-a-aps?" Her expression, with eyebrows arched and head cocked once again, was as seductive as Cleopatra's.

"That would be fun."

"Splendid! We'll keep it in mind."

After another cup of tea and small talk spiced with secret little smiles and sidelong glances out of delicately mascaraed eyes, I made my escape, pleading I had examination papers to grade. Her handshake as I went out the door was caressing and clinging. "Goodbye, dear sir," she said softly. "And do come back again."

The first semester continued to flow along at a stately, academic pace, and I gained confidence steadily in my teaching skills. November blustered into southern Illinois with winds that whipped Lake Kanaka into a foaming froth, and the walk from the apartment to the science building was a struggle against buffeting winds. But inside the classroom and the biology laboratory studious calm prevailed, or what passes for calm, that is, in the assemblage of twenty high-spirited and voluble young females. I had grown somewhat accustomed—hardened perhaps is a better word—to the shrill chirping of the girls before class began, a decibel-loaded keening that would daunt any male and sometimes made me momentarily quail before going through the door.

But one day during a laboratory session devoted to dissecting a mollusk I thought more concentration and less chatter would be beneficial. Then, as I often did, I recalled the acerbic words of Bill Byer and I said, "Ladies. The word *laboratory* can be divided into two quite different words: *labor* and *oratory*. Let's have more of the first and less of the second." Then, to pique their scientific curiosity and possibly some other biological interests as well, I said, "If you look carefully at the lower portion of your specimen you can see a rudimentary penis." There were a couple of titters and then a hush descended until Myra Pickens raised her hand and said, "Sir, I can't find the rudimentary penis. Could you point it out to me please?" Again, there were titters but they subsided as I went to Myra's bench and pointed to the tiny organ on the microscopic slide.

Altogether a satisfactory teaching day, I thought as I walked home through the November dusk. I also amused myself by trying to weigh how much of Myra's question had sprung from scientific curiosity and how much from hormonal drives. Over sherry I put the question to Roscoe, being careful, after my previous experience, to leave Myra Pickens' name out of the account.

Leaning back against the book-lined wall behind the low sofa, he said, "About fifty-fifty, I would say. If she's a serious student."

"I guess that's right."

"But, Stephen, this whole business of mammalian sex is strange, don't you think?" His sharp face was serious, his eyes behind the glasses narrowed. "You as a biologist must find this system of inserting the sperm inside the body of the female where the egg rests to be a mighty strange arrangement."

"It's certainly more efficient than the system many fish use, having the female lay the eggs on the bottom and the male spraying sperm over them. The male mammal delivers his sperm right to the egg."

"How about birds? Don't they do it better?"

"Well, maybe. But I sure would not want to be a female duck. The drake hammers her on the back of the head until he knocks her silly and then half drowns her while copulating."

Roscoe shook his head grimly. "Well, I certainly would not want to be a female mammal either. Just the thought of having my body penetrated makes my skin crawl." He shook his head again. "Surely the revulsion against having your body penetrated must be universal."

"Well, perhaps," I said dubiously.

"Well, it certainly is revolting to me, and I believe it is a fundamental reaction. That being so, can you imagine how powerful the instinct to mate must be to cause females to submit to the violation of penetration? Can you imagine how strong that force must be to overcome that basic human revulsion?"

"I believe you are leaving out of account some emotional and hormonal factors, but when you put it that abstractly, no. No, I can't."

Roscoe stared at me for a moment and then chuckled ruefully. "Abstractly is the only way I know about human sexuality so far," he said. "My only other guide to thinking about it comes from lines by William Butler Yeats.

'And love has pitched his tent,/In the place of excrement'."

Eight

Slush, sleet, and gloomy days invaded the Kanaka campus in early December. Wading from house to laboratory and back again became more and more irksome, and the students began to droop like caged birds as the semester droned to a close. They yearned to fly home to family and friends and Christmas parties. Roscoe announced he was going home to Connecticut, "Though God knows why." And I was trying to decide between going back to Ithaca for the holidays or staying in Hochdale. Staying put had the twin advantages of saving money and impressing Dr. Brandenwein with my devotion to science if I spent some of those days in the laboratory.

In this state of ennui and indecision I sat with Roscoe one evening listening to music. At my request he was playing the Brahms Fourth Symphony which I remembered liking at a Boston Symphony concert I had attended with Meg Satterlee. We sat silently through the first movement with its lovely arching and swooping theme, but then as the symphony moved on I noticed Roscoe frowning and shaking his head. Finally he sat up straight and burst out, "Listen to that bastard! He's scared shitless like the rest of us but instead of facing it he bluffs and blusters, as though mortality does not exist or is escapable."

I was baffled as I had been at other times by Roscoe's sudden flights on unexpected tangents, some of which I later found deeply insightful. I knew there was probably more to come so I kept silent.

"Mozart, you see, by contrast has guts," he went on. "Mozart walks right up to the brink of the abyss called mortality, looks down into its depths without flinching, and then says, 'Life is lovely while it lasts. So let's live it joyously'." He hoisted himself off the low sofa. "I'll show you what I mean. Let me play the second and third movements of Mozart's Piano Concerto in A Major, Koechel 488."

He set the pickup on the record and the music began with piano and orchestra playing a slow stately theme followed by other grave and solemn passages. The themes were lovely, sweet but not sentimental, not at all funereal. Instead, they were serene, bespeaking thoughtfulness and philosophical reflection. At least that is what I felt, guided by Roscoe's comments. The following movement was lively and joyous with piano and orchestra capering and dancing delightfully. In a way, it reminded me of Benny Goodman's "Let's Dance!" At least in spirit.

"See what I mean, Stephen?" asked Roscoe earnestly as he took the record off the turntable and slipped it in its jacket. "See the difference from Brahms?"

"Yes, I think so."

He shook his head, mouth twisted in a wry smile. "God, it's hard work civilizing a scientist. But it is a worthy cause."

"No harder or more worthy than making a literary man scientifically literate."

"*Touché.*" He grinned at me. "Speaking of culture, the movie theater in Herrin is showing a rerun of Laurence Olivier's *Henry the Fifth.* I'd like to see it again. Why don't we go tomorrow night?"

"Fine with me."

The next night we walked to the little garage behind the house—a shed barely large enough to house the car—and got into Roscoe's Chevrolet coupe. As before, I found

Roscoe's driving technique trying. His procedure was to push hard on the accelerator until he reached forty-five or fifty and then take his foot abruptly off so that we advanced over the road in a series of lurches. As usual, though, his conversation was diverting.

"Tell me, Stephen," he said above the drone of the Chevy engine, "what is the evolutionary value of hairlessness for humans? All our near relatives, like chimpanzees, are totally furry, hair from top to bottom. Being without fur certainly has been no advantage. Man has had to kill other animals for their furry skins and resort to all kinds of other strategies just to keep warm enough to survive. We'd all be much better off if we were as furry as dogs or apes. So why are we not?"

We droned on through the night for some time while I ransacked my mind for possible explanations. But all I could come up with was a blank. How *could* there be any survival advantage in being hairless and exposed to deadly cold? I finally had to admit I was stumped. "It's a good question," I said. "I don't know."

"Hmmmm," said Roscoe.

Throughout most of "Henry V," I was deeply engrossed with the swift-moving drama and the soaring language, especially when Laurence Olivier, his tenor voice flaring like a golden horn, cried, "Once more unto the breach, dear friends, once more!" But during one of the scenes with Fluellen, the Welsh captain, whom I could scarcely understand, my mind reverted to Roscoe's question about man's lack of fur and suddenly it struck me: a neutral mutation. I nudged Roscoe beside me. "I've got it, Roz. It's a mutation—"

"Later," he hissed. "*Later!*"

As we slowly made our way up the aisle amidst the murmuring crowd and the smell of popcorn, Roscoe exclaimed, "What a patriotic paean! I was all ready to go fight the bloody French myself!" Later, just as we were getting into the car Roscoe turned his head suddenly and said in a low voice, "Did you see that?"

"See what?"

He turned the key and started the engine. "I'll tell you in a minute after I've extricated us from this parking lot." Shortly later, when we were on the road back to Hochdale, he asked, "What was it you were trying to tell me about mutation?"

"Oh, a possible explanation for man's lack of fur. You see, not all mutations improve survival capability. Six toes, for instance. Some cats produce a sixth toe. Doesn't enhance or diminish survivability."

"My grandmother had a sixth finger."

"Survive okay?"

"Obviously."

"Well, there you are. Hairlessness may have been a mutation that came along fairly late in human evolution, maybe after he had learned to use tools and weapons. By then he could clothe himself by killing and skinning other animals, so he no longer needed fur."

"Hmmmm. Not bad, Stephen, not bad."

We drove in silence for a while until I asked, "What was it you saw in the parking lot?"

"Oh, Professor Barbara Harris."

"She told me she often comes here to the movies."

"Her being there is not surprising. Who she was with, *is*."

"Who?"

"Pete Domenico, the young mechanic at Springdale Chevrolet. He services my car so I recognized him."

"Well, maybe he also services Barbara's—uh, chassis?"

"Never mind, Stephen," Roscoe snapped. "Never mind." He made those clicking sounds with his tongue against the roof of his mouth that are usually expressed as "tsk, tsk."

When we got home I found on my desk a letter, a small blue envelope addressed in Meg Satterlee's feminine hand. Roscoe must have picked it up in the afternoon mail. Inside, I found bits of village news and then: "Stuart"—this had to be Stuart Price—"asked me to tell you he would like to talk with you about the nature preserve project and hoped you might come this way during your Christmas vacation. He said he would put you up for a few days. But, dear Stephen, if you do come, Mother and I would love to have you stay with us too. You could have your old room back while Miss Patton, our roomer, goes home to Providence for the holidays."

My indecision about Christmas vanished. I went into Roscoe's room, letter in hand. "Hey, Roz, I'm going to Massachusetts for Christmas."

He turned back from the bookshelf he was facing. "Wonderful, Stephen. We can go together. We'll take the Greyhound to Chicago and the New York Central Wolverine Express from Chicago to Boston. That's great."

Seeing Meg again, seeing her standing in her doorway before me, blithe and comely, I was taken by surprise. Somehow, in the six months or so since I had seen her last, I had stylized my mental image of her. She had become in my mind almost nun-like, with gentle blue eyes, pale coloring and a meek expression—rather like one of those Victorian prints of a medieval lady pining for her departed knight. But here she stood before me, vital and vibrant in her Christmas-red dress, face bright with color and eyes merry with delight.

And her greeting surprised me too. On the trip back East, lying in my Pullman upper berth as the Wolverine Express devoured the miles across New York State and the sleeping car swayed and jounced and the steel wheels reiterated their cheerful clickety-click, clickety-click, clickety-click, I had wondered once again about our relationship. It seemed that Meg had been giving me ambiguous signals, sometimes almost sisterly in her affection, and other times teasingly amorous, like her suggestion about visiting my observation shed again, "rain or sleet notwithstanding." Today, she rushed up, threw her arms around my neck, pressed her body hard against mine saying, "Stephen, you old darling!" and kissed me hard on the mouth. Still pressing close, she threw her head back and said, "My goodness, am I glad to see you!" Then she released me and stepped back. "Let's look at you. Have you changed?" She cocked her head quizzically and then nodded. "Mmmm, I'd say yes, a little. A bit more professorial. But still the same sweet Stephen." She took my hand. "Come in and say hello to Mother while I make some tea and bring in the brownies I baked for you."

Despite Meg's gay, open warmth I could not help at first feeling stiff and uncertain around her, not really at ease. And quite soon Meg noticed and confronted me. "Stephen, my dear, you seem to be holding back somehow, keeping your distance. What is it?"

I hesitated. "I'm sorry, Meg. I don't quite know myself—I feel disembodied almost, as though I were not here." I knew this was somewhat disingenuous, although true in itself it was not the whole truth. I went on: "It may be just the sudden change of place, from Illinois to New England. The tremendous contrast."

"Ye-s-s-s," she said dubiously. "But there seems to be something more to it, something more physical. You seem shy about being close to me, touching me. Are you uncertain about you and me, our relationship?"

"Ye-s-s, I guess, in a way. It seems ambiguous to me."

"Ambiguous? Why?" She narrowed her eyes, puzzled. "Oh, because of that stormy afternoon at the shore?"

I looked down into her calm blue eyes. "Well, yes."

Smiling, she put her hands on my shoulders. "Listen, you silly old thing. That was a lovely, impulsive incident between two adult, willing people. It created no obligations and for me, no regrets." She shook my shoulders. "Now, you'll have to stop acting as though being close to me would give you poison ivy. I don't intend to let you make love to me even if you want to." She stepped back and chuckled. "Not unless you get me sopping wet again and chilled to the bone."

Sunday morning, the day before Christmas 1952, was a classic New England winter's day, and I was happier than I had been in months, being in Clinton Avery's familiar old skiff, again, heading down the Yare River toward a white gold sun lifting over the ice-decked salt marshes. I had asked Meg to join me in a nostalgic visit to my observation shed on Stuart Price's knoll, the place where I had spent so many happy and fruitful hours watching ducks living their lives on the ever-changing waters of Beach Plum Island Sound. Meg sat facing me, bulky in a down-filled parka with the fur-lined hood framing her glowing face. A skein of golden-eyes lifted off the glittering water ahead and a merganser came whistling past just above the surface. In the diamond-studded sun path ahead the black silhouette of a harbor seal's head jutted through the water for a moment and then sank tracelessly from sight.

Inside, I was virtually singing with joy. Once again I had that glowing sense of being embraced by New England, resonating in response to its splendid landscape—the intricate seacoast and the rock-studded hills—and its sustaining traditions, burnished by time and the generations. More immediately, I savored the salt marshes—vividly alive and ever-changing in the flush and flow, the in-and-out, of the ceaseless tides. The marshes and their residents, the clamoring, raucous ducks, had been my companions on long, solitary days. And today it seemed, as Avery's venerable Seagull outboard chugged down the river, that they were welcoming me back. To add to my mood of happy reunion I had sitting before me sweet Meg whom I found more delightful than ever.

"I can see the roof," shouted Meg above the clamor of the outboard. "Your shed is still standing."

I beached the skiff, her bow crunching up on a thin layer of ice at the water's edge, and we clambered ashore. About four inches of crusty snow lay glistening in the slanting sunshine, and small animals and birds had left their imprints on the white surface. A red fox had inspected the place, with two forepaw prints on the cinder block before the door recording his visit. I opened the door and stepped over a small drift of snow on the sill. I stood for a moment looking around at this monument to my previously untried building skills. Gazing at the accurately placed studs, the cleanly cut rafters, and the tight, solid flooring, I could scarcely believe I had done all that work. But there the little building stood, sturdy and shipshape.

"Does it feel like home?" asked Meg behind me.

"Astonishingly so. As though I had left it yesterday. Illinois and Kanaka College seem like a dream I had last week. Or last month."

Meg sat down at the cot facing the window looking out on the Sound. "Tell me about Kanaka College. You haven't talked about it at all."

"That's true." I sat down beside her gathering my thoughts. "I guess that's because I don't quite know what to say."

"Do you like it?"

"Some things about it, yes. I like the teaching."

"What about the people, your associates?"

I shook my head. "Mixed bag. I've got a bear of a department head, Dr. Brandenwein, a Prussian martinet. Some of the people are strange, unlike anyone I've met before, but the man I'm sharing an apartment with, Roscoe Bilder, is fascinating. Brilliant and fascinating."

Meg put her hand on my knee and patted it. "You seem mixed in your mind. Uncertain."

I turned toward her and put my arm around her shoulders. "More than uncertain. Suspended in thin air. When I'm not in Hochdale it's as though it does not exist, and even when I'm there it's shadowy."

We sat silently for a moment and I watched a large raft of goldeneyes and whistlers bobbing on the choppy water. They made me nostalgic for those long hours I had sat taking notes.

"You remember, dear, that Stuart is coming by this afternoon to take us to his house for dinner," Meg said.

"Yes, I remember. Shall we start back?"

"Yes, we should." She turned her head toward me, blue eyes crinkling at the edges and a small secret smile on her lips. "But before we leave here," she said, "I think it would be nice if you kissed me. For old times' sake, you might say."

I put my hand under her chin, tilted her face up to mine, and expressed in my kiss a mix of warm affection and the joy of returning to this special place. It became somewhat protracted, but soon Meg put her hand beside my face and pushed me gently away. "That will do just fine," she said. She smiled lovingly up at me. "For now, at least."

Nine

"As I remember, Stephen," said Stuart Price standing before me with a bottle of S.S. Pierce bourbon in one hand and a jigger in the other, "you like yours on the rocks with a splash of water."

"That's right, thank you." I was sitting beside Meg on a large leather sofa facing the stone fireplace where oak logs blazed and crackled. Two other guests, Benjamin Coffin, a fortyish man with glasses and the shoulders of an athlete—introduced by Price as "my lawyer"—and his wife Nancy, a quietly handsome, brown-haired woman, sat on either side of the fireplace.

"I know how you like yours, Meg dear, and I promise not to make it too strong this time."

"Good man, Stuart," said Meg smiling sweetly up at him. "We remember how fatal that can be."

Price handed us our drinks in wide mouthed, heavy bottomed glasses and turned to Mrs. Coffin. "And you, Nancy?"

"Might I have a scotch and soda?"

"Scotch and—," he turned back to the drinks cabinet. "Whups, no soda here." He turned to Meg. "Meg, my dear, would you mind fetching a bottle of soda while I make Ben's martini? You know where it is in the pantry."

"Of course." Meg set her glass down on the low table before us and went to the kitchen. I watched her slender, shapely figure departing and silently weighed how much intimacy this small exchange between Price and Meg reflected. Conclusion: rather more than I found comfortable.

Later, as the conversation began to take shape and gather momentum, I savored the atmosphere of this traditional New England room, its small-paned windows, dark panelled walls, oriental-carpeted floors, and tall mahogany chests bristling with gleaming, ornate brass pulls. The tables bore bronze statuettes of crouching tigers and rearing horses while the walls displayed oil portraits of earlier Prices. I sipped the robust whiskey and mused over the contrast between this tradition-laden room and the apartment I shared with Roscoe in Illinois. Here the multilayered past seemed to embrace the visitor, to make him part of a rich continuum peopled by generations of earnest contributors to history and tradition. In Illinois, by contrast, the visitor felt—at least, I felt—solitary, a lone individual in a broad, nearly featureless landscape.

Stuart Price brought me back into the conversation, saying, "As I told you, Ben, Stephen gave me the idea for making my place a wild bird sanctuary."

Coffin nodded in recognition. "I remember."

"How have you decided to set it up in legal terms?" Price asked.

"I think making it a trust, a land preservation trust, is the way to go. But before we can start filing legal documents we need to establish exact boundaries, have a land survey, and get a precise statement of the functions and purposes of the trust."

Price turned to me. "That's where I hope Stephen can help while he's here."

"I'll do my best, but this is really outside my range of competence."

"But you know what to ask," Price said, nodding at me.

As he turned back to Coffin, Meg slyly slid her hand across the leather cushion and gave mine a squeeze.

Next morning over a mug of blistering coffee as we breakfasted in his snug, kerosene-stove-warmed cottage in the salt marsh, Stuart Price said, "I've got neighbors on two sides willing to join me in the project, each putting up somewhere between fifty and seventy-five acres. With my holding, that amounts to something like five hundred acres along the Sound north of the Yare. One question is, do we need to fence in all that? That's a helluva lot of fencing."

"I don't think so. Maybe along the western edge running beside the highway, but otherwise probably not."

Conversation about the nature conservancy went on throughout a breakfast of sausages and fried eggs, with Price asking detailed questions and I answering as best I could with a combination of half-knowledge and guesswork. After our second cup of rich coffee—S.S. Pierce's special brand, of course—he said, "Let's take a look around. See who is visiting us just now."

Late December offers two kinds of weather on the New England seacoast: leaden days with heavy skies and brilliant days that pierce the eye. This morning was one of the eye-piercing kind with the sky a diamond blue and the sun flashing dancing sparkles across the snowy marshland. The sharp air went down to the bottom of my lungs with every breath, and the snow crunched and creaked beneath my feet. Out on the Sound, gabbling and jostling were my old friends, goldeneyes, whistlers, ruddy ducks, bluebills, and, of course, the bustling, marauding widgeons.

"There they are," said Price. "Your charges."

"*My* charges?"

He turned to me, a confident smile on his strong, ruddy face. "Having launched this project with your suggestion, you're planning on seeing it through, aren't you?"

"In what way?"

"By advice and counsel for the present and later by—" He broke off and pointed out at the ducks? "Did you see that? What's that widgeon doing, snatching weeds out of the bluebill's beak?"

I looked out at the familiar event. "It's a constant pattern, a kind of symbiosis between the diving ducks and widgeons who stay mostly on the surface."

"Never saw it before in all my years here."

"My account of it in my master's thesis caused quite a hot argument among my professors at the examination. But you were saying—"

"Oh, well, I was saying that once we get this conservancy set up it will need some kind of continuing supervision, and I'm hoping we can find some way to involve you in that."

"Pretty hard to imagine how I could do that while teaching in Illinois."

He turned to me and nodded. "True, but maybe we can work out something to bring you back here."

That seemed to me a possibility too remote to consider, but I said nothing. Later, as we were walking back to the cabin, Price asked, "How does Meg seem to you these days?"

My wariness system immediately went on full alert. During the dinner party the night before I had observed an intimacy between Price and Meg that had grown considerably since I had left Brixton. Watching the way they spoke and smiled at each other awakened in me proprietary feelings about Meg, feelings considerably stronger than I had thought existed. So, wariness suggested I counter the question with a question. "Why, do you think she has changed recently?"

"Well, yes, I guess. In a way." We continued to crunch across the snowy ground where stiff spikes of marsh grass stabbed now and then through the glistening crust. "It seems to me she is beginning to reach out more from that narrow life she has lived so long with her mother. To break out of that cocoon."

"Oh? Less attentive to her mother?" I knew the answer to that question but I wanted to draw Price out.

"No, never! But she must be aware that her mother is failing considerably."

I decided to ease off a little. "Yes, I'm sure that's so. Her mother does seem to have aged greatly since last spring."

We had reached the front door of the little cottage resting on its knoll. As Price put his hand on the knob, he turned to me with a confident smile on his face. "Meg will be relieved of that responsibility sometime in the next year, I fully believe, and when that occurs I intend to do what I once told you I would—ask her to marry me."

"Did Stuart say anything about your taking on supervision of his nature preserve after it's established?" asked Meg. "He told me at dinner last week that he intended to ask you to do it."

We were sitting on the maple-armed sofa in the snug low-ceilinged living room with small glasses of sherry before us. Meg had helped her infirm mother up the stairway to her bedroom and had come back down wearing fluffy bedroom slippers. She had turned the radio on to the Boston classical music station and the evocative sounds of Debussy's "La Mer" flowed softly through the room.

"Yes, in a general way."

"And what do you think, dear?"

"It's too vague an idea for me to think anything. I certainly can't supervise—whatever that means—a Massachusetts nature preserve while teaching in Illinois."

"Oh, no, of course not. But I think Stuart had in mind your coming back here." She set her sherry down and laid her warm, firm hand over mine. "And I can't think of anything nicer than that." Her serene blue eyes looked deep into mine, and I leaned over and kissed her gently. She placed her hand softly beside my mouth, and I put my arm around her shoulders and pulled her close. Inside me was a powerful surge of affection reaching toward desire. My recent conversation with Stuart Price had made Meg infinitely more precious to me, more desirable to possess, than ever before. In a moment Meg pushed me gently away. "Not now, Stephen darling. Not now." Her blue eyes were beseeching. "Too many things are bearing in on me at present. Mother's failing condition and—and several other things. I can't deal with any more just now, dear, Not just now."

Ten

"Here's one for you Stephen," said Roscoe emerging from the steam-filled bathroom wearing only a towel, his thin chest and torso glowing pink. "What causes your fingers to get wrinkled from being submerged in water?"

Six months of living with Roscoe had accustomed me to the unceasing questing of his mind, but also I had learned to recognize in these questions the bright 12-year old boy who spends an hour with the encyclopedia and then says to the nearest adult, "Did you know that the incubation temperature of alligator eggs determines the sex of the baby alligators? Low temperature produces females, high temperature, males? Why do you suppose that is?"

Still, I felt, as Roscoe intended I should feel, obliged to come up with an answer. And I had learned to make my answer sound authoritative whether I knew what I was talking about or not. "The skin softens and stretches during immersion and that produces wrinkles," I said with greater vocal assurance than inner certainty.

"Mmmm. I suppose you're right."

By the calendar, mid-March, winter was nearing an end but blizzard flurries and grey slush declared that winter's death was not imminent. The first two months of the college spring semester are always the dreariest. My students worked hard, as usual, but it seemed to me doggedly and cheerlessly. My own state of mind resembled theirs but with an added nagging uncertainty about my future. Dr. Brandenwein had made no mention of extending my contract another year and the Cornell department was silent about calling me back as a graduate assistant. As for that other alternative, Stuart Price had made only vague allusions to my returning to Brixton in some capacity although Meg's affectionate letters always expressed hope I would.

So I attended classes, prepared and graded examinations, read term papers, and held student conferences. One gleam of brightness in this grey was the blossoming of some of my students, those who displayed unfolding questing minds. Foremost was Myra Pickens, Roscoe's honor student, who invariably asked the acute question that illuminated the discussion.

Myra also began visibly to take greater care with her personal appearance, wearing discreet makeup, even including a little eye-liner. Coincidentally, I seemed to see some subtle changes in my housemate: brighter ties and fresh shirts daily. His conversation, though always brilliant, was sunnier and less mordant. I did not make a connection between these two observations until I happened to be passing Roscoe's office door one day just as Myra Pickens was leaving. She was looking back over her shoulder with a beguiling smile while he leaned against the door jamb, his eyes soft with affection.

When he saw me he straightened quickly and said crisply, "Oh, Stephen. Going back to the house? Wait up and I'll walk with you."

Walking across the campus, stepping around slushy puddles and dodging glops of wet snow as they fell from the trees, Roscoe said, "I'm very impressed with Miss Pickens' work on her honors essay."

I wanted to say something similar about her work in Biology I but I recalled Roscoe's explosion when I had mentioned that Myra was in my class. So instead I asked, "What's her subject?"

"William Morris, the Victorian figure. She's analyzing fallacies in his socialist theories."

"Oh," I said, thereby exhausting my views on William Morris.

"She's beginning the writing phase, and I've suggested she come to the apartment Friday afternoon so we can work on her draft without interruption."

Again, the only contribution I could manage was "Oh."

As it happened, on that Friday afternoon I met Barbara Harris as I was emerging from the College post office where I found my usually empty letter box, empty. "Oh, Mr. Aspen," she said, a bright smile dimpling her cheeks and displaying white teeth, "what a coincidence that I should run into you! I was just thinking about you in connection with a film that is showing over in Herrin. You remember we talked about joining forces sometime, and this is a film I'm certain you would enjoy."

"Oh?"

Before I could come up with some other stalling gambit she pushed on, "Yes, it's an Alec Guiness comedy called 'The Captain's Paradise.' I'm told it's slightly naughty"— she simpered and cast her eyes down for an instant and then raised them slowly to meet mine—"the captain has two wives in the film, you see, one in each port—but I understand it's very droll. And he's such a splendid actor, don't you agree?"

To answer that seemed safe enough, so I said, "He certainly is. I remember him in 'The Lavender Hill Gang'." I halted, asking myself whether I had that title right. Was it "Gang" or "Mob?" Probably "Mob."

When I turned my attention from looking inward to the upturned face of Professor Harris, she was earnestly saying, "and the English have such a delicious sense of humor, don't you find?" She nodded and added, "Just."

Here again, no visible snares so I said, trying to seem to be entering into the spirit of the discussion, "Oh, I agree." But just ahead, I knew, lay the crunch, the answer-demanding question. And then it came.

"Then shall we make it a twosome tonight?" she asked, cocking her head and smiling beseechingly. "Shall I come by and pick you up in my car about seven?"

Trapped but determined to break free, I said, "Oh, Professor Harris—"

"Barbara."

"Well, uh, Ba-Barbara, I really can't tonight. I—"

"Oh, dear. I was so hoping you could join me." Her voice was low and pleading, and as I looked down into her upturned face, her blue eyes earnest and entreating, I wavered and nearly weakened. After all, what was I afraid of? Was I concerned that this fortyish woman, struggling to retain the beauty and appeal that had once been hers, and desperately seeking the company of a man, would somehow assault me or entrap me? No, not exactly, but still I sensed something like a web, a tissue of involvement, that reached out from her, an entanglement it seemed prudent to avoid. "Well, really, Profess—"

"Barbara."

"Ba-Barbara. I know I would enjoy going to the Alec Guiness movie with you tonight, but I'm afraid duty calls. I've got a stack of midterm reports to read and an exam to prepare." As I spoke I could see her expression changing from disappointment to hope, her mouth opening with indrawn breath as though about to speak, and I sensed she might be going to suggest some other night on the weekend, so I rushed on, "I'm really going to be working like a beaver the whole weekend."

Immediately she released her indrawn breath and her expression changed back to disappointment. "I'm so sorry. I was so hoping we could enjoy this lovely little film together." She paused again then and laid her hand on my arm. "Do let's try again." She cocked her head and mustered up a small smile. "Don't forget now, sir. We have a date to see a film together sometime in the future." She made a little sidestep and then walked mincingly on, head held high.

Relieved but disturbed, troubled by the visible chagrin I had caused this lonely woman, guilty only of reaching out to me, I hurried on across the campus. As I climbed the steps to the apartment I could hear murmuring voices in Roscoe's room and then a tinkle of feminine laughter. I went quietly into my own room and hung my overcoat and hat in the closet. Just as I was sitting down at my desk I heard Roscoe and Myra Pickens out on the landing. "This was a good session, Myra," he said. "We'll meet here again next week when you finish that next section."

"I'll have it ready, Mr. Bilder. And thank you for that lovely sherry. It will fortify me against the cold." She laughed a somewhat artificial, adolescent laugh and skipped down the stairs. "Bye-bye," she called back.

In a few moments Roscoe strolled into my room almost visibly glowing with satisfaction, his narrow face creased in an uncharacteristically warm smile. "I've just had an excellent conference with My—Miss Pickens," he said, rubbing his hands together in a washing motion. "What a rewarding student she is. So responsive!"

I gazed at the gangling figure before me, twining his legs together like vines, without responding. Most of the things I could think of to say would not be appropriate, nor appreciated.

But Roscoe was too full of euphoria to notice, and he pushed on, "You know, Stephen, here it is Friday night of a good week at the teaching factory, and I think we ought to celebrate. There's an Alec Guiness movie on in Herrin that I'd like to see. I think he's funny as hell. The way he rolls his eyes, feigning innocence while loaded with guile, puts me in stitches."

"I can't, Roscoe. I turned down Barbara Harris just ten minutes ago. She asked me to go with her tonight but I fobbed her off. We might run into her there, and I'd feel like a louse. I already feel guilty."

"Barbara Harris, that posey, affected female! Why do you care what she thinks? Besides, she probably won't go to-night. I just looked outside and it's sleeting again. She won't drive in this stuff."

I protested some more, telling Roscoe I had no desire to cause further pain to that lonely woman, but I did not protest long and hard enough. Eventually, it seemed a choice be-tween disappointing an exuberant Roscoe or running an unlikely risk of meeting Barbara Harris. I gave in against my better judgment.

But after two hours of chuckling over Alec Guiness' artful portrayal of a ferry boat captain with a wife on each side of the Straits of Gibralter—savoring his austere de-meanor with his staid English wife in Gibralter and his dashing abandon while cavorting with his Moroccan dancer wife in Tangiers—I found myself, while leaving the sud-denly bright movie theater, amidst the aroma of spilled popcorn and the hubbub of the chattering throng, walking side by side with Barbara Harris. When I noticed her she was looking up at me with reproachful eyes. She said noth-ing, shook her head once, and turned away, but the hurt in her eyes was sharp and stabbing. At her side was the Chevrolet mechanic we had seen her with before, Pete Domenico.

When we reached the sidewalk, Roscoe who had appar-ently not seen Barbara, said to me, "Let's have a beer at the hotel bar before we start back." Then he turned and asked, "Wasn't that a delightful picture?" His euphoria which had begun with his afternoon session with Myra Pickens had not lessened and bonhomie exuded from him. I was too troubled by the pain I had found in Barbara's eyes to re-spond but I followed him silently to the shabby hotel bar and dutifully downed a beer.

It was about three miles out of Herrin, where the road jogged around an ancient and massive oak, that we came upon the wreck. Barbara Harris' immaculate green Chevrolet had bent itself into a U around the tree and steam was still geysering out of the radiator and broken lines. The left headlight shot a white glare out through the night mists but nothing was moving inside the car.

"My God!" muttered Roscoe as he slowly braked the car to a stop. Then he said, "Jump out and see if you can help them. I'll go telephone from the nearest farm house."

As I stepped out onto the road my foot skidded sideways and I saved myself from falling only by grabbing the door handle. The surface was a thin sheet of ice, sleet that had frozen as it fell. I cautiously made my way to the wrecked car while Roscoe slowly drove away. On the driver's side, the glass was unbroken. Pete Domenico sat slumped over the wheel. Beyond him, on the passenger side in the shattered glass and twisted and torn steel I could make out Barbara's smashed head with blood oozing from her left ear and dripping drop by drop from her earring.

I tried to open the door beside Domenico but the impact had so deformed the body of the car that it was jammed shut. I considered breaking the window behind him but I still would not be able to open the door, and I could not drag him out through the window. So, what to do? Pondering, I thought I smelled gasoline, and as I looked under the back wheels I could see a steady drip, drip of fuel. The idiotic thought occurred that the car was losing its life's blood just as Barbara was, and at about the same rate. But still there seemed to be nothing I could do except wait. Wait and perhaps pray. Pray that a spark or hot metal would not ignite the gasoline and create an instant funeral pyre.

At long last Roscoe came back and at longer last a rescue truck and ambulance arrived. With crowbars two men forced open the door and lifted Domenico out. He was unconscious but alive. Barbara was not. I turned away as they pulled her body out by her heels across the seat, her blood-soaked dress riding up over her hips and revealing black satin panties above her starkly white round thighs.

I turned to Roscoe standing silently beside me. "Let's go," I said and climbed into his car, too sick at heart to speak again or to respond.

Eleven

Maytime in southern Illinois brought soft air and flowering meadows, blossoming orchards, and honey-suckled hedgerows. The romance of my housemate and his honors student blossomed in harmony with the season of cherries, apples, and peaches. Several times when I came home on those springtime afternoons I heard the unmistakable rustling and murmuring of a man and a woman in "the lists of love" as Shakespeare phrases it. And later, after Myra Pickens had tripped lightly down the stairs, Roscoe had come into my room flushed and wearing the vaunting air of a conqueror.

Roscoe and I never discussed his liaison openly. In fact, we discussed very little in the weeks after we encountered the steaming wreck and the smashed body of Barbara Harris. Because of my involvement, though indirect as it was, guilt hung over me like a thick black cloud, blocking out the sunshine and dimming my responses to the outer world. Try as I might, I could not erase from my mind two shattering images: the sharp hurt in Barbara's eyes when we met in the movie theater and the blood dripping drop by drop from her earring as she lay dead in her crushed car. After several expostulations, like "For God's sake, Stephen, it's not your fault that idiot Domenico hit the ice on that curve at fifty-five" and other well-intentioned efforts, our conversation dwindled to monosyllables.

The hubbub of scandal that erupted over the incident— "Can you believe it, a college professor dating a car mechanic? One would think she might have found a more suitable companion among her colleagues"—engulfed the atmosphere of the isolated woman's college which tended in the confining winter to take on the tone of a nunnery. Once or twice it seemed to me that meaningful glances, perhaps imagined, were aimed at me when the phrase "suitable companion" was murmured. The endless raking over of the details of the fatal accident, which I heard every time I had coffee in the faculty lounge, kept the wound of my guilt open and bleeding. Meanwhile I took what solace I could in the solid academic achievements of my students.

All the while, I watched with increasing unease the burgeoning intimacy between Roscoe and Myra Pickens. I knew that this was his first genuine liaison, his virgin assumption of the lover's role, and I knew how deeply committed this shy and inexperienced man was becoming. I was less concerned about Myra who was soon to graduate and leave Kanaka College for the outside world where broader experience and new relationships would probably weaken and gradually dissolve her attachment to Roscoe. Soon it would probably become to her merely a pleasant episode in her maturing young life. It was, I knew, far, far deeper and different for Roscoe.

After idyllic May came warm June and lovely, lazy weekends. The college year was drawing to a close, and the girls took on bright spring plumage—leaf green and butter yellow dresses in class, white and navy blue shorts while strolling under the arching campus trees, and glistening bathing suits as they lay sunning on the college boathouse dock. Roscoe and Myra took long afternoon picnics, paddling in his bottle green canoe to secluded coves, and coming back languid and bright red with sunburn. And once Roscoe returned with a rash of poison ivy on his buttocks which he acknowledged to me by asking my guidance as he applied unguent salve on his bottom. Another time he came home soaking wet when they had been caught in one of those sudden rain squalls that frequently came sweeping down the lake when the hot June sun had superheated the Illinois plain and created towering thunder clouds.

On the Saturday afternoon the week before Commencement, Roscoe and Myra set out on one of these expeditions. It was a brilliant day, cloudless but humid with the promise in the atmosphere of another of those surprise squalls. I spent the afternoon in the apartment reading term papers, sweating gently and plucking pages off the underside of my arm as I rested it on the desk. I was only dimly aware of the storm when it approached around six o'clock, but then there came the sharp, percussive crack of a nearby lightning strike, followed by a roar of wind and the thrashing of rain against the frame house. I went on reading papers, trying to finish the task before I broke off for supper, but I became increasingly aware that this was an unusually violent storm, something more than a passing squall. Through the window I could see the graceful elm trees swaying and dipping in response to the slashing wind. And the gutters alongside the curbs ran flush with streams reaching out toward the center of the roadway. I told myself that Roscoe would once again come home sopping wet.

But Roscoe did not come home at all, not for hours, and the rain had stopped and darkness was nearly total when I at last heard his slow, heavy step on the stairway. When he appeared at my doorway, his face was dead white and his eyes burned with agony. He stood with one hand high on the door jamb, his mouth slack, and stammered, "Stephen, I lost—I *lost Myra*." Then he put both hands to his face and sobbed, "Oh, my God! My God, my God!" He turned then and reeled toward his room and threw himself face down on the bed.

I followed him, bewildered. What did "lost Myra" mean? Had he lost her love or lost her in the storm? I stood beside the studio couch staring down at the shoulders of the sobbing man. "Roscoe, tell me, what do you mean, you 'lost Myra'?"

He rolled his head back and forth, face down, and said in muffled voice, "I lost her, Stephen. Lost her. She's gone."

Prolonged uncertainty erupted into anger. "God damn it, Roscoe! What do you mean, 'gone'? Where has she gone? *Where is she?*"

He rolled over, his face ravaged with grief. "She drowned," he said in a flat, expressionless voice. "We capsized in the storm. Got separated." He put his hands to his face. "Oh, *God. God!*"

I waited impatiently a moment for the spasm to pass, and then he said, "I righted the canoe but in the storm I capsized again, and when I finally was able to look for her she had disappeared."

It took a few seconds to absorb the shock but then I knew we had to take action. "Roscoe, for Christ's sake, we've got to notify the sheriff's office and the rescue squad. Right now!" I started for the telephone. "And the dean's office. We've got to notify the College."

In the same curiously flat, laconic voice, he said, "It won't do any good. They won't find her."

"Nevertheless." And I made the calls.

It was three o'clock under a moonless but star-encrusted sky when the rescue squad finally gave up. For over five hours they had scanned the rough, rolling water of the lake with searchlights on rescue launches and scoured the stony shoreline and the nearby brush with their high-powered lanterns. Finally, the sheriff, a lanky man with a black-holstered pistol on his hip, approached as we stood watching. He shined his light down at our feet and said, "I'm afraid we'll have to give up for the night, Professor. We'll start again after daylight." He turned to walk away and then stopped, his face dimly visible in the starlight. "Oh, yes. I'd appreciate it if you'd stop by my office tomorrow to make a statement. Say about ten."

"All right," said Roscoe. We walked slowly and silently in the dark to his car, and when we got home he turned into his room without speaking and closed the door.

I was exhausted from the long hours of tension, and I quickly undressed and fell into a profound sleep. Some time later I was dragged out of a bottomless unconsciousness by a hand shaking my shoulder. Dazed and thick-tongued I rolled over, "Wha-a-a-t? What is it?"

It was Roscoe, speaking with great urgency. "Wake up, Stephen. Wake up! I've got to talk with you. I can't sleep until I do."

I rubbed my eyes with the heels of my hands and sat up on the edge of the bed. "I was sound asleep," I muttered plaintively, "but what is it?"

Roscoe sat down on the chair by my desk. "I've got something to tell you. I've *got* to tell somebody."

Full wakefulness was beginning to take over, and I stared searchingly at the deeply troubled man before me. His eyes were terrible to see. "All right, Roscoe. I'm awake. Tell me."

He looked sternly at me. "It's not easy, Stephen. It's terrible but I've got to tell you."

"Yes."

He paused for a moment, looking down at the floor, and then raised his stricken eyes. "You see, Stephen, I'm afraid I did not search very hard for Myra."

"Oh, come on, Roscoe! You *did!* You searched for hours."

"Yes, but not at first."

"What do you mean?"

Again he paused, silently staring at the floor, and then spoke in a low flat voice. "We had had a terrible disagreement. Myra said she wanted to break off our relationship. But I told her I could not bear that. I wanted us to become engaged and then get married after six months or so. She said no. Flatly no. She told me I was too old for her. She said she was not ready for marriage. Instead, she needed to leave here after graduation and live her own life."

"I see."

"I was very upset, crazy with hurt and anger, and we argued fiercely. And then in the middle of it, the storm struck. I had not been paying attention while we argued and before I could get the canoe headed up into the wind we capsized."

"When you surfaced after capsizing, could you see Myra?"

"No, but I didn't try. I was half out of my mind, savage with hurt and anger, and for the moment I had the insane thought I wanted to get rid of Myra, to hurt her as she had hurt me. I concentrated entirely on righting the canoe and retrieving jackets and picnic things that had fallen overboard. Some time passed. I don't know. Five minutes, maybe longer. Not ten, I don't think."

"But then you looked for her."

"Yes. I paddled around and around in the driving rain and through the white caps, circling the place where I thought we had turned over. And as I did my anger dwindled and transformed into panic. I became frantic."

"Could Myra swim?"

"Yes, she was a strong swimmer. But the waves and the wind were so violent she may have swallowed water and choked. And she was in the water a long time without help. Without *my* help."

"But you might not have been able to save her anyway, Roscoe. You might not have been able to get to her, or even to find her, in all that wind and rain."

"But I'll never know for certain. If I had tried and failed, that would have been different. But not to have tried—oh, God!"

I sat on the edge of the bed, staring at him. He sat bent over, head down and hands clasped between his knees. Then I remembered his interview with the sheriff next morning. "You know, Roscoe, you ought to think very carefully about how you phrase your statement to the sheriff tomorrow."

He raised his head sharply. "I have. I will tell him the truth."

"But, I don't think you really *know* what is true. In your disturbed state of mind the time that passed may have seemed longer to you than it really was."

He shook his head. "I know what happened. I know what is true." He got to his feet. "The trouble is, I don't know how I can live with that truth." He came over to me and put out his hand. "Thank you, Stephen. You've been a true friend." He walked out the door and as he went through it without looking back, he said, "Goodnight."

Tired as I was I had no difficulty in falling asleep again. But as usual my built-in inner alarm clock clicked my eyes open at seven o'clock, and I washed and dressed and walked across the dew-laden campus to my laboratory. Roscoe's door was closed as I left, but I let him sleep, thinking he had plenty of time before his meeting with the sheriff. I spent the morning making out final grades and straightening up and putting away equipment in the laboratory.

It was nearly noon when I walked back to the apartment with the hot June sun casting black shadows through the campus trees and the broad lawns glistening an intense green. As I came to the grey wooden steps of the house I thought I heard a humming noise coming from the backyard. I turned toward the sound and then realized with a sudden rush it was the sound of an automobile engine running. And it was coming from behind the closed door of the small garage where Roscoe kept his car.

I ran and opened the broad, swinging door and went to the driver's side of the car. At first I could not see him but as I opened the car door I found Roscoe lying down across the seat. I yelled at him, "Get up, Roscoe! Wake up!" He did not stir and I was beginning to feel light-headed in the exhaust-filled shed. I ran outside, coughing. Bent over, I took a half dozen deep breaths and then went back to the car to pull Roscoe out. It took several tries to untangle his angular body from the narrow space, and I had to break off twice when I felt close to passing out. But at last I freed him and dragged him out onto the grass in the backyard. He lay limp, his mouth sagging open in his ghastly face. I felt for his pulse and found as I expected, his wrists still and his hands cold, the cold of death. Then I noticed a folded slip of paper in his shirt pocket. It read, "Stephen: it was the only way. Thanks. R.B."

I put the note back in the pocket, walked to the front door, climbed the steps to the apartment, and for the second time in twenty-four hours called the sheriff's office.

Interlude: Summer 1994

*L*ooking back now, I realize that the summer of 1953 was the most crucial time of my life. In that summer my future was balanced on a knife edge of uncertainty. I had no clear pathway to a career in view and no positive perception of myself as a man, a person. The triple tragedies of Barbara Harris, Myra Pickens, and Roscoe Bilder had done great violence to my inner security, to my personal set of standards and my confidence that there was some order and rightness in human affairs. Barbara's senseless death shamed me and left me with a crushing weight of helpless guilt. With just a little forbearance, a slight willingness to overlook Barbara's grasping for male company and the courage to take the small and harmless risk of entanglement, I could have accepted her invitation that sleeting and icy night and could probably—being a conservative driver—have avoided the accident that caused her death. My puny reasons for refusing her invitation, when placed beside the enormous fact of her death—her once lovely head smashed and blood dripping drop by drop from her earring— battered my self-esteem and undermined my confidence in my personal values.

For Myra Pickens I felt only the normal regret one feels over the untimely death of a young person of charm and great promise. Perhaps I could have tried to warn Roscoe that his attachment to Myra might greatly exceed hers to him, that she was really an immature woman who was perhaps only momentarily infatuated with her professor, but to have done so, I knew, would not have deflected him in the slightest and would not, in any event, have prevented the accident on the stormy lake.

But Roscoe's death had far deeper meaning for me. My feelings for him were complex, even contradictory. In part, I was his disciple. He had taught me so much, opened so many new vistas, broadened my span of appreciation and understanding in so many ways. At the same time, I had almost a paternal feeling for him. Despite his brilliance, he was a great innocent, a babe in the wood, the wood of the real world. And for that reason, I felt protectively affectionate toward him. The loss for me was multilayered and deeply, deeply painful.

In this damaged and unsettled state I left Kanaka College immediately after Commencement. I left because I could no longer stay. While I was packing to leave, Dr. Brandenwein called me in and told me that the College had decided to renew my contract. "Of course," he said in his harsh Germanic accent, "we would prefer for you to acquire your Ph.D. degree if you wish to stay here permanently. But for the present we will renew your contract. At no advance in stipend, of course."

It seemed pointless to explain to him that I would not—could not—stay at Kanaka under any circumstance that might occur to the mind of man, so I thanked him and left. At Cornell Bill Byer had nothing to offer so I drifted on east to Brixton where Stuart Price had said he wanted my help in establishing his nature sanctuary. From the start I knew that Price had nothing permanent to offer me—six months consulting, at best—but no one else was seeking my services for any purpose whatever, and for the moment I did not especially care whether anyone did or not. My sails were furled. I lay dead in the water. Adrift.

The one positive note in my life at that time was a steady glow of affection for Meg Satterlee. Meg's letters throughout my year in Illinois had been unwavering in their tender, thoughtful concern, a steady stream of sweet, undemanding affection that had added certainty to my attachment to Meg. It was true that I had come back to Brixton to work with Stuart Price, but it was even more true that I had returned in order to be near Meg. And *though my outlook was as uncertain as uncertainty itself, deep inside me was the hope that my future might in some unforeseen way include Meg.*

Twelve

A little after five I heard them coming, the buzzing outboard driving Stuart Price's lap-straked skiff down the
tidal creek toward his cabin in the Brixton salt marshes. I got
up from the bench beneath the scrub willow in front of the
house and sauntered slowly toward the dock to greet them.
I had spent the afternoon, just as I had for the previous week,
sitting and doing nothing, gazing idly and without purpose
out across the Sound where ducks in their hundreds flapped
and bobbed and dove beneath the rippled surface of the sea.
The afternoon onshore breeze had been cool and steady,
strong enough to keep the greenhead flies off balance.

Stuart Price had cut the engine just as I walked out onto
the dock in the late afternoon sunshine and Meg Satterlee
was standing in the bow ready to toss me the bowline. She
stood smiling broadly, trim in white blouse and fitted blue
jeans, her blond hair pulled close to her shapely head. "Hi,
Stephen!" she called as the boat glided silently toward me.
"We've got the lobsters and the beer!" I took the line and
fended the boat off with my right foot. I reached a hand out
to help Meg onto the dock but she turned back toward Stuart
and asked, "What can I carry?" While they helped each other
gather up the duffle bags and the packages, I noticed again
as I had before—Meg and Stuart had become a couple.

Stuart handed me a large aluminum bucket. "Here you go, Steve. Collect some fresh seaweed along the shore over there and then dip an inch or two of sea water in the bucket under the seaweed." I looked quizzically at him as I took the bucket. "The seaweed makes a bed for the lobsters so they get steamed, not boiled."

"I see." I turned and followed Meg up the dock, watching the supple lift and shift of her hips as she walked.

Stuart proposed we have drinks on the grass in front of the house. "So long as the breeze keeps the damned greenheads at bay." Meg and I arranged the deck chairs while he was inside making the drinks, and after we sat down I asked, "How's your mother doing, Meg?"

She smiled brightly. "Today was a good day. When I visited her she was listening to the radio, and when she looked up she *recognized* me. Most times she doesn't."

"Ummm."

"But it's *so* hard, Stephen. She's so frail. Wispy. She's just slipping away, day by day."

"That *is* hard."

We sat silently for a moment, and then Meg turned to me. "But how are *you* doing, Stephen?"

"Hmmp. All right I guess." Pause. "Surviving."

Meg shook her head. "That's not good enough." She reached over and took my hand into her lap. "I worry about you, my dear. You're not the same Stephen you were last year." She squeezed my hand and held it close against her firm thigh.

"I've got a few things to sort out."

"I know. I know." She squeezed my hand again. "Why don't we talk about it sometime when we can be quiet—and alone?"

"Umm, maybe. But mostly it's something I must do myself."

Again the squeeze. "I can help, you stubborn old darling. I can help."

Just then we heard the screen door slam behind us as

Stuart came with the drinks and Meg quickly dropped my hand. I watched the faces of the two as drinks were being handed about and saw again the subtle signs of agreement and understanding between them. But still, it seemed to me, Meg's affection for me had not changed.

"Your health." Stuart raised his glass. "Oh, and before I forget, Steve, I've got all the bids in hand for the fencing along the highway. Come up to my office tomorrow morning and we'll make a decision."

"What time?"

"About ten?" He frowned, cocking his head. "Let's see, will the tide be right?" Pause. "Yes. Rising tide. I'll see you at ten."

"Fine."

Next afternoon, after a handsome lunch at Stuart Price's club—a dark mahoganied, oriental rugged, brass lamped, Havana-cigared institution—I was drumming back down the tidal creek in Stuart's small skiff. We had made our choice among the firms bidding for installing a mile and a half of galvanized security fencing along Route 9, the western border of the nature sanctuary. Afterward, Stuart had left lunch hurriedly to catch the afternoon Boston and Maine train to attend an evening business meeting in Boston and then spend the night.

And so I was alone once again. Alone and still rudderless. Even so, I was somehow vaguely aware of some new stirring within. It was as though a nameless flow was slowly seeping into me, accepting me, dissolving the alienation that had never left me in Illinois, absorbing me, bestowing a feeling of once again belonging. It was only beginning, merely the leading edge, but New England's charm seemed to be reaching out to embrace me once again.

My wrist watch, vibrating on the hand holding the outboard tiller read 2:40. Still early. I had a sudden impulse to go find Meg. I passed by the tributary creek leading to

Price's dock, sailed out to the Sound and down to the Yare River and up against the flowing tide of the Yare to the Brixton town dock. It was well after four when I walked up the front steps of the Satterlee home.

Meg met me at the door, her face a portrayal of grief. "Oh, Stephen, I'm so glad you're here. The nursing home just telephoned. Mother died in her sleep while napping after lunch. I'm on my way there now."

"May I come with you?"

"Oh, *do! Please do!*"

There seemed little to say as we drove the five miles to the Fairweather Retreat, a handsome white building standing amidst a park of sweeping lawn and broad-branched trees.

"Beautiful place," I said as Meg pulled into the parking lot.

"Yes, beautiful. And dreadfully expensive. We could never have afforded it ourselves but dear Stuart made it possible." We got out of the car and walked up to the white-columned portico. "Mother has lived her final days in the greatest luxury she has ever known."

A white-haired woman stepped out from behind a desk near the door. "I'm so sorry, Miss Satterlee. So sorry. But your mother passed away so peacefully. She was sleeping quietly and then she was—well, *sleeping*. What a lovely way to leave us."

"Yes," said Meg. "May we see her?"

"Surely. She's in her room."

We found Mrs. Satterlee in bed in her high-ceilinged, wide-windowed bedroom. One window was slightly open and a gentle breeze stirred the white curtains. The old lady seemed to be serenely sleeping, her hair neatly combed and her old hands resting on the white coverlet. Meg stood silently a moment and then leaned over and kissed the lined, white forehead. "Goodnight, Mother dear," she said and turned and walked to the door. I followed her as we walked down the corridor. The woman at the desk said, "The Retreat will make all the arrangements, Miss Satterlee, in accordance with your previous instructions."

"Thank you. I'll come by tomorrow."

Back at her house Meg tossed her purse in a chair and turned to me. "I would like a drink of some kind, Stephen. Be a dear and see what you can find in the cupboard. Stuart has left some bottles here."

In the cupboard I found Chivas Regal scotch and Remy Martin cognac. "Scotch or cognac?" I called from the kitchen.

"Cognac for me, please." I found suitable glasses and poured a stiff slug of cognac for Meg and a hefty glass of Price's Chivas for me.

Silent, sipping our drinks, we sat across from one another as the August afternoon light slanted in through the small-paned windows. I reflected that death and I had been close companions over the past three months, this being the fourth in that span. This one was different though. This was the normal, peaceful termination of a long and useful life, not the sharp, tragic—

"You know, Stephen, I can't seem to feel sad about Mother's death. It was time for her to go."

"I think that's right."

She mused, sipping her cognac. "Mostly at the moment I am trying to think about the change this will make for me. Caring for Mother has until now been the determining fact of my life. For years there has been only one path for me. Now lots of ways are open. Almost too many."

"How about Stuart?"

Her head jerked up, and she looked intently at me. "One of the ways, certainly." She tilted her glass and finished her drink. "Make me another of those, Stephen, and I'll go heat up some clam chowder."

"I ought to be getting back before flat low tide or I'll have to wade a half mile through mud."

"Oh, no! You must not leave! I need you, Stephen." She got up and came to me arms outstretched, and we hugged close. Still clinging, head buried against my chest, she said, "You're very dear to me."

Later I sat in the kitchen while Meg prepared supper.

After we had eaten, I again made a move toward leaving and again Meg insisted I stay. "I really don't want to be alone tonight. You can sleep in your old room."

After an evening of rambling conversation, Meg doing most of the talking, reminiscing, we went upstairs and Meg kissed me gently goodnight. I undressed down to my underwear shorts in my old room and waited until I heard her leave the bathroom. Some minutes later I was walking from the bathroom when I heard what sounded like sobbing. It was Meg, face down in her bed. I went in and bent over her. I put my hand on her shoulder. 'Meg?"

She rolled over. "Oh, Stephen. Without thinking I went into Mother's room to see if she was all right. And her bed was so *empty!* So empty!"

I put both hands on her shoulders and she reached up to me. "Hold me, Stephen. Hold me close!"

I lay down beside her and took her lovely, firm body in my arms. Close, as she asked, and then closer and closer, until finally she said in muffled voice, "No, darling. Please, no. Not now, Stephen dearest, not now."

I released her then and lay back, wondering whether to stay or go to the other bed. Meg decided that by rolling next to me and laying her arm across my chest. "Goodnight, Stephen darling," she murmured, "I can't tell you what it means to me to have you with me tonight." I patted her arm softly and said nothing. We lay together then the rest of the night, sleeping the innocent sleep of young children.

After an early breakfast next morning I pushed off in the skiff and headed down river on the rising tide. Meg had prepared breakfast while wearing a blue, white-trimmed dressing gown and had kissed me gently goodbye. "We won't mention to Stuart that you spent the night here with me," she said as I went down the front steps. "I see no need to mention it."

With that instruction in mind I was prepared for Stuart

Price's question when he pulled into his dock just behind me. "I thought I heard your outboard," he said. "Where have you been?"

"Just out on the Sound looking at the ducks."

"Well, jump out of that rough gear you're wearing, my lad, and put on your best bib and tucker. You are going to have an interview this morning that will set you up handsomely for life."

"What do you mean?"

"Go on along. I'll tell you the whole story while you are changing clothes."

Mystified but in no position to quibble, I walked down the dock and climbed up the worn path to the house. Behind me, Price said, "At the Sloate board of trustees meeting last night, our Headmaster, Matthew Makepeace, told us the biology master had unexpectedly accepted a post teaching at Milburn College. School opens in two weeks and they have no one to teach biology. So I stepped up to the plate and said I had just the man. I told a few lies about you and said I would have you up at the school for an interview sometime before noon today. So get a move on! We've got fifty miles to drive."

Thirteen

Sloate Preparatory School for Boys sits snugly on a wooded tract above the Nashua River north of Worcester. Stuart Price and I drove through a gateway of white, square wooden columns and down a winding gravel lane toward a large white building distant among the widely-spaced oaks, elms, walnuts, and hickories. The morning air had that tawny late August scent of browning grass newly mown. Rounding a bend halfway down the long driveway we came upon a man driving a horse and red cart. The man was small, a gnome, probably in his middle sixties, and he wore a black broad-brimmed, flat-crowned hat. He held in his right hand a long, willowy whip. We both stopped.

"Ah, there you are, Price. I was just giving Gertie a little trot before lunch. Go on along up to my office. I'll join you shortly."

"Right you are, Mr. Makepeace," said Price with the forced jollity of an old schoolboy in the presence of his headmaster. "This is Stephen Aspen here."

"Mornin' to you, Aspen." He crinkled his bright, bird-like eyes. "Be with you in a shake of a lamb's tail."

We found Headmaster Makepeace's office just inside the entrance on the right of a broad center hallway. A large square room, it was crammed with academic clutter: books and pamphlets stacked atop one another within floor to ceiling bookcases and piled atop the desk and tables. Over the doorway hung an oak-framed portrait of Josiah Makepeace, great-great-great grandfather of Matthew. He was the founder of Sloate School, Stuart Price told me, which was named to honor the maternal family. Broad small-paned windows looked out front and side onto mossy grass beneath tall, spreading trees. On its tripod beside the window was a spotting telescope, and when I walked over to examine it I found on the window seat below a copy of Roger Tory Peterson's bird guide.

Shortly Mr. Makepeace skittered into the room, looking even smaller on his feet than he had perched on the cart. His face set in a chirpy smile and his eyes darting and quick, he motioned us toward a maple settee in front of his desk. "Sit down, gentlemen, please." He himself sat down momentarily in the wooden armchair at his desk and then, apparently having difficulty looking over the broad desk covered with books and papers, jumped up and squatted on the chair seat, again perched like a bird.

"Glad to have you back at the old place, Price. I didn't get a chance to ask you last night. Are you still cluttering the natural landscape with tall office buildings?"

Stuart Price's strong face took on an unnaturally shy grin. "No, sir. Just now I'm designing a school in Waltham."

"Good for you. That's good!" Mr. Makepeace switched his sharp gaze onto me. "Welcome to you, Aspen. Price tells me you might help us out in biology."

"Yes, sir. I would like to be considered for the position."

"All right." He picked up a long, yellow pencil and placed it momentarily between his upper lip and his nose, then took it away and cocked his head, like a robin staring at the ground. "Mind if I ask you a question or two?"

"No, sir."

"For starters, where do you come from?"

"Michigan, southern part. Grass Lake."

"Westerner, eh? Rancher?" He chuckled, sort of a cackle. "That's a New England joke. Bad one. We get a lot of good boys from those parts—Adrian, Battle Creek, Grosse Pointe." He looked intently at me for a moment. "Schooling?"

"Just the Michigan public schools through high school then Cornell for bachelor's and master's degrees."

"Mmhuh. And Price tells me you majored in biology with a minor in ornithology?" He gestured toward the spotting scope. "I'm a bird watcher myself. Might be handy to have someone around who really knew something about birds."

"I'm afraid I'm better on ducks than songbirds."

"That's all right, that's ducky." He snickered. "Another bad joke. Comes from spending a lifetime in the company of twelve year old boys." He got down off his perch and stood at the desk, tapping it with the end of his yellow pencil. "Let's get serious." He squinted to one side toward the window and then directly at me. "Price tells me you spent the past year teaching at a girls' college in Illinois."

"Yes, sir. Kanaka College."

He nodded briskly. "Now, then, tell me. What makes you think teaching college *girls* qualifies you to teach prep school *boys*?" He put his hands on the desk and rose up on his toes, staring at me like a fierce sparrow hawk.

I paused a moment, trying to determine how serious his question was. Then I said, "I think teaching consists mostly of getting the attention of a student, using that attention to impart knowledge, and then finding ways to get the student to make that knowledge work." I paused. "I think that approach applies to either sex." While I waited for Mr. Makepeace's response, I saw no reason to tell him I had just spouted a capsule version of the teaching philosophy Bill Byer had hammered into me for four years.

Mr. Makepeace's stare remained fixed for a moment while his expression slowly softened. I heard Stuart Price beside me shift his position in the settee. "Well, now, young man," said the Headmaster, "that's a pretty good answer.

Pretty darn good." He clasped his hands behind his back, head down, and flitted back and forth behind his desk. Then he darted around it and stopped before me. He held out his hand. "Aspen, I like the cut of your jib and I'd like to offer you a position teaching biology at Sloate School."

I stood up and took his hand. "Thank you, sir."

He nodded briskly at Price. "Now, for the business part. We ordinarily start our masters at—" He named a figure roughly two-and-a-half times my Kanaka salary.

I was startled and almost gulped and I guess it showed because the Headmaster hurriedly added, "But in your case, because of your teaching experience, we'll make it—" And he added another $1500.

Of course I accepted. Mr. Makepeace pressed on. "Now, when can you come up and move in?"

"Tomorrow, if you wish. I would like some time to study your syllabus before classes begin."

"Syllabus?" He grinned a sideways grin. "We have no syllabus here. I expect the syllabus to be up there between your ears." He grinned again, a sharp little grin. "But fine. Move in tomorrow if you like. I'm going to make you the house-master for Sudbury Hall, the Fifth Form dormitory, and you can take over the quarters there." He turned then to Stuart Price. "My thanks to you, Price. I'm happy to see the good judgment instilled by a Sloate education still survives."

Price smiled boyishly. "Thank you, sir. This is a happy day for all three of us and for Sloate School."

Mr. Makepeace nodded briskly. "Oh, one more thing before you go, Aspen. What about athletics? We like our masters to handle one of the sports in our program."

"Only college intramurals, I'm afraid. Touch football, squash. I won the Cornell intramural squash singles championship."

His small eyes sparkled. "Great! That's simply great! You can coach our squash team."

After another round of handshakes, with Mr. Makepeace

hopping and twittering about like an exultant sparrow, Stuart Price and I went to his car and drove away. Price was jubilant. "Stephen, my lad, you're fixed for life! You'll love the school. I spent four of the happiest years of my life there."

Given Price's euphoria, it did not seem useful to point out that being a carefree student at an institution and serving as an employee are worlds apart.

We passed through the white-pillared gate and turned out onto the country road. "The other bonus," he said as his big Buick sedan smoothly picked up speed, "is that you can go on playing a role in the nature sanctuary. I'll put you on a retainer, maybe five thousand—I'll have to check with the rest of the committee—and you can come down a couple of times a month and keep track of things."

"Fine, Stuart. I'll be glad to lend a hand, but I don't want to be paid. The salary from Sloate will have me rolling in money."

"Nonsense! I believe in giving a fair return for services rendered." He stared ahead as we droned down the road, the big car cushioning the bumps with a sort of billowy motion. "Oh—just thinking—you're going to need a car to get back and forth. Go down to the dealership tomorrow and pick one out. I'll finance it until you start drawing your salary."

"You're making me hopelessly obligated to you."

"Nonsense! Just helping a friend and colleague."

But while Stuart Price was jubilant, Meg's responses were mixed. "Oh, Stephen, I'm delighted for you, of course. But I'm going to miss you terribly. I count so much on your support, your sane judgment. And I feel I need it especially just now. You know—all the things I have to sort out with Mother gone and my future uncertain." She put her hands on my shoulders and leaned her head against my chest. "You are so dear to me, Stephen, and Sloate is so far away."

"Just fifty miles. I feel certain I'll be able to slip away now and then."

"Promise me you will," she said and held her face up to be kissed.

"Promise."

The housemaster's quarters at Sudbury Hall barely escaped being sumptuous. The living room was paneled in rich dark mahogany, with brass-handled cupboards below. The sofa and chairs were dark green leather and beneath them lay a deep red carpet. Behind the sofa facing the small fieldstone fireplace was a long mahogany table bearing two tall brass lamps, red shades matching the carpet. A short hallway led from the sitting room past a Pullman style kitchenette to a blue-tiled bathroom. Across the hall from the kitchenette was the doorway to a handsome bedroom. I walked over to the broad, small-paned window and looked out. The boughs of a willow oak hung low close by, and through them spread a view of broad green lawns. I took a deep breath, reveling in the happy rightness about the place—my deeply comfortable rooms, the aged, gently nurtured grounds, the solidly handsome buildings—and the prevailing ambiance of permanence and tradition. Momentarily a comparison hovered on the edge of my mind—Sudbury Hall and the apartment with Roscoe at Kanaka College, the plain rooms in the frame house in a small Illinois town—but I dismissed it quickly as unworthy. Living with dear old Roscoe, which had such deep meaning for me, did not have to be demeaned in order to make the present seem a piece of stunning luck.

Walking out the doorway of Sudbury Hall, I stopped for a moment to admire my new car. It glistened in the sunshine, a spanking new 1953 Ford convertible, charcoal grey with red leather interior. I had set out at the dealership to buy a conservative dark blue coupe but the salesman, after looking me over, had said, "A young fellow like you ought to have something with a little more splash. Have a look at this nifty convertible. We got it on special order for a fellow," he explained, "but before he could take delivery his wife told him she was going to have their third child and they needed a station wagon. In this old town we don't get many calls for a car like this so I'll let you have it for a hundred dollars more than that coupe."

I could not resist. Who could? Besides, I reasoned, in my new surroundings a car with "a little splash" would not look out of place. Actually, during the next week, when parents began arriving with their sons in Cadillac limousines and long Lincolns, my "nifty convertible" looked almost plebeian as it sat modestly by the curb.

As I passed the little car I patted it on the rear fender and headed for a stroll around the grounds. The academic buildings, including Edison Hall, the science building which was to be my center of activity, were all white, generously spaced around a large grassy quadrangle. Set back against a wooded hillside was a steepled chapel, a perfect model in miniature of a traditional New England Congregational Church. Off to one side, on flat terrain near the Nashua River, stood the athletic field house and the football, soccer, and baseball fields. Inside the field house I located the squash courts. There were six, all newly painted, the walls gleaming white and the marking stripes bright red on the freshly varnished floors. I walked outside and stood for a moment on the steps in the late August sunshine. Again, I took a deep breath. Everything about Sloate School bespoke long established grace and plenty, generous abundance reined in by good taste. As I stood musing, I realized, with some surprise, that I felt entirely at ease amidst this affluence. It all seemed so *right*, so exactly as I would have it, that I felt at home within it. Then, in the midst of this moment of epiphany I thought of Meg Satterlee and wished she were here to share the moment with me. My dear, sweet Meg. Then came the jolting afterthought: *My* Meg?

The following days, the opening of school, and the weeks

and then the month that followed, substantially reduced my euphoria. What I came to appreciate as day followed day was the vast difference between college and boarding school teaching. At Kanaka College I taught my class or monitored my laboratory and then went back to the seclusion of my room. I was with my students two or three hours a day. The remaining twenty-one or twenty-two were mine to be spent alone or not as I wished.

But at Sloate I was with students, many not even mine to teach, virtually twenty-four hours, day in and day out. All day long and most evenings my door leading out into the central hallway was open, and boys went trooping and frolicking by, sometimes stopping to ask a question about a school program or regulation. In the morning I followed the last stragglers down the walkway to the chapel, and at breakfast, lunch, and dinner I sat at the head of a dining table and did my best to maintain civility and decorum. From time to time I would be awakened with a knock at the door by a student proctor who came to inform me that Bradshaw or McIlhenny or someone was keeping everyone awake by coughing constantly and seemed to have a fever. Then I would bundle up the sufferer and take him to the infirmary. In general, the situation of a boarding school master was summed up aptly by Brickson Jaeger, a bulky voluble Kentuckian, who asked me one day, "Do you ever get the feeling you're up to your ass in boys?" I nodded silently but could as easily have shouted, "Yes!"

But as the weeks went by and I became adjusted to my role as housemother, etiquette monitor, athletic coach, as well as teacher, the teaching became more and more satisfying. Again, the difference between teaching prep school boys and college girls was substantial. At Kanaka, the sustained interest of the girls in the classroom was so intense it took getting used to. But at Sloate, the interest of the boys in the classroom and the laboratory was grasshopperish, to say the least. Now sharply focused, now wandering. Three of the boys in fifth form biology were, when they wished to be, brilliant: Woods Jefferson, son of a Williams College professor; Clinton Wiener, son of a Wall Street broker; and Boynton Ross, son of a constitutional lawyer. They enjoyed competing with one another, at times striking sparks of real brilliance. They often startled me with their acute perceptions. Myra Pickens, my best student at Kanaka, was bright and delightful but never to my mind brilliant.

Another difference between my classes at Sloate and at Kanaka struck me early on. The girls were invariably receptive, almost always willing to accept my view in a discussion. Too willing, I felt at times. The boys, especially the very bright ones, easily and quickly took up confrontational positions, and sometimes clung tenaciously to an untenable view until one of their peers shot them down. Characterizing the difference in terms of another species—at Kanaka I was a patriarchal stag leading a herd of docile does. At Sloate I was an older stag surrounded by muscular young bucks.

But that analogy does not describe the difference entirely. One day, I decided to give the rough side of my tongue to Brent Caxton, a large, sleepy-eyed boy and star halfback on the football team, who was being deliberately obtuse. In an instant, I had the whole class in full cry against me. The boys banded together like a pack of wolves and voiced in chorus their displeasure over my treatment of one of their fellows. At Kanaka, a girl singled out in like fashion would have been frowned upon by her sister students who would take it for granted the rebuke was deserved. No pack mentality for them.

After several weeks of adjusting and accommodating, I began to take great satisfaction in the hours I spent in the classroom and laboratory. I found the clash and challenge of the young male minds not only invigorating but, carefully used, a productive teaching tool. Just so long as I did not single out one of the young stags for scorn and transform the herd into a wolfpack.

I had also discovered very soon at Sloate that a sprightly social life existed among the faculty and staff. The first week

I found in my mailbox a tiny square envelope with an invitation to supper at the Makepeaces. On that evening Mrs. Makepeace met me at the door, bright red hair tousled and curled above her small grey eyes and gaunt face. "Come in, come in!" she said in a husky, tobacco-hardened voice. "I'm Cordelia, and Mattie will be down shortly." She laughed a dry, hoarse laugh. "Oh, dear, dear, dear! Isn't it frightful having the little urchins back so soon? I scarcely feel we've had any summer vacation at all!"

I did not really share her sentiment about "the little urchins," so I merely smiled and said, "Hello."

Two other guests arrived, an English teacher, Roger Altby and his wife, Eve. Mrs. Makepeace greeted them much as she had me, "Come in, come in, fellow sufferers. The school year has begun again."

"Back to the old grind," responded Altby. I had decided when I first met him that he was the very model of the traditional New Englander. Slender, a plain, expressionless face, he wore the mandatory tweed jacket, grey flannel slacks, high-collared striped shirt and tiny knotted foulard tie with the aplomb of a ninth-generation scion of an ancient New England family. It was two months later that I learned he was a native of Kokomo, Indiana and had graduated from Ball State College.

His wife, Eve, small, quick-eyed, and luxuriously shaped, seemed to have more in common with the bright lights of Chicago or Detroit than the wooded hills of New England. When we shook hands her grasp was soft and clinging, and she looked me over with slyly appraising eyes. Then, with one of those seductive looks that begin with deeply lowered eyes and end with uplifted melting gaze, she said, "Well, here's our new master. Welcome to the bosom of our little family," and ending with a gentle squeeze and a girlish giggle.

While we smiled at each other, a newly arrived guest, a compact, handsome man, slid quietly past us and greeted Mrs. Makepeace. "Oh, Gil, darling," she said, "how good to see you! *Now* the evening can begin! Come meet our new science master, Mr. Aspen. This," she said while holding him by the hand, "is Gilman Brooks, our fine arts teacher."

Brooks turned to me holding out a firm hand. "Hello, I'm Gil Brooks." He spoke in a slightly husky voice, and somehow, even in those few words, conveyed gentle charm. I had never before met a man who at first glance exuded such an aura of modest grace and silken charm. His instant appeal was like that of a young colt, sleek and glossy.

At this point, Headmaster Makepeace, resplendent in an English pink hunting jacket and black silk pants, skittered into the room balancing a tray of sherry-filled glasses, and the party began. "Hello, everyone! Snatch a glass and drink up!"

At supper, whose main dish was a casserole of somewhat uncertain mixture dominated by tuna fish, the conversation was lively, consisting mostly of a monologue by Cordelia Makepeace who told a steady series of tales about her well-to-do family during her youth in Westchester, New York, the exploits of her younger brother, the manager and *maitre d'* of a swank New York bar, and the exciting people "Mattie and I knew when we were at New Haven." During this scarcely interrupted flow, Matthew Makepeace said nothing, addressing himself seriously to his plate and making little quick nods of assent now and then. Roger Altby, I noticed, had perfected the role of conversational accompanist which consisted of interjecting, with exquisite timing in a thin, nasal voice, such words as "Imagine!" or "Lovely" or "Glorious" whenever a small crack in the talk-stream flowed by. Eve Altby and I, sitting side by side, said nothing, but now and then her knee snuggled gently against my thigh.

After supper, Cordelia moved to the grand piano and began to play Broadway show tunes, one after another. Most were by Cole Porter, "whom Mattie and I partied with at New Haven," (I made a mental note: never say "Yale" but always say "New Haven"), and Headmaster Makepeace, sitting in a nearby easy chair, sang chorus after chorus of Porter's "Let's Do It." When she finished the song Cordelia said, "Cole was *so* naughty! 'Demure young mules feeling low, do it.' Oh, dear, dear, dear! And those *double entendres*. 'Baby, if I'm the bottom, you're the top.' Dear, dear, dear!"

She turned back toward Gilman Brooks who was standing behind the piano bench, "Come, take over, Gil. You play much better than I."

"Nonsense," he said with a winning smile. But she insisted and slid over to the end of the bench to make room. He began to play "Let's Do It" again, playing it as Cordelia Makepeace had suggested far better than she had, and in his faintly husky voice he led the Makepeaces in singing five or six more choruses, including "Old sloths hanging down from twigs do it, though the effort is great." When at last they finished, Cordelia Makepeace put her hand on Brooks's shoulder and said, "Oh, Gil, remember those wonderful parties we used to have in New Haven?"

"With great pleasure, my dear," he said with a charming smile. "With great pleasure."

And so the evening passed, lively and entertaining in a bizarre way. When the time came to leave, Eve Altby took my hand in both her soft ones. "We must see more of you, Mr. Stephen Aspen. And you can be sure we will."

"Goodnight," I said. "And thank you, Headmaster and Mrs. Makepeace for a delightful evening."

Then, in the crisp air of the early autumn night as I walked across the campus where the tall trees held their bare arms high and stars prinked and glistened, I thought of Meg and wished the evening had been spent with her.

Fourteen

The Thanksgiving goose, carved with surgical precision by Stuart Price, golden crusted and crammed with oyster stuffing, lay on the sterling platter circled by a wreath of scarlet cranberries. Mashed potatoes mounded into a snowy peak in a nearby bowl and emerald peas and glazed carrots stood near. After serving us all, Price circled the table pouring champagne from a bottle wrapped with a linen napkin and then raised his glass, "To my dear mother and to my dearest friends!"

The gorgeous dinner was topped of with mince pie mixed and baked according to the traditional Price recipe. Replete, we left the table and seated ourselves in a semicircle before the log fire in the living room. Coffee and cognac followed, with cigars for Price and Coffin. "Stephen is in training," deadpanned Price. "He's coaching the Sloate squash squad." Conversation flowed gently on, low-keyed and contented.

Soon it was four o'clock and the afternoon light was fading. The Coffins made signs of leaving—"I've got to walk our two setters before it gets dark," said Benjamin Coffin. They made their goodbyes and after seeing them off, Stuart Price turned to me, "I've got to run Mother down to Haverhill. Meg of course lives quite the other direction, so would you be a good chap and take her home? You and I can meet back here later for a light supper of leftovers."

"Happy to do it." I turned to Meg whose face wore a mixed expression, seemingly suppressing something, a look I could not read. But I followed her as she got her coat. Then I kissed Mrs. Price's offered parched cheek and turned to Meg, her face framed by her fur collar, "Shall we go?"

Crimson and gold streaked the western sky above the setting sun, and a light breeze hinting faintly of the sea drifted by as we walked out to my car. Meg opened the door and slid across the leather seat close beside me. Shortly later, when we had passed the outskirts of the town and reached the open road, she slipped her glove off her left hand and took mine in her warm, firm one. "Stephen, I've got to talk with you."

"I'm here and listening."

"Not now. After we get home. I've got to organize my thoughts first."

"Organize mine too while you're at it."

We drove the rest of the way in silence. When we stopped before her house, Meg jumped out and I followed her up the steps and into the house. We dropped our coats and I sat down in the corner of the sofa. Meg sat close beside me and then turned so that she was in my arms across my lap and facing me.

"Stephen," she said earnestly after she had finished wriggling into place, "Stuart has asked me to marry him."

"I'm not surprised."

"Nor am I. I've seen it coming for months, but I'm no more certain now of what to say than I was six months ago."

"Hmmm. Why are you uncertain?"

Long pause while Meg stared at her knees resting against the back of the sofa. Then she looked directly at me. "Partly because of you and partly because Stuart has been so good and so kind. I'm torn."

"Torn between Stuart and me? But I haven't asked you to marry me."

"I know. Why haven't you?"

"Well, partly because until very recently I was in no position to and—"

"But now you are. Rich as Croesus."

I kissed her fragrant hair. "Don't interrupt, my sweet. I'm coming to the sticky part."

"Which is—"

"Stuart Price has been as good and kind to me as he has to you. I'm obligated to him in more ways than I can count."

"That's true." She lay in my arms quietly for some time, pondering. "So what does that make me? The prize that goes to the most generous man?"

"That's not a very charitable way to put it."

"I know." She shook her head as though to dispel the thought. "Forgive me. But, damn it, I feel trapped!" Then she put her face up to mine. "Oh, Stephen, I don't want to lose you! I can't give you up. I just can't."

I bent and kissed her, gently, and then, responding to her intensity, more strongly. Then we parted and I looked down at her sweet, troubled face. "Meg, you know I love you. I truly do. But I know how much it means to Stuart to have you as his wife, and I could not live with myself if I took you away from him. It would destroy everything he has built his hopes on for the past several years. He would regard it as a breach of trust. And in fact so would I." I paused, looking down at her face, eyes narrowed and forehead creased in a frown. "Ask yourself, Meg. Could you feel right telling Stuart you would not marry him because you planned to marry me?"

She hesitated, then sighed and shook her head. "I would give anything in the world to be able to say 'yes.' But you know I can't." She shook her head and sighed again. "I'm afraid you're right—right again, you and that wonderful sane judgment I've always trusted." She lay quiet for several minutes and then looked up at me. "So you think the answer is clear-cut. I should tell Stuart I'll marry him."

"With reluctance—*deep* reluctance—yes."

She studied her knees again for several minutes. Then she said in a low voice, "You know, I really am very fond of Stuart, quite apart from his generosity. He's a wonderful companion and we have great times together. He's gentle and thoughtful and sweet. In fact, I guess I *do* love him. But—" She turned her face up toward mine. "Not the way I love you. You make me tingle He only makes me purr."

I hugged her gently and said nothing.

She lay quietly again for a long time while the grandfather clock in the hallway solemnly noted the passing seconds. Then she raised her eyes to mine. "If I am to say 'yes' tomorrow or the next day or next week, then tonight, Stephen, may be the last night you and I can be together as we have been in the past." Her blue eyes looked intently into mine, a soft smile on her lips.

Perhaps I was a little slow on the uptake. I looked at her questioningly.

"Kiss me," she said. And the open-mouthed fervor of her kiss cleared my mind of doubt.

"Meg," I said when our mouths parted, "you and I were lovers long before Stuart asked you to marry him. So, as far as I am concerned, until you give him your answer you are more mine than his."

"Yes," she said. She disentangled herself from my arms and held out her hand. "Come with me."

In her soft bed under the slanting ceiling of the snug little house, her smooth firm body yielding to mine, we made pent-up, loving love. Then we parted, languorous and tender, and then made love again. Afterward we lay quiet, intertwined, until at last Meg said, "Stephen, my dearest, you must go."

I drove back through the night to Stuart Price's big house under a black sky winking with stars while my body and mind glowed with love. At his front door, Stuart Price greeted me cheerfully. "Get the dear lady home all right?"

"Yes, indeed."

"Did she seem upset that I did not take her home myself?"

"No. She seemed to understand."

"Good." He shook his head in admiration. "She's a wonderful girl, isn't she?"

"She's all of that."

He leaned toward me and peered closely at my face. "You look flushed. You're not catching cold or coming down with a bug, are you?"

"No, I'm fine, Stuart. Just fine."

He took my coat as it slid off my shoulders and hung it in the closet. "Did Meg tell you I've asked her to marry me?"

"Yes she did."

"God, I hope she accepts. She asked for a few days to think it over."

I looked directly into his firmly cut, forthright Yankee face. "I think she'll probably say 'yes,' Stuart. I really think she will."

His face creased into a warm smile. He took my hand in his strong one and shook it. "My God, you're a hell of a good chap, Stephen. Let's have a scotch nightcap on that!"

As we walked into the living room to the liquor cabinet, he said, "You know, old friend, I think this is the best Thanksgiving I've ever had."

"It's the best for me too," I said.

Alone with Meg on Thanksgiving night I had found it easy to be magnanimous in advising her to accept Stuart's proposal. And then later, face to face in his living room, I had been easy, relaxed, in the company of the man whose wife-to-be had just been my loving partner in bed. But in the quiet of my room in Sudbury Hall, after the bell for lights-out had rung for the boys, and I was alone with the silence it was not the same. My feeling for Meg had deepened and strengthened over the past several years and she had become a pole star in my galaxy. In giving her up I was accepting a keen loss, both for the present and for a vaguely conceived future. We had both felt that our night together on Thanksgiving night was a final liaison, the last forever. That finality and the loss of any possible future day-by-day intimacy with Meg I found devastatingly hard to accept.

I took refuge in concentrating on my classes and laboratory sessions, and perhaps even more helpful, on dealing with a new and challenging undertaking, coaching the Sloate squash team. I had played very little squash the previous two years, and besides, being self-taught, I was apprehensive about my ability to coach a school team. But I had beaten several pretty good prep school guys in winning the intramural championship at Cornell, and these kids seemed no better than they had been.

I had loved the game from the time I first played it, the speed of the action and the strategy. Squash resembles tennis in that you use a racket but differs in that both players use the same court and instead of a net there is a front wall in a rectangular room. Squash somewhat resembles billiards too in that you can angle shots into corners, and you can hit the ball toward any of the four walls, even the back wall, the only requirement being that the ball must strike the front wall before hitting the floor.

During my graduate school year at Cornell I had played squash now and then with Bill Byer. We used to meet at the Law School building where there was a good court and then walk up to Willard Straight Hall afterward for lunch. Bill was a "cute" player. He loved to play soft little wristy shots up in the corners—rather like drop shots just over the net in tennis—and they were very hard to get. The strategy I worked out to combat him was to drive the ball as hard and as low as I could close along the side walls, a shot rather like a passing shot in tennis. To return such a shot, if I got it right, Bill had either to lunge sideways and volley the ball as it rocketed off the front wall or run back and scrape the ball off the side wall as it bounced out from the back wall. Either way, it was impossible from those positions to play one of his dinky little drop shots in the corner. On my good days I soon had Bill, who was ten years older than I, panting from dashing back and forth across the court and mumbling hard words under his breath.

During the Sloate team practices in the preseason I saw a situation similar to mine with Bill developing between Aram Akajanian, a wiry little scholarship boy from New York's East Side, and Brent Caxton, the large halfback. Like Bill Byer, Aram loved those little corner shots and Brent, despite his considerable athletic ability, was having great difficulty in moving his bulky body fast enough to reach the ball. As I watched, Brent became more and more frustrated, and I began to be concerned, as his face grew redder and redder, that he might explode and begin using his racket as a weapon against his tormentor.

So I took the big, angry kid aside. "Brent, there is a way to beat the game Aram is playing. Drive the ball as hard as you can along the side walls. Just hammer the hell out of it." (One of the things I learned early on is that prep school athletic coaches are entitled to use "damn" and "hell" occasionally with the boys. It is considered manly and consistent with athletic toughness.) "Come into this court with me and let me show you."

For the next ten minutes I tried my best to drop dinky little shots in the corners—admittedly not one of my best skills—while Brent drove the ball from one side to the other. He frequently got the shot too high, making for an easy return off the back wall, but toward the end he was getting the hang of it. "Gee, Coach," he said, blue eyes alight and sweat trickling off the end of his nose. "I see what you mean. With more practice I'll be able to beat that little bas—uh, excuse me—that little twerp."

Fortunately for me, the squash season opened happily for Sloate School as we beat Berkshire handily, winning both singles matches and one of the doubles. As the season wore on, we won three more matches and lost two. The final match was against Sloate's arch rival, Grantly Hill School. We had to travel thirty-five miles there by the athletic department's bus, and as we rode along it was clear the boys were tense and keyed-up. There was little banter and there were several snappish returns like, "Can it!" or "Knock it off."

My two best players, Aram Akajanian and Brent Caxton, played well and won their singles matches and teamed up successfully for the doubles. But the other kids, less talented, lost all their matches, and when the results were put together, the meet was a draw. The coach for Grantly Hill, a blonde, somewhat porky fellow named Ted Malone, came up to me. "Seems we got a tie here, Coach," he said. "Why don't you and I play two out of three and decide the winner."

Akajanian and Caxton, who had been sitting beside me in the gallery watching their teammates lose their matches, immediately said, almost in chorus, "Go ahead, Coach! Take him on! We'll be rooting for you."

There was no way I could gracefully refuse. I borrowed Caxton's racket and slipped off my Sloate School sweatshirt and white, side-striped trousers. I was otherwise prepared to play since it seems to be an inflexible tradition that all school coaches wear jockstraps and athletic shoes to every practice and game. Perhaps it is the way they psych themselves up for the competition.

Malone and I volleyed for several minutes, and I could see he had a nice, easy action, lots of wrist in his swing. He also moved well despite his somewhat portly figure. Then I said, "All right, let's go."

The first game we felt each other out, and Malone finally won it, 15-13, making his last two points with nifty little corner shots that dropped like rocks off the front wall. During the second game he apparently decided that he had the touch for those pesky little dinks in the corner and began to use them repeatedly. So I resorted to the strategy I had found worked against Bill Byer and began driving the ball hard and low along the side walls, hitting the shot with all my strength so that the ball came screaming off the front wall, usually past Malone's outstretched racket. Then he had to rush back to the corner to pick the ball off the sidewall in a saving, indecisive shot that I was able to put away out of his reach. That game ended in my favor, 15-11, and Malone's chest was heaving and his face beet red.

The third game was a continuation of the second except that Malone, trying to thwart my hard drives, began to crowd in front of me as I was hitting the shot. In squash you are entitled to claim interference if you cannot get an unobstructed swing. You cry "Hinder!" and the point is played over. After three claims of "hinder" and he was still crowding me on every shot, I tried the next tactic, usually effective. I drove the hard black ball with all my might into his broad, plump back. He yelped and let the air out of his lungs with a "whoosh."

"Sorry," I said, "but you need to give me a little more room."

"Okay," he said, pacing around the court for a minute or two while the sharp stinging and cold chills subsided. "All right, let's go."

The score then was 11-11 and we went up the range a point at a time, 12-11, 12-12, until we reached 14-14. Here the scoring in squash resembles tennis in that two consecutive winning points are needed after deuce is reached. For the next ten minutes we seesawed back and forth, each winning one point and losing the next. By this time my right arm was leaden with all the blasting I had done, and Malone was almost staggering as he lunged from side to side or rushed back to the corners to retrieve the shot. In the gallery above, my boys and Malone's were shouting encouragement, and I could hear Brent Caxton above the rest yelling, "C'mon, Coach, drive it past him!"

The end finally came when I had won a point and during the next volley Malone, after three or four exchanges, dropped one of his dinks in the right corner. I made a dive for it, got my racket under it and flipped it into the opposite corner where it dropped dead. My point, game, match, meet!

The Sloate boys were jubilant and in the bus on the way home, they sang the Sloate School song, "Fight on for grand old Sloate, mother of boys and maker of men," and repeated choruses of "For he's a jolly good fellow!"

"Gee, Coach," said Caxton, "that driving strategy of yours really works. You had that fat ole guy really sucking wind."

Walking up from the field house after showering and dressing, I allowed myself a little self-congratulation. In a small world small triumphs loom large. I was a campus hero for the next several weeks. The Sloate student newspaper, *The Clarion Call*, ran an interview and a two-column picture of me on the front page. The student photographer insisted on taking my picture in the squash court, in game regalia (although I decided it was not strictly necessary to wear a jockstrap for photographic purposes). Headmaster Makepeace called me into his office and, hopping around like an enthusiastic chickadee, wrung my hand and patted me on the back. "Aspen! Do you realize, Aspen, we haven't been able to beat Grantly Hill at anything except fencing for three years? You're a hero, my boy, and I expect a flock of letters from the alumni telling me to give you a raise in salary. May have to do it."

The night of my triumph I paused at my mailbox before going to my apartment and found a small envelope bearing Meg's feminine handwriting. My heart did a little useless flutter, and I went to my green leather easy chair and read the letter.

"Dearest," she began. "Some bad news and some good. But first let me tell you I still cherish Thanksgiving night. I touch those memories with tender fingers again and again. As long as we live we will have that night to remember.

"Now the bad news. Molly's husband, Charles, died last week after an illness of about three months. Cancer of the liver. Molly is with me now—this is the good news part—but her plans for the future are uncertain. She may stay here indefinitely.

"This next bit you are honor bound to regard as good news. Stuart and I have fixed the date for our wedding for Christmas Eve. You will be receiving an invitation to be a part of the wedding party as an usher, and Stuart has asked me to invite you to stay on in the house over the holidays while we take our honeymoon trip to Antigua.

"There. Bad news and good, but aside from poor Charles, mostly good. The really bad news is that I miss you terribly. And I always will."

I put the letter down and gazed across the room at the bookcases and the mahogany cupboards below. But all I saw in my mind's eye was emptiness, the emptiness that I felt was to keep me company the rest of my life.

Fifteen

On the day the term ended and the boys spread far and wide to their homes for the Christmas holidays, a round of faculty parties enlivened the Sloate campus. The Altbys held a party the first night, and Eve Altby met me at the door, eyes dancing. She was wearing a bright, red dress that clung close to every hill and dale of her luxurious body. "Happy holidays, Stephen!" she said, lifting on one tiptoe to brush her soft lips against my cheek. "Come in and help us make merry."

Brickson Jaeger, the large voluble Kentuckian who taught English, was standing nearby. He leaned over and asked "Did you say something about making merry? That reminds me of the one about it was Christmas Eve and all the boys were making merry. Mary got sore and went home." He bellowed loudly at his joke, and Eve merely said, "Brickson!"

I moved over to a group of men standing with the host, Roger Altby. He greeted me with his dry, reserved manner and poured me a bourbon in an old-fashioned glass bearing the seal of Sloate School. Gilman Brooks reached a hand out to me. "Hello, Stephen," he said in his suave manner, and once again I was struck by his boyish charm and the image of a sleek colt came to mind.

Altby took my arm and pulled me aside. "May I ask a great favor of you, old fella?"

"Sure, Roger. What is it?"

"My brother has just had a major operation, cancer of the lung, and his prospects don't look too good. So I've got to go out to Indiana for a few days. Would you be good enough to drive me to Worcester to catch my train?"

"Sure, happy to do it. When?"

"Tomorrow afternoon. Another thing. Would you look in on Eve from time to time? She gets pretty jumpy when she's left alone."

I looked across the room at his hot-eyed wife who was flouncing around and showing off her appetizing figure. "Sure, my pleasure."

In a moment I went over to a group including the Makepeaces. Cordelia was wearing a brilliant green cockatoo feather in her flaming red hair while Headmaster Makepeace was again wearing his red hunting jacket and black pants. "Greetings, Mr. Aspen," said Cordelia. "We're just hearing a naughty story by Brickson."

"Ah, the champion squash coach, the hero," said Matthew Makepeace as he took my hand in his small bony ones.

"Well, at this point," said Jaeger, "the wife comes up behind her husband who has his back to her while he is bending over the bathtub and says, 'They're not hanging Wright tonight.' Get it? Not hanging *right*? And he says, 'Nag, nag, nag.'" And Jaeger's whoops of laughter bounced off the ceiling and the panelled walls around the room.

"Oh, Brickson, you're so *bad!*" said Cordelia. "So *bad!*"

The Headmaster pursed his lips and said nothing. Gilman Brooks who had also just joined the group rolled his eyes as he looked at me with a wry smile.

I drifted away and found Eve Altby before the fireplace. She greeted me with one of those upward swooping seductive looks and then moved close to me so that her breast nuzzled the back of my hand as I held my drink. "I think it's wonderful how you beat that Grantly Hill squash coach. You must be very good."

"Not all that good. He was pretty porky and slow." She narrowed her eyes alluringly and leaned even closer while the back of my hand pressed more firmly against her plushy round breast. I said, "Eve, Roger tells me he's going out to Indiana for a few days. I'll drop by and check on you now and then while he's gone."

For a flicker of an instant I thought I saw something like a flash of fright in her eyes, but then she smiled and said, "That will be kind of you."

Brickson Jaeger approached us again, chuckling as though he had a joke too good to keep. "I was just telling the Makepeaces about my class on 'Romeo and Juliet' last week. You know it really is one of Shakespeare's bawdiest plays. That fellow, Mercutio, knocks out one horny crack after another. Like greeting Romeo after he has spent the night in Juliet's bedroom, 'Here he comes, without his roe! A dried herring!' And then telling everyone the time is twelve o'clock with the quip: 'the bawdy hand of the dial is now upon the prick of noon.' Of course, I had to point those things out to the little innocents—they never would have got it otherwise.

"But what really sent me off so that I could not speak for five minutes was when little Brookmeyer asked me to explain what the Nurse's husband meant when he said to three-year old Juliet who had just fallen down on her face, 'Thou will fall backward when thou hast more wit, Wilt thou not, Jule?' And Brookmeyer asked, 'What's so witty about falling down on your back, sir?' And I told him, 'If you are a girl it can lead to some very interesting consequences about which many witty remarks have been made'." And Jaeger bellowed again, a high hooting laugh that ricocheted around the room. "Oh, God, what a task it is to explain the real world to these innocents!"

"But you're up to it, Brickson," I said evenly. Then, bringing to mind something good old Roscoe had told me about "Romeo and Juliet," I said, "Tell me, did you know that the very first words Romeo and Juliet exchange form a perfect fourteen-line Elizabethan sonnet?"

Jaeger's broad, oafish face took on a startled look. "No, where did you get that?" He frowned, "In fact, I don't think I believe it."

"Look it up. Act I. You may have missed it because it's not one of the bawdy passages."

Eve looked at me admiringly. "You're wonderful, Stephen! You're a scientist. You're not supposed to know things like that."

"Something I picked up along the way," I said, watching Jaeger's broad receding back as he sought out new listeners to impress, perhaps to shock, with his sophomoric naughtiness.

I circulated around the room for another fifteen minutes and then found my host. "See you tomorrow, Roger. Thanks."

"Right you are, fella."

I found Eve near the door and took her warm, soft hand in mine. "Goodnight, madame hostess."

"Goodnight, dear sir." She rose again on one tiptoe and pressed her full lips against mine. Then she dropped quickly down again and looked quickly over her shoulder. "Goodnight, you lovely man."

Next afternoon Roger Altby and I headed down Highway 34 toward Worcester. Snow had fallen during the past several days and the ridged fields glistened white in the clear winter light, and bluish shadows lined the hollows. The trees made dark charcoal strokes against the white background. We rode in silence for a time and then Roger began to speak in low tones, almost as though talking to himself. "Sometimes I get slightly concerned about the impression people get about Eve. In a party, among a group of people, she is very vivacious, seems self-confident. Maybe a little too outgoing. But—" He let his voice trail off.

"Eve is a very attractive woman. She *should* be self-confident."

"Ye-s-s-s. But—" Again his voice trailed away.

"You used the word 'jumpy.' You said she sometimes got 'jumpy' when you were away."

"That's right. And I admit I don't quite understand it." He turned toward me, his plain, almost expressionless face wearing the tiny edge of a smile. "Anyway, old fella, I'd be grateful if you'd stop by and check on her once or twice. She admires you very much."

"Be happy to."

During the following day and much of the next I was busy in my office grading term papers. Once again, I was startled by the excellence of one or two papers and mildly depressed by the ineptitude of several others. The average, though, was higher than I remembered of my own performance in Grass Lake High School.

Walking back to Sudbury Hall I decided to look in on Eve Altby as I had promised Roger. I must admit that something besides my promise and neighborly compassion was in my mind as I approached her door. Those sultry looks, clinging hands, and gentle nudges with knee and breast when we had been together had more than awakened my curiosity. Had those touches been a preamble to something? Or were they mere flirtations of the moment, without further implications?

I rapped the knocker several times with no answer and then waited in the silence. At last Eve appeared. She was wearing a fluffy white bathrobe and her face and throat were rosy pink and she was fragrant with a musky bath oil. She also looked thoroughly frightened. She held the door open only about a foot. "Oh, hello."

"I just stopped by to see how you're getting on." She offered a thin smile.

There was a pause while we looked at one another through the slightly opened doorway. Then I said, "I thought maybe you'd offer me a glass of sherry on this wintry afternoon."

She looked dubious. "I've just got out of the bath. I'm not very presentable for company."

"You look presentable enough to me. You look lovely."

A ripple of fright moved across her face. Then she smiled that thin smile again and said, "Well, come in then, if you want to. I'll go put on something more decent." She turned and walked away, her white legs slender beneath the fluffy bathrobe and her slippers clip-clopping on the oak floor. "The sherry is on the sideboard," she called as she disappeared.

I poured sherry into two glasses and set them down on a low coffee table before the leather sofa where I took my seat. I waited expectantly. Finding Eve dewy fresh from her bath, rosy and fragrant, seemed to strengthen that other interest I had for my visit.

In a moment Eve reappeared, wearing a gaily flowered housecoat that zippered up the front. She picked up one of the glasses and sat primly in a chair across the room from me, knees close together and legs crossed at the ankles.

"Have you heard from Roger since he left?"

"Last night. He arrived safely but his brother is very bad."

"I'm sorry to hear that. But you've been getting along all right?"

"Ye-s-s-s." She hesitated. "I'm all right." She looked as though she would be happy if I did not ask more questions.

There was a pause while we sipped our sherry. It was quiet in the room, and the absence of boys and the normal activity on the campus made it seem as though Eve and I were isolated from the rest of the world. I had a thought. "It seems a little dark and chilly in here. A fire would be nice. Did Roger leave firewood in the box?"

"Yes. But I can't build a fire. They all smolder and go out."

"I'll build one. An old Boy Scout from Troop 20, Grass Lake, can always start a fire." I grinned knowingly at her with the notion she might think I had more than one kind of fire in mind.

She returned my glance, blank-faced, and looked away.

I gathered wood from the woodbox and soon had a cheerful blaze in the small stone fireplace. I went to Eve and took her hand. "Come sit with me facing the fire, Eve. It's lovely and snug on a winter afternoon."

Reluctantly, it seemed, she got out of her chair, holding my hand out at arm's length, her eyes like a frightened fawn's. She sat down at the opposite end of the sofa from me, her feminine fragrance wafting over me while her body language bespoke defensiveness and resistance. I was baffled, piqued, and slightly irritated. I had a perverse desire to break through Eve's resistance and find out how far she was willing to go. What sense was there in this stand-offishness after all those nudges and come-ons? I watched the crackling blaze for a moment. Then I said, "You don't look very comfortable over there by yourself, Eve. Come sit closer beside me."

She looked at me, eyes wide with alarm. "I'm fine here."

"Then I'll come sit beside you." I slid down the sofa until my thigh brushed hers and took her free hand in mine. "Isn't this better?" I asked and slid my right hand down her leg and squeezed her knee.

"Don't," she said and twitched her leg away.

"But, Eve," I said, throwing myself thoroughly into the part, "I'm terribly attracted to you. You're a lovely, desirable woman, and you've been so sweet to me when we've been together at parties." I bent and kissed her mouth and found it cold and ungiving.

She gasped, whipped her head away and said, "Please don't. Please!"

I released her and leaned back against the sofa. I decided to stop playing the game. "All right, Eve, I give up. I'm baffled. Every time we've been together at parties you've come on to me like Cleopatra to Antony. Looks that would start a fire in the rain and soft nudges and caresses. Tell me, what in the hell has been going on?"

"I don't know what you mean."

"Stop fencing, Eve. You know exactly what I mean."

"I was just being friendly."

"*Friendly!* Seductive is more like it. Any other man, finding you fresh out of the bath this afternoon, would have thrown you over his shoulder and flung you down on the nearest bed."

"I'm afraid I've given you the wrong impression."

"I believe that's possible. What were you trying to do?"

"Oh, I don't know." Then she sighed and turned her face earnestly toward me. "Promise me you won't tell anyone else what I say."

"Promise."

"Wel-l-l." She sighed again. "Well, the truth is I'm not comfortable around the people here. They scare me."

"Scare you? Why?"

"I guess because they're all Easterners and rich and from old families. Roger and I—and especially me—are just a couple of nobodies from Kokomo, Indiana. My father was a salesman in a shoe store and never finished high school. I'm always scared to death I'll say the wrong thing and ruin things for Roger."

"He seems to be able to handle things all right. He's fitted in perfectly."

"Sure. Roger's smart. He's as smart as any of them. But me, I'm just dumb. Kind of pretty but dumb."

"Eve, you badly underrate yourself But tell me. What made you decide to pick on me?"

She turned a shy smile toward me. 'I wanted you to like me. You seemed like a nice guy. Friendly and from Michigan, the Middle West, like me. I thought if you liked me I would have at least one person to feel comfortable with at the faculty parties."

I looked thoughtfully at the troubled, artless woman beside me, so thoroughly attractive and yet so misguided, so ill-equipped to deal with the milieu in which she had been placed. All I felt then for this ingenuous woman beset by circumstances not of her choosing was gentle sympathy. I reached over and patted the back of her hand. "You suc-

ceeded, Eve. I would have liked you without all those feminine wiles. I like you because you're sweet and attractive
and fun to be around."

"Those are kind words."

"Genuine. Now that we understand one another, you
know you have a friend. From now on I'll be looking for
you at all the faculty parties." I stood up. "More sherry
before I go?"

"I don't think so. But must you go? Stay and tell me
more about yourself."

"Another time. How about the fire? Shall I put another
log on?"

"That would be nice. Yes, thank you."

I positioned a big log on the fire so that it would draw
and walked to the front door. Eve followed and as I put my
hand on the latch I said, "If you need anything, call me."

"I will, Stephen." She reached up then and gave me a
gentle, sisterly kiss. "Goodnight."

The wedding party gathered for dinner the night before
Meg's and Stuart's wedding. We had walked through a
rehearsal at the First Congregational Church that afternoon.
It was to be a formal but not grandiose ceremony with three
bridesmaids and three ushers. An uncle of Meg's from Ip-
swich was to give the bride away. Benjamin Coffin, Stuart's
lawyer, was best man.

At dinner and afterward over cognac I sat beside the
recently returned Molly. I had expressed my condolences
which Molly received matter-of-factly, and by the time we
were sipping cognac we were just about back to where we
were when I had watched her riding off in Charles's car to
take up her marriage once again. Molly had changed, but
only a little. She seemed calmer, slightly less bouncy, but
she was still tight in her skin and gave off that indefinable
lure of a desirable female.

"You know, Stephen, as well as I," she said quietly as

we sat side by side on the couch, "my marriage with Charles never was much of a love match. Oh, I miss him. Of course I do. Miss the solid everydayness of our lives. But thanks in part to you I feel I made Charles the best wife I could so I have no regrets. But now I've got to decide what to do with myself next."

I watched across the room as Meg, radiant in turquoise blue, moved around the room to talk with one person after another. "What do you think that might be? Will you stay around here?"

"Might. Meg offered me the house in Brixton and thinks I might be able to take over her job at the library."

I grinned at the thought. "Molly, the librarian? Doesn't seem exactly in character."

She turned quickly toward me, her eyes saucy. "Not the bookish type, you mean? Just what would you say I am qualified for?" she asked with a witchy smile.

"My innate sense of decorum prevents me from answering truthfully on this solemn occasion."

In response, she jabbed me in the ribs with a sharp finger. "Beast!" she hissed.

But aside from these exchanges with Molly I found watching Meg, glowing with womanly beauty and playing convincingly the role of a woman about to enter into a happy marriage, a devastatingly unhappy experience. Once or twice Meg and I exchanged long glances, but in the main she held her head high and moved among us serenely. I tried my best to appear to be a man happy that his friend and benefactor was marrying the woman of his choice.

But my best apparently was not good enough to deceive the knowing eye of Molly. Once during the dinner party she asked me in a low voice, "Do I detect the aroma of a lost love?"

I looked into her questioning eyes. "Meg and I have been close friends. I'm going to miss our intimacy."

She grinned knowingly. "Sounds like the first paragraph of a more honest confession." She reached over and patted my hand. "After the wedding you'd better come by and have a long talk with Sister Molly."

On Christmas Eve, the wedding day, the First Congregational Church reposed on fresh, white snow and seemed a factual replica of a thousand postcards depicting New England in winter. And Meg with her small, neatly featured face and Stuart with his strong-jawed, prominent-nosed countenance seemed as thoroughly New England as the church. The interior of the church was spare and the ceremony short and almost terse. Afterward there was a brief reception with cake and champagne and then we were all standing in the doorway waving goodbye to the wedding couple as they were whisked away for a train to Boston, a night at the Parker House, a train to New York, and an airplane to Antigua.

I stayed for a few days at Stuart's house as had been planned, and then, bored with nothing to do and weighed down by the knowledge that I was living where Meg would soon be mistress—passing by the doorway of the master bedroom with its large, four-posted bed grew daily more painful—I packed up the convertible and drove back to Sloate School and Sudbury Hall.

Sixteen

In the days before school resumed I worked in the laboratory, organizing, reorganizing, and restoring order. Even with the best of daily attention, a laboratory gradually falls into disarray. Solutions get used up, specimens are returned to the wrong tray, and dissecting tools are mislaid. I acquired from my father a passion for neatness and organization, so I spent several enjoyable days getting my laboratory shipshape once again.

Then, after reading the term papers and the final examinations taken just before the term ended, I turned to making out grades. I found few surprises. The three stars, Woods Jefferson, Clinton Wiener, and Boynton Ross deserved and were given A's. Then came a middle group, including Brent Caxton, who fell into the B and C range. I finally gave Caxton a C+. Then I turned to the two boys at the bottom of the class, Billy Reston and Jimmy Dixon. Their term papers were skimpy and shoddy and their examinations were a full grade below the others.

The choice lay between a D, a passing grade without credit, or an F for failure. I worried over the decision for a long time. I got up from my desk and looked out the window at the snow-laden, deserted campus, the great oaks and hickories standing stark against the winter sky. No teacher—

or at least no *good* teacher—wants to give a student a failing grade, if only because it raises the distinct possibility
that the teacher has not taught well. But at the same time,
no good teacher wants to reward laziness or inattention. Back
and forth I went in my mind, trying to assess the impact on
the boys of either grade, and at last I decided to fail them
both. If nothing else, to have passed them would have been
unfair to the other boys who had worked for the most part
up to the level of their capabilities. These two clearly had
not.

With the grades made out and the grade sheets completed for the registrar, I left my office about four o'clock.
It was a crystalline afternoon with a sharp wind knifing out
of the northwest. As I walked along the curving pathway
toward Sudbury Hall, the wind stinging cold against my
cheek and the slanting sunlight casting sparkles on the crusty
snow, I suddenly decided to stop by Eve Altby's. I had not
seen her since my return from Meg's wedding. At that time
I had felt my own state of mind required all my attention
without involving myself further with Eve's problems. In
that first week I had not wanted to see or talk to anyone.
I needed time to regain my equilibrium.

As a consequence, when I walked up to the Altby's door
I was feeling guilty for having neglected Eve, especially since
the clerk at the school post office had told me a day or two
before that Roger had not returned because his brother in
Indiana had died. I knocked at the front door and listened
to the silence that followed. After several minutes, I knocked
again. And then again. And waited. Finally, I tried the door
and found it unlocked. I opened it a foot or so and called,
"Eve!" Silence. I called again, "Eve, it's Stephen." Again I
listened and heard the sound that defines silence like no
other: the steady ticking of a mantel clock. I stepped inside
and closed the door behind me. As I walked across the living room toward the bedroom I called again, softly, "Eve?"
The bedroom door was open, the bed neatly made. Eve was
not there. The bathroom door was closed but there was no

sound of water running or toilet flushing. I knocked gently on the door. "Eve? It's Stephen." I waited, reluctant to open the door and possibly embarrass her. I knocked again and then in the waiting silence I opened the door and found Eve.

She lay on her back, a pool of pink water shrouding her body except for her head leaning against the back of the bathtub and her breasts rising slightly out of the pink sea like mounded islands. I reached for her wrist and through the blood oozing from the slashes I felt a faint pulse.

I ran back to the bedroom, taking my pocket knife out as I ran, ripped the bed open and cut two long strips out of the sheet. Then I ran back to the bathroom and put a tourniquet on each arm, a procedure I had learned for a Boy Scout merit badge.

I took off my jacket and my wrist watch, reached into the tub, got my hands under Eve's armpits and eased her slowly up the back of the tub. Hefting an inert hundred pound bag of cement, which I had done as a teenager on a summer job, is difficult enough, but hoisting a limp and floppy naked woman is far worse. Besides, she was slippery, and I was concerned not to drop her back into the tub or down onto the tile floor. At last after wrestling several moments with the dripping and bleeding woman I got her into a position where I could get my shoulder under her waist. I straightened slowly, holding her in place by the backs of her knees and carried her into the bedroom. I laid her gently on the bed, and covered her with a blanket. Then I went to the telephone.

On the desk beside the telephone was the Sloate School directory. I looked up "Infirmary," fairly certain no one would be there, but beneath that entry was: "In Emergency: Dr. Reuben Featherstone, tel 692." Dr. Featherstone, the school's attending physician, lived in Adams, the nearby village. When he answered, I said, "Mrs. Altby has had an accident. Can you come at once to her quarters in Welbury Hall?"

"Be there in ten minutes."

I went to the bathroom and looked in the medicine cabinet for bandage material. All I found was small band-aids and a roll of adhesive tape. I also saw, standing on the flat end of the tub near the faucets, a bottle of sleeping pills and a safety razor blade. I took the cap off the bottle and saw that only a few pills were missing from a nearly full container. Probably not enough to be lethal.

I hurried back to the bedroom and used my knife again to cut broad strips out of the sheet. These I folded into two oblong packets and made compress bandages for both wrists and secured them with the tape I had found. Then I eased off the tourniquets and watched to see whether renewed bleeding was staining the bandages. While I watched I put my finger against the carotid artery in her throat (more Boy Scout lore) and felt a faint, steady pulse. I pulled up a chair and sat beside the bed watching. Eve's face was ghostly white and her nostrils pinched and ashen at the edges, but the blanket over her was gently rising and falling as she breathed.

In about ten minutes I heard a car door slam and I went to the front door to let Dr. Featherstone in. "Suicide attempt, Dr. Featherstone," I said. "I found her in the bathtub."

"Dear God! Pills, poison?"

"No, slashed wrists. Probably a few sleeping pills also." I pointed to the bedroom door. "She's in the bedroom."

The round-bodied little man, wearing a red stocking cap and a shiny black overcoat, trotted across the living room carrying his black satchel. I walked behind him to the bed-room door. "I'll wait out here unless you need me." He went in and during the long silence that followed the mantel clock steadily beat the pulse of passing time. I went over to the desk and picked up a copy of the *Publications of the Modern Language Association*, a thick grey paperbound book with a table of contents on the cover. My eye fell on a title, "Problems in Punctuation in Thomas Campion's Lyrics." I put it down.

Dr. Featherstone came out of the bedroom. "I think you caught her in time. Saved her life." A small smile crossed his red-cheeked face punctuated by a short, bristly moustache. "You're the new master, Mr. Aspen, aren't you?"

"Yes, I am."

"Well, sir, she's lost a deal of blood. She's going to need a transfusion. And right soon. We'd best get her down to the County Hospital.

I frowned, shaking my head, "I would hope we could avoid that."

"Why?"

"Publicity. The poor woman's got enough problems without it being known she attempted suicide."

He looked at me quizzically. "But I can't treat her here."

"How about the Infirmary?"

He cocked his head. "S'pose that's possible. We've got a small blood supply stored there. May not be the right type."

"Well, if we can't, we can't. But it's worth a try."

He stood studying my face for a moment. "All right. Let's bundle her up. Can you carry her?"

"Sure." He nodded and as he turned toward the bedroom, I said, "You see, my notion of what happened, Dr. Featherstone, is that Mrs. Altby fainted in the bathroom while taking some pills, dropped the glass she was holding, and fell on the shards and cut her wrists."

He looked back over his shoulder. "That's neat and almost plausible."

"While you're getting her ready I'll go in the bathroom and smash a glass."

In a moment we had Eve bundled up tightly. As I lifted her off the bed I thought I heard a slight murmur, but as I carried her out to Dr. Featherstone's car her head lolled loosely against my shoulder. He opened the rear door, and I slid her onto the seat, then ran around and got in the other side. I pulled her against me and again I seemed to hear a tiny murmur. "All set, Doc," I said.

When the car stopped in front of the green-shuttered Infirmary, Dr. Featherstone said as he got out, "Let me open the door and turn on some lights before you bring her in." I sat waiting in the car with Eve slumped beside me while the cooling engine ticked quietly. Then the doctor, standing in the lighted doorway, waved to me. I slid across the seat until I could get one foot on the ground and pulled Eve toward me. The next few moments of wrestling with her inert body to position it so I could carry her reminded me sharply and painfully of that terrible noontime in Illinois when I struggled frantically to pull Roscoe Bilder's already dead body out of his car.

At last I got her where I could get both arms under her and lift. There was a split second when my foot slipped on the icy road and I expected us both to land in a heap but I managed to recover and stagger toward the doorway. "Put her on the examining table there," Dr. Featherstone said, gesturing toward the brilliantly lighted white-tiled room. "I've got to draw a little blood to get her blood type."

I laid her carefully on the taut sheet of the table. "I'll wait outside." I walked out into the hallway and strolled slowly up and down, gazing at the bright-colored posters chronicling the medical feats of Hippocrates, Galen, and Harvey.

Shortly later, the doctor appeared in the doorway. "Bad news. She's Type O Positive and we don't have any in the blood bank."

"Hold on! *I'm* Type O Positive."

"Are you sure?"

"Absolutely. I had to learn it for my First Aid merit badge."

The cherry-cheeked little man with the stubby black moustache looked at me speculatively. "Are you willing to give a fair amount of blood? I'm going to need more than one pint."

"Whatever you say. I'm in pretty good condition."

The doctor directed me to roll up my left sleeve and lie

down on the other examining table. Deftly he hooked me up and pulled out a pint of blood. "Just lay there a minute," he said. Then he hooked up Eve, lying still and white-faced, and after a few minutes he took her blood pressure and shook his head. "We'll have to go for another one," he said and quickly hooked me up again.

"You seem to have done this procedure a few times before," I said as I watched his dextrous motions.

He smiled a wry smile. "Serving eighteen months in the Massachusetts General Emergency Room gives a man a lot of practice." Again he transfused my blood into Eve, waited, and then took her blood pressure. He looked up from his sphygmomanometer anxiously. "I hate to ask this, but are you game for one more? You'll feel pretty lousy and may pass out."

"Let her rip. It's in a good cause."

Again he made the transfer of blood from my artery into Eve's arm. When he had taken her pressure he said, "That's about as good as we can do for now." He squinted at me. "How're you doing?"

"The lights in the room seem to be getting dimmer."

"Just as I thought. Let me help you into the next room where you can stretch out on the bed. Also we need to get some fluids in you."

He took my arm and swung it around his neck, half carrying me, while I with legs like cooked spaghetti stumbled beside him and flopped onto the bed. By this time the room was becoming totally dark.

When my eyes opened sometime later I was staring at the acoustic-tiled ceiling, and I tried without success to make patterns with the holes in the tiles. They persisted in running in straight lines, vertically and horizontally. Dr. Featherstone appeared, took my hand in his, and wrapped my fingers around a glass. He placed a plastic straw in my mouth. "Sip this juice," he said, "and tomorrow keep on drinking all the liquids you can." He stood watching me, his round belly cinched with a black leather belt touching the edge of the hospital bed. "I've got hold of a nurse in Adams. She'll take care of the lady overnight. And I'll come back and check on her in the morning." He turned around and started packing his little black satchel. "I've got to leave as soon as I'm sure you're not going to pass out again. I have office hours from four to six and my waiting room is probably jammed to the gills."

"I'll be all right, Doc."

"You haven't tried to get on your feet yet." He patted my shoulder. "I'd wait until Nurse Bundy gets here before doing that." He started to leave, then turned back. "The lady will probably be coming around in a little while."

I lay looking up at him. I was beginning to feel a little more solid, a little more knitted together. "You know, Doc, something I've noticed. You haven't asked me how I happened to be alone with Mrs. Altby."

He chuckled. "Well, I guess I've been around long enough to know not to ask questions when a man is alone with another man's wife." He glanced sideways at me out of his shrewd little eyes. "Especially when the lady's as good to look at as Mrs. Altby."

"Her husband is in Indiana attending his brother's funeral. He asked me to check up on her now and then."

"Danged good thing you did. Saved her life." He picked up his black overcoat and hunched his shoulders up a couple of times to get it on. He looked back at me. "You take it slow and easy. Don't try to get up until Nell Bundy gets here."

"Okay."

I heard his rubbers shuffle as he walked down the hall. Then the door slammed, and shortly I heard the grinding of an engine starter and then the diminishing sounds of a car leaving. My eyes preferred to stay closed against the glare of the white ceiling and I soon fell into a halfway state, neither asleep nor awake, but just drifting. I came to with a start when I heard a woman's voice, saying something plaintive but indistinguishable. It was Eve.

I knew I had to get to her despite the doctor's admonishment to stay in bed until the nurse came. I swung my legs over the side of the cot and pushed down on the bed with my hands as I straightened my knees. I almost made it up and then my knees buckled and I plopped back down. My heart was beating like I had just finished a fast game of squash and my head seemed filled with air. I could hear Eve murmuring in the next room, and I knew I had to try again. This time I turned so that I was bent face down toward the bed with my arms extended. I got my knees straight and then slowly pushed up until I was erect. The room swirled around briefly, then steadied, and I managed to totter to the doorway and grab hold of the door frame. Then, after a pause, I lunged several steps forward and caught the edge of the examining table.

At the sound Eve turned her face toward me and gazed with unfocused eyes. She frowned with the effort to see clearly, and then looked surprised. "Stephen?"

"Yes, it's me, Eve. It's Stephen."

She frowned again. "But, where—?"

"You're in the Infirmary, Eve. I found you and got the doctor to come and you're going to be fine." I was talking fast because I was racing against imminent collapse.

Eve stared at me for several seconds while comprehension slowly gathered. Then she turned her head sharply away, and in a faint voice said, "Oh, Stephen! I'm so shamed."

Shamed? Now it was my turn to struggle for comprehension. "Shamed" because I had found her naked in the bathtub or "shamed" because of her bungled suicide? But the effort of keeping upright while clinging to the table was enough of a challenge without adding the burden of thinking so I gave it up. "You'll be fine, Eve," I muttered.

Then I heard the front door swing open and in bounced apple-cheeked Nurse Nell Bundy with a bright red woolen scarf over her head. "Well, well. How's everybody in here?" she asked cheerily while shedding her coat and scarf. "Oh, I see you're awake," she said to Eve. She turned to me. "And what about you, young man? You look a little peak-id."

"Just a little woozy."

"Well, let's get you back in bed over here." She took me firmly in hand with a strong arm around my waist and steered me back to the bed. "You just sip on this juice while I find a nightgown and robe to make the lady comfortable."

Lying down again was bliss and I sank back into that drifting state with relief. Some time later I came wide awake again, and this time I felt quite solid. I got to my feet, a little wobbly but head clear, and found Nurse Bundy sitting in a chair beside a sleeping Eve. She was knitting something with heavy dark blue yarn. "I'm going to go home."

Then with the nurse's anxious instruction to take it easy, I put on my coat and left. I was kitten-weak but not light-headed, and the first breath of outside air, Arctic air that had recently left Manitoba on the wings of a northwest wind, swept my head clear of any lingering wispiness. The wind, like a cold hand on my back, pushed me up the walkway. I went to the Altby apartment and let myself in. On the small desk in the living room I found an address book and placed a call to Roger's brother's house in Kokomo.

After passing through several hands, I got Roger. I told him that Eve had had an accident and was in the Infirmary and was going to be all right. "But it's essential that you come home immediately, Roger. Tomorrow."

There was a pause while Roger absorbed this information. Then he said in his measured way, "Can't make it tomorrow, old fella. Couple of things to finish up here. Maybe day after tomorrow."

In my present state I was very short on patience. I shouted back in the telephone, "*Tomorrow*, Roger. You've got to come back tomorrow!"

There was silence from his end. Then he said, "I don't quite understand the urgency. You said Eve was going to be all right."

"Never mind what I said. You get your ass back here tomorrow!"

Again a period of silence. Then, "All right, my friend,

I'm baffled, but I'll be on that train tomorrow that gets in from Albany about 5:30."

"Good. I'll be there."

Back in my apartment I half ran to my bedroom and fell into bed without undressing. Next morning I felt loose in my joints but clear in the head and I could sense that normality was on its way. I went through my normal teaching routine in the morning. After lunch I went back to the Altby apartment and scrubbed down the blood-spattered bathroom and gathered the soaked and bloody bedding into a bundle for the laundry. Then I set out in the convertible for Worcester and Roger.

He came into the waiting room looking his usual imperturbable self. Once in the car and headed back for Sloate I gave him a play-by-play account of the previous evening. When I finished he said thoughtfully, "I told you she might be a bit jumpy in my absence, but I didn't think it would come to this. She must have been upset about something else too."

I dimmed my lights in response to a flash from an oncoming truck. "Eve is very uncomfortable here at Sloate. She feels out of place, lonely, alien." I went on to recount the conversation I had had with her several days earlier.

Glancing sideways, I could see in the dim glow of the dashlights a slight frown on Roger's face. "I don't understand that. I'll admit I found the Yankee way of looking at things a bit strange too at first but I adjusted to it."

"You've adapted completely. You've become as Yankee as the Yankees. But not Eve. She feels out of her element here."

He shook his head. "Oh, she'll snap out of it. Something temporary must have set her off."

Exasperation swept away all my sympathetic patience. "Goddammit, Roger, don't be so mule-headed! Your wife tried to kill herself last night. A healthy young woman does not go to that extreme unless she's deeply troubled. I'm telling you right now, you're either going to get Eve out of Sloate or lose her through suicide or separation."

He turned his long, solemn face toward me. "You're in dead earnest, aren't you?"

"Yes, Roger. *Yes!*"

He sat quietly for a moment while I watched in my rearview mirror as a Greyhound bus that had been gaining on us for several minutes started to pull out to pass me. "You make my leaving Sloate sound easy. Where do you suggest I might go?"

"Back to Indiana or somewhere in the region. Somewhere where Eve will feel more at home. With your teaching credentials you ought to have no trouble finding a job."

He gazed at me for a moment and then looked straight ahead. "As a matter of fact, the dean at Ball State, Jesse Baxter, friend of my brother's, talked to me at the funeral about an opening in the English department. Said he'd like to see me come back."

"Manna from Heaven, Roger. Manna from Heaven."

After that we both said little for the rest of the way until we reached the white gates at the entrance to Sloate School and Roger said, "I'll talk it over with Eve and then decide what to do." He reached over and patted my hand on the steering wheel. "Anyway, I sure want to thank you for everything you've done. You've been a true friend to Eve and to me."

"Eve is a lovely woman and a good wife, Roger. You ought to take good care of her."

Seventeen

The second week of January 1954 brought the boys streaming back and daily life at Sloate School regained normality with its boisterous commotion outside my hall doorway, the uncertain decorum at mealtimes, and the monitored quiet of the classrooms. It also brought about that false promise of spring, the annual January thaw in New England—brilliant sunshine, gentle breezes, and temperatures in the middle fifties. In a region where, as one cynic observed, there are two seasons, winter and July, this gentle caress was like a frigid woman's kiss—promise without result.

But false or not, fine weather in January in New England is to be enjoyed while it lasts, and I walked back from the dining hall after breakfast with my coat open wide and a smile on my face. Just before I reached the entrance to Sudbury Hall I was intercepted by Julie North, Headmaster Makepeace's secretary. "Oh, Mr. Aspen. Headmaster wants to see you right away."

"Okay, Julie. I'll just stop by my place first and pick up my briefcase."

"Mr. Aspen. He said, *right away.*"

"Oh?" I looked at her questioningly. "Well, okay."

In his office, I found Headmaster Matthew Makepeace

pacing up and down with a fierce scowl on his sharp face. "There you are, Aspen!" he barked. He glared at me like an enraged sparrow hawk. "I suppose you know you've got me in a goldanged mess with our most important trustee, Trevor Reston."

"Who?"

"Trevor Reston, that's who! Our best fund raiser and next chairman of the board of trustees. You flunked his son, Billy. Trevor got me on the horn at 6:30 this morning, hot as a firecracker, breathin' fire and brimstone. Wants me to fire you within the hour."

"Oh, *Billy* Reston. Yes, I did fail him in biology."

The Headmaster glowered at me. "Don't you understand we're here to *educate* boys? Teach 'em—not flunk 'em?"

"Yes, I understand that. But, Headmaster, Billy did not do the work. His term paper was a disgrace and his final exam was a full grade below the rest. He did not perform anywhere near the level of his capabilities."

The Headmaster jerked his head up and down several times expressively. "Your job, mister, is to make certain he *does*. In this school you take 'em by the back of the neck and push their nose deep down into the book. You don't flunk 'em. You *make* 'em work."

"Yes, sir." I stared at the angry little man, his blue eyes snapping and his lips twitching with emotion. "Well, Headmaster, I'm sorry about the situation this puts you in. What do you want me to do now?"

"*Do?*" he snapped. "Withdraw the grade. Make it a D, if you like."

I shook my head. "I'm sorry, but I can't do that."

His eyes popped incredulously. "You refuse to do as I ask?"

"If you are asking me to withdraw a grade based on my best judgment as a teacher, then, yes, I refuse."

He scowled at me for a long moment, and then turned away and paced up and down in jerky little steps behind his desk. He stopped and faced me. "Goldang it, Aspen, you know danged well I don't want to fire you. Matter of fact, couldn't do it in midyear even if I wanted to." His expression changed from angry scowl to near pleading. "But you got to understand, son, I'm in a helluva—pardon my French—spot." We stood for several minutes confronting each other in the high-ceilinged office while the large Seth Thomas clock on the wall ticked off the seconds. Finally, he said, "So, you see the fix I'm in. Just what do you suggest I do about it?"

I thought for a moment, firm in my determination not to change young Reston's grade but seeking some way to ease Headmaster Makepeace's problem. Finally, I said, "I would be willing, Mr. Makepeace, to have Reston's work and the grade I assigned to it reviewed by a competent judge."

"You'd be willing to abide by the decision, whatever it was?"

I hesitated. "Yes, I would."

He gazed at me thoughtfully. "I guess the logical thing to do then is to refer the review to the Scholastic Standards Committee of the faculty. Let them decide."

"That's fine by me." I waited for him to say something or to dismiss me. He was standing sideways to me, staring out the window. "Just one thing we ought to have understood, sir. If the committee rules against my decision, I will resign at the end of the school year."

He wheeled quickly around. "Now, now. Let's not jump the traces. We'll face that when and if it comes." He nodded briskly. "Meanwhile, I'll tell Mr. Reston we're reviewing the matter."

"All right." I turned then and left.

On my way to Edison Hall I met Roger Altby. "Good morning, fella!" he said cheerily. "Join me in the lounge for a cup of coffee?"

Coffee, I felt, might help settle me down, so I agreed and we strolled over to the faculty lounge. Fragrant cups of coffee in hand we took a table near a window looking out at the bright and deceitful morning. Roger, unlike me, was clearly in an upbeat mood. "Eve is feeling fine again," he said, "and she asked me to express her undying—whups, unconscious pun there—her tremendous gratitude when I saw you."

"Glad she's all right."

"Yes, she's fine." He sipped his coffee. "We've had several good talks recently about her state of mind."

"Great." I gazed at his self-satisfied, complacent face. "Have you gotten in touch with your friend, the dean, at Ball State?"

"Not yet. I thought first I'd find out for sure whether Eve is really that dissatisfied."

I exploded, "For Christ's sake, Roger! Aren't two slashed wrists convincing enough for you? What do you want her to do, cut her throat at high noon in Sunday chapel? You damn well better write or telephone the dean before that job vanishes. It's the perfect answer for you and Eve."

He looked at me curiously. "You seem a little edgy or upset this morning."

"Never mind that. We're talking about the serious problem you and Eve have." I scowled at him for a moment and then said, "As a matter of fact, I *am* upset. I've just come from a bad session with the Headmaster." Then I told him about the matter of Billy Reston's grade and my discussion with Headmaster Makepeace.

"You say he's asking the Committee on Scholastic Standards to review the grade? *I'm* on that committee."

"Oh? Who else?"

"Well, Brickson Jaeger, Schofield in chemistry, Matthews in history, Dunlap in political science, Arnold in classics." He counted with his fingers on the edge of the table. "That's five, there are six. Oh, and myself." He looked thoughtfully out the window for a moment. "I think the chances are pretty good the committee would back a teacher up in a case like this. But I'm never certain which way Jaeger is going to jump, he's so damned full of himself and erratic. Well, Dunlap, either, for that matter."

"That's not entirely reassuring." We sat quietly for a few minutes finishing our coffee. I put my cup down on its saucer. "Well, I've got to make *something* good out of this day before it's over." I got up and tapped Roger on the shoulder, "Meanwhile, I wish you'd write your dean today." He nodded. "I guess I will. I'll tell him I may be interested."

"Tell him you'll take the goddammed job," I growled.

That afternoon I got hold of Billy Reston and sat him down in my office for a talk. He was an attractive boy, somewhat undersized for his age but remarkably handsome with an elegantly shaped head, bright blue eyes, and dark, close-cropped hair. "Well, Billy," I said, "you and I were not too successful working together last semester, were we?"

He gazed at me without expression. "Guess not."

I looked at him kindly. "Any idea why not?"

He stared down at his hands. "I guess I did not study hard enough."

I chuckled. "That's a pretty good answer, Billy. An honest answer." I sat looking at the small, withdrawn boy whose every aspect declared he was very unwillingly in my presence. I decided a change of subject was needed. "How was your Christmas vacation? You went home to Westchester, didn't you?"

His expression became sullen. He shook his head. "No, sir."

"Oh?"

He squirmed a little sideways in his seat. "You see, my father has a place at Hobe Sound in Florida. He had me and some of his friends down for Christmas."

"And the rest of your family?"

His face twisted and for a moment I thought he was going to cry. "My brother and sister were with my mother in Westchester."

I gazed forbearingly at the unhappy child, my attitude quickly shifting from reproving teacher to friendly counselor as Billy's answer gave me insight and understanding.

Billy's poor school performance was clearly related to his family situation—a family in which at Christmas time, of *all* times, a father divided himself and one son from the rest of the family, from his wife and two other children. I could hardly imagine the hurt which that separation inflicted on a teenage boy who had spent the three previous months in a boarding school separated from home and family.

In a try at lightening the situation a little, I offered, "Well, Billy, you probably had some fun sailing or surfing in Florida."

"No, it was lousy. Cold and rainy."

We sat silently for a moment, I contemplating the handsome, disturbed boy while he looked down at the floor. Then I said, "Well, Billy, I'll tell you what we're going to do about biology. We'll get together with Jimmy Dixon for an hour or so each week and go over the assignments."

He looked up earnestly. 'I don't think that will be necessary, sir. I just need to work harder."

"Well, let's try it for a while anyway."

"All right, sir."

I smiled encouragingly at him. "Another thing, Billy. I remember you tried out for the squash team this past season, didn't you."

"Yes, sir. But I didn't make it. I wasn't good enough."

"Well, look, Billy. We're going to lose Bobby Powell this spring when he graduates and there'll be an opening on the team. Why don't you and I work out together now and then? Maybe we can sharpen up your game for next year."

For the first time a broad grin swept over the handsome face. "I think I'd like that, sir. That would be neat."

That afternoon Jason Dunlap, the chairman of the Scholastic Standards Committee, came by to pick up Billy Reston's term paper and his finals blue book. "We'll need examples for each of the higher grades, too," the robust, full-bearded man told me. "Perhaps several examples at the C level."

I sorted through the files and provided him with the

papers. "This is a bad business, you know, Aspen. It pays to find out who the parents of your students are. Makes it easier to avoid crises like this."

I gazed at him evenly. "I thought academic grades were awarded on the basis of merit and achievement."

He gave vent to a loud guffaw. "Well, yes, certainly. But now and then it's wise to trim around the edges a little, so to speak." He packed up the papers in his briefcase and turned to leave. "Headmaster has asked us to complete the review by Friday. We know what he wants and plan to give it to him." As I watched his broad back pass through my office door, I reflected that those parting words had an ominous ring.

Mid-morning the next day I was down on the coastal marshland, buzzing down the tidal creek in Stuart Price's lap-straked skiff. It was Wednesday, the 15th, the day of the month Stuart Price usually convened his meeting of the nature sanctuary supervisory board. Stuart of course was still honeymooning in Antigua and no meeting would be held. But I had scheduled myself to be absent from school every 15th of the month, so I decided to spend the day looking around the sanctuary for problems, such as a break in the fence along the highway or evidence of poaching, maybe a concealed duck blind. Whatever else, it gave me an excuse to break away from the cloistered atmosphere of school and the Billy Reston problem and to breathe the vigorous air and savor the tangy smell of the salt marsh. The wind against my face as I moved easterly down the creek had swept directly off the North Atlantic, but I was wearing heavy winter gear and ski mittens and the raw breeze felt invigorating. For the moment, at least, I was far from the uncertain threat of Jason Dunlap's review committee. The creek was at half tide, incoming, and though the banks were crusted with ice the channel was flowing clear and sea green.

I turned in at the entrance to Price's dock and cut the outboard. The skiff glided silently alongside the rough wooden pilings until I caught hold of one, stopped the boat, and tied up. The path up the slight rise to the little cabin was six inches deep in crusted snow, snow that had melted on the top several times and frozen again. But no tracks of any intruder marked the path, and the little house had apparently been visited only by a curious red fox whose tracks led away across the marsh.

Back in the boat I cruised on down the tidal creek to the Sound and then pointed the bow north toward the Marker River, the upper boundary of the sanctuary. Flocks of goldeneyes, redheads, and buffleheads lifted off the water as I approached and wheeled around and plopped down again in my wake. The black head of a harbor seal surfaced briefly ahead and then sank again without a ripple. Out again in the flatness and seeming desolation of the salt marsh amidst flying ducks and the flooding tide, I seemed to be reliving those strenuous but lighthearted hours I spent researching my thesis. Memories of those days went hand in hand, however, with other memories dear to me, and simultaneously remembrances of Meg came rushing back as well. I had been fairly successful since the wedding in keeping thoughts of that endearing woman at bay but Meg's associations with the marshland and the ducks and the tides were too strong to withstand isolation. And then along with those memories of Meg came a renewed sense of deep loss.

After cruising slowly up the Marker River as it curved and twisted through the marsh, scanning the shore closely as I ran the Evinrude outboard at half throttle, now and then poking the nose of the bow into a small tributary that could have concealed a blind, I turned back to the Sound. When my old lookout site came abeam, I turned in toward shore and beached the boat below the observation shed. I stepped gingerly across a sheet of ice left by the previous tide and walked up the slight rise to the little building. Like Price's cabin, it appeared unmolested and sound. I opened the door, which stuck at first because of an ice ridge under the door-sill, and stepped inside. Directly in front of me, of course, stood the cot where Meg and I had made love while the storm raged outside. I stood for a moment as I remembered lying with Meg on the cot, her body sodden at first beneath mine, and then warming from the glow of my body covering hers. And I smiled as I remembered her murmuring at one point, "Would it be all right with you if I took a breath?" But the memories which were sweet when first recollected quickly turned sour as the reality of the present reasserted itself, and I turned away. I closed up the little shed, went back to the boat, and pointed her down the Sound toward the Yare River.

The Yare marked the southern boundary of the sanctuary and as I putted slowly up it I looked for signs of poaching on the north bank. I found none and shortly I arrived at the Brixton town dock where I tied up and strolled up to Avery's general store. Mrs. Avery, wearing a grey apron over her blue gingham dress, greeted me noisily, "Hey, Clint, come and see this stranger."

Clinton Avery extended a bony hand in greeting, and we stood chatting for a few minutes amidst the boxes, bins and cluttered shelves and the mingled smells of spices, fertilizer, ground coffee, and galvanized nails. We commented at some length on the weather and exchanged information about each other. "Been a few changes around here since you left," said Mrs. Avery. "Meg Satterlee married that rich fella, Price, I s'pose you know, and moved up with him. The sister, Molly, has come back—a widow now, I hear—and she's taken over the family home. Also taken over Meg's job at the library."

I nodded, "I guess while I'm here I better look in on her." I turned to Clinton Avery. "Business holding up all right?"

"Lousy as ever," he said. "But we're survivin'. Guess that's about all you can ask for these days."

"That's the truth," said Mrs. Avery as I moved toward the door and we said goodbye.

Molly, wearing a tan camelhair overcoat and a paisley

scarf over her head, came out of the door of the library just as I walked up. Her face lighted with a broad smile. "Stephen! What a delight to see you!" She reached up and pecked my cheek.

"I've been out in the boat all day inspecting the nature sanctuary and decided to stop by."

"I couldn't be happier. Come have some tea. You probably could enjoy hot tea after your day out in the weather, and I'm badly in need of company." She glanced out the corner of her eyes. "Especially male company." She took my arm and we walked along under the bare-boughed maple trees. "You know," she said with a chuckle, "the only available men here are Hank down at the filling station—he chews tobacco and spits—and Junior Naylor, the clerk at the post office who has acne."

"Severe deprivation," I said. "*Especially* for you."

"Right!" After several steps, she asked slyly, "Under these circumstances, do you think you'll be safe having tea alone with me?" She glanced up with that familiar saucy look.

"I'm wearing a chastity belt."

She chuckled again. "I'll just bet you are. A mental one, at least. Still carrying a torch for my married sister."

"Faithful Stephen. Faithful to the memory."

"That's not all bad, you know."

Inside the Satterlee house we dropped our outer coats and Molly put down a package she was carrying. "I brought home a new record I just bought for the library. I'm trying to build up the record collection. This is a recent release of the Boston and Koussevitsky playing the Sibelius Sixth Symphony. I'm looking forward to hearing it. Do you know the Sibelius Sixth?

"I don't know *any* Sibelius. My musical mentor never got me beyond Mozart."

"So far so good. But Sibelius lives in a different universe. Charles used to love to play Sibelius with the orchestra. There are some marvelous passages for double bass,

especially in the Fourth. The Fourth gave him a real work-
out, he used to say. But I'm especially fond of the Sixth. It
has a kind of ethereal quality. Would you like to hear it
with me?"

"Yes, I guess so if you'll bring me that hot tea you
promised."

"That's my plan." She started for the kitchen. "Make
tea and then play the record." She glanced back over her
shoulder with that inimitable Molly look. "It will keep my
mind off your irresistible masculine charms."

"Any help I can get," I said.

While she ran water in the tea kettle and rattled tea cups,
I sat musing once again about what made Molly so femi-
ninely alluring. She was saucy and flirtatious, of course, and
she was beautifully made—the lingering image of the lovely
curves of her womanly back as she vanished through the
kitchen door reminded me of that—but there was something
else, a lure, not a fragrance like musk, but as strong and as
compelling.

Later, after Molly had made the tea and poured our cups,
she took the shiny black record out of its tan envelope and
placed it on the turntable of her Magnavox phonograph.
Then we sat side by side on the sofa, sipping and listening
to the first movement of the Sibelius Sixth Symphony. The
music began with an unaccompanied choir of violins playing a high keening almost eerie sound that slowly descended
until suddenly there was a low growl from the bass. Then
woodwinds entered, and they seemed to be dancing and
prancing in curlicues of tight, near-dissonant harmonies. The
movement flowed on in a swirling, advancing stream as the
reeds took over alone and then were joined by the brass in
ensemble. As Molly had said, it was a different musical
universe, strange and mysterious in structure and instru-
mentation but arresting and compelling. It had that quality
of a good mystery story, it created that sense of wonder—
what will happen next? And throughout, an indefinable
northern quality seemed to pervade the sound, like north

winds sweeping through the needled boughs of spruces, pines, and firs. I sat captivated until the record ended. "That was marvelous, Molly," I said. "Really wonderful." "I thought you'd like it. Sibelius makes wonderful music. And it's like no one else. Shall I play the rest of the symphony?"

"I'd love to hear more, Molly, but I really should leave now. I want to get back upriver to Price's dock before dark."

"Of course." She reached over and took my hand. "Stephen, dear, I'm so glad you came. It *is* pretty lonesome here, and I'm still getting adjusted." She smiled at me appealingly. "Please do come back."

"I will, Molly," I promised. "I will."

As I walked down the village street toward the Brixton town dock I said to myself it was characteristic of Molly to like Sibelius. Just like his music, compelling but elusive in its appeal, Molly always had me wondering what was coming next.

Eighteen

When I ran into Roger Altby Friday morning on my way to class he told me the meeting of the Committee on Scholastic Standards had not completed its review—"ran into a snag"—and the scheduled meeting that day with Headmaster Makepeace had been postponed.

"Thanks for telling me, Roger." I wanted to ask what the snag was but decided that would be an inappropriate question from "the defendant." As we walked on along on the pathway I turned to him. "Did you write that letter to Ball State?"

"I did. Mailed it Tuesday afternoon."

"Good man." I wanted to ask him what he had said in the letter, but I decided there were limits to my right to push Roger around in handling his own affairs and just possibly I had already exceeded those limits. We came to Edison Hall then and I dropped off to go to my office. "See you soon," we both said, not quite in unison.

That afternoon I sent for Billy Reston. He arrived at my door, eyes wide with apprehension. "Billy," I said, "I need a little exercise to work up an appetite before dinner. How about going down to the field house with me and playing a few games of squash?"

The broad grin I had seen earlier spread across the

handsome face. "That would be neat, sir. I mean, if you really want to."

"Let's go."

On the squash court Billy was not very strong, but he had quick feet and was remarkably nimble. He could reach nearly every shot I hit but the returns were not very decisive. Once or twice he managed to flick a little wrist shot into the corner that had me floundering as I scrambled to reach it.

After the first game we stood in the center of the four-walled court, both panting and sweating slightly and had a talk about his game. "You know, Billy, my best game is to drive the ball hard and low along the side walls. You don't hit the ball as hard as I do, so I don't think that's a particularly good strategy for you. But you've got those quick wrists for dinks in the corner and they can be sure winners. Let's practice those for a while."

"Okay, Coach," he said jauntily. "I'll do my best."

For the next half hour, amidst the sharp popping of the black ball as it rocketed off the walls and the screech of our rubber-soled gym shoes gripping the varnished floor, I hit reachable shots for Billy to flip into the corners. He really had a knack for it—something I never had—and toward the end of the session he was laying down corner shots that no player of any skill could have reached.

Later, side by side in the shower room, with Billy turning his back shyly toward me in the hissing shower in order to shield his small, prepubescent loins, I said, "I think you ought to build your game around those cute corner shots, Billy. You're damned (once again I was using the license granted prep school athletic coaches) good at it. If you work on them, you'll probably have those big strong guys falling all over themselves."

He turned his head toward me, grinning broadly. "I'll work on them, Coach, and maybe I can make the team next year."

"I wouldn't be surprised, Billy. Not at all surprised."

Later, at dinner in the teeming dining hall as I was

shepherding my exuberant table members into their places, Roger Altby came up to me. "Eve and I would like you to stop by for coffee and brandy after dinner."

I looked questioningly. "Anything special?"

"No, just a little winter weekend cheer."

We all sat down after Headmaster Makepeace led us in prayer, and I got my boisterous charges through dinner with only two flipped butter pats and one teaspoon-of-water toss. After a few parting words by the Headmaster from his table at the head of the hall enjoining the boys to use their upcoming weekend wisely—"Enjoy both study and play but remember study comes before play"—they filed out, table by table, in good order. But once outside the hall they made the frigid night ring with whoops and yells.

Eve met my knock at her front door in a long-sleeved blue velvet dress. She looked brightly pretty and she was smiling the shy, timid smile of a little girl. "Stephen," she said, taking my hand, and said no more.

"Come in, fella," called Roger. "Coffee's ready there on the cocktail table, and I'm pouring the brandy." After we all three gathered on the sofa before a crackling fire in the stone fireplace, Roger handed me a yellow sheet, a Western Union telegram. I unfolded it and read, "OFFER ASST PROF ENGLISH AT $6500 START 1 SEPT STOP PROMOTION ASSOC PROF LIKELY 1-2 YEARS STOP REPLY SOONEST STOP SGD BAXTER." I put it down and turned to Eve and Roger, both of whom were beaming wide grins at me.

"Terrific," I said. "Just wonderful. Have you given your answer yet, Roger?"

"I sent it this afternoon. 'Accept offer.'"

I raised my brandy glass. "Then here's to great success and much happiness in Indiana!"

We all sipped and grinned at one another. Then, Eve put her hand lightly on my knee. "There's so much for me to say to you, Stephen, that I cannot say it."

"Consider it said, Eve. Please consider it said." I patted her hand on mine.

"I'll never forget what you did for me."

I raised my glass in toast to her. Then for another half hour we sat together companionably, drinking coffee, sipping cognac, and chatting in the snug living room while the fire snapped and blazed cheerfully in the stone fireplace facing us. And much of the time Eve burbled happily about having "a house of my own and having dinner alone with my husband and sometimes with old friends."

Then I suggested it was time for me to get back to Sudbury Hall before it was demolished by my fellow occupants. At his doorway as I was leaving Roger said, "Things have gotten a little sticky in the Standards Committee, but I still have hope it will turn out all right."

"Is that all you can tell me?"

He hesitated. "Yes, it is. But I'm still hoping for the best."

We shook hands, I kissed Eve on the cheek, and then under a sky teeming with diamond-bright stars I walked back in the bitter night to the building I shared with sixty rollicking young males.

After Tuesday morning classes I stopped by the school post office to pick up my mail. Usually it was a useless exercise, but today there was a surprising total of three pieces, two envelopes and a penny postal card. One envelope bore Meg's firm, neat hand, the other envelope was Sloate School business stationery and simply addressed, "Mr. Aspen." The postal card was written in the twisted, squiggly hand of Bill Byer, my Cornell professor.

Walking back to Sudbury Hall with head down I nearly mowed down several students as I opened Meg's letter and read, "We're back and I am dying to see you. Please come as soon as you can get away." I looked up from the page and noticed, as I had not earlier, that the sun was a glory of golden fire in the bright blue sky.

The other envelope contained a brief note: "Meeting of the Committee on Scholastic Standards in the Headmaster's office at 2:30 pm today." Nothing said about my presence, but since I was the defendant at the trial I assumed my attendance was required. It is unlikely that the sun actually dimmed as I read the summons but my outlook on the brilliant day certainly did.

I tried to read Bill Byer's card as I walked but the handwriting was too cryptic so I put it away until I got inside. Then I slowly deciphered, "Aspen: Situation opening up here for which you might be suited. Involves new research. Like you to come to Ithaca during spring break to discuss possibilities. Byer." Well! I looked up from the scrawled message and seemed to find the sun had resumed its former luster. Bill's card offered the prospect of returning to the splendid Cornell campus looming high over Cayuga Lake, working once again amidst the vibrant stimulus of a great university, and channelling my energies into research advancing the frontiers of knowledge instead of tutoring strident young males. At the very least, this put the imminent decision of a not entirely friendly faculty committee into a fresh perspective.

The six members of the Committee on Scholastic Standards sat in chairs facing Headmaster Makepeace's desk. I sat off to one side with my back to the large window. The Headmaster took his seat behind his huge, cluttered desk and then, apparently feeling he could not view the committee adequately stood up on the chair and squatted like a bird on a perch. "Well, gentlemen," he chirped, "let's have your review."

Jason Dunlap, the chairman, unfolded a sheet of paper he was carrying and cleared his throat loudly. "I regret to inform you, Headmaster," he rumbled, "that the Committee has been unable to reach a united conclusion. We are divided, three by three, into two camps."

"No conclusion!" the Headmaster squawked. "What in hell—pardon my French—kind of review is that? How can I tell Trevor Reston our review came to no conclusion?"

"As I said, Headmaster," Dunlap rumbled on, "it is regrettable. What I propose is that speakers from the opposing views present their separate cases and then let you decide. If that is satisfactory, Mr. Altby will present the 'pro' side, if I may put it that way, and I will present the 'con.'"

"Well, that's a right funny way of presenting a review." The Headmaster shook his head. "And a neat way of passing the buck, besides."

"I don't know what else to suggest, sir."

Headmaster Makepeace picked up a yellow pencil and chewed on it briefly. Then he got down off the chair and sat on the seat. "All right, fire away. You go first, Altby."

For the next hour and a half I sat and listened while the two spokesmen presented their cases. Roger standing straight and looking solemn and sartorially correct in his tweed jacket and high-collared striped shirt with tight-knotted tie, spoke for himself, Don Schofield, and Sam Matthews. He made the case that Billy Reston's work was substantially inferior to the general class level and did not deserve a passing grade. "We cannot maintain high scholastic standards," he concluded, "by accepting as passable work that is unacceptable."

Jason Dunlap, his full greyish beard and huge body giving him the appearance of salty sea dog, then presented the "con" view for himself, Brickson Jaeger, and Bentley Arnold, the doddering, old classics master. The group accepted that Billy's work was below the class average, but argued that to fail him was poor pedagogy. Better, they said, to give him an Incomplete or possibly a D and then counsel the student independently. "As I've heard you say many times, Headmaster, 'We're here to teach them, not flunk them.'"

Headmaster Makepeace nodded vigorously. "That's right, Dunlap. That's right. It's what I've been saying for twenty-five years." He looked at me sternly and then pressed his lips tight together and nodded again. "Well, now. You got anything to say at this point, Aspen?"

"The only thing I would point out, Headmaster, is that

both sides agree that the student's performance was well below the class level and that is the basis on which I gave him a failing grade."

The Headmaster shook his head in exasperation. "But Aspen, that doesn't solve my problem with Trevor Reston. I've got to give some answer that will satisfy him."

Roger Altby spoke up in his solemn, measured way. "With all respect, Headmaster Makepeace, our unanimous agreement *does* enable you to tell the father that the Committee on Scholastic Standards has reviewed the case and unanimously finds the boy's work substandard. Then you can offer any of several remedies for the future."

"Hmmmph! Shows what you know about fathers! This father in particular. Try telling any man his son is below your standard and he'll— Well, I'll tell you this, Trevor Reston would make us regret the matter ever came up." He looked out the window and then looked at me and said, almost plaintively, "I like the idea of giving him an Incomplete for the semester and then working with him individually. What do you say to that, Aspen?"

I was on the verge of recounting my conference with Billy Reston and the fine relationship he and I had subsequently established. I was also going to suggest that there can be pedagogical value in a failing grade when it shocks the student into working harder as it seemed to have done with Billy. But at this point Brickson Jaeger broke in with his bullyboy style, "What you suggest, Headmaster, is the only *intelligent* thing to do."

I clammed up immediately. Looking at the Headmaster I slowly shook my head.

He looked away and stared out the window for a moment. "Well, gentlemen," he said. "I guess this is as far as we can go today. I'll give the matter some thought and then make my decision." He looked sternly at me. "I'll call you in when I've made up my mind, Aspen."

Walking back to our quarters together, Roger said, "I'm sorry it's turning out this way, fella. I did the best I could but that bastard Jaeger and that muddle-head, Dunlap, just wouldn't listen. And of course, dear old Bentley Arnold, who hasn't flunked one boy in forty years of teaching classics for fear of hurting their feelings, was hopeless."

"Ah, well, Roger. Nothing's been decided yet. It may turn out all right still."

Roger shook his head. "Afraid not, friend. I've been around that old geezer, Makepeace, long enough to know which way he'll jump. I can tell you he started wetting his pants the minute that benefactor and trustee telephoned and he hasn't stopped since. Right now he's trying to figure out the best way to tell you he's going to take the 'con' side and change the boy's grade."

"If he does, I'll resign. I told him I would."

Roger turned an earnest face toward me. "Are you sure you want to do that? You've got a great future here, you know."

"I think I must. I weighed the decision to fail that boy very thoroughly, and I can't accept having it overturned arbitrarily. Incidentally, I find it very ironic that I failed another boy in the class, Jimmy Dixon, and not word one has been said about that."

Roger shook his head. "I don't know whether it would have hurt or helped if that had come up before the committee, but it shows you what's got the old boy fired up. Money." We walked on along as he said, "Well, let's hope it doesn't come out the way I'm afraid it will."

Midnight that same day found me driving back to Sloate from dinner with Stuart and Meg in Buryport. My headlights sliced white beams through the blackness on Highway 16 and the heater in my convertible blew hot air at full blast to match the stabbing cold of the New England night. But as I watched the racing shafts of light glint off the icy snow banks along the edge of the road, my mind was luxuriously fondling the memory of a brief moment alone with

Meg. For a few seconds after dinner we were together in the hallway, out of sight of the others—Stuart, the Coffins, and Molly—and Meg took my hand and said in a low voice, "Come see me some afternoon soon. I need to see you."

"Anything wrong?" I whispered.

"No, no. Nothing. I just miss you terribly."

I squeezed her hand and we moved on to join the others. Even without that interlude, the evening had been very enjoyable. Molly was in a frisky mood and once, when we were side by side on the sofa and she caught me looking at Meg with loving eyes, she jabbed me in the ribs and said, "The blaze from your torch is hurting my eyes."

"Oh?" I pulled my eyes away and turned to her, saucy-eyed and handsome in a knitted suit that left no dip or swell unnoted. "I seem to be having trouble dimming the flame. Any suggestions?"

"Sure. Try gazing at me awhile, the original wet blanket."

I chuckled. "Hardly. In that suit you could light a torch or two yourself."

She leaned back in mock surprise. "Why, you old flatterer, you. I didn't think you'd notice."

I patted the hand resting on her moulded thigh. "You're hard to miss, my dear."

Later, in a more serious moment, I asked her how things were going for her in Brixton. "Actually, quite well. I'm beginning to enjoy my work at the library, especially building up the record collection." She smiled companionably. "How's it going for you?"

I made a face. "Just now I'm at a critical point." I recounted briefly the situation involving Billy Reston's failing grade. "If it turns out as I'm afraid it will, I plan to resign at the end of the school year."

"Whoa! That's serious. Are you sure that's what you want to do?"

"I think I must."

"What then?"

"I don't know. I may go back to Cornell and do research."

She gazed at me, her greenish eyes earnest and sympathetic. "I do hope it doesn't come to that. For lots of reasons." Then after several minutes of sitting silently beside me, she said, "Call me when you know the decision." Then, that mischievous light came into her eyes as she added, "And come and see me. Wear that chastity belt, if you like. I enjoy the challenge."

With a frown on my face that was half smile, I said, "Molly, you're incorrigible. You could melt an iceberg."

Later, as I recalled that conversation as the Ford hummed quietly northwestward with the speedometer on the green-lighted dial registering 60, I grinned, thinking fondly of Molly's unquenchable sauciness. And then, with greater fondness my mind slipped back to Meg's whispered words in the hallway.

Next morning on my way to meet my eight o'clock class I met Julie North waiting for me in the doorway of Edison Hall. "Headmaster wants to see you when you've finished your class," said Julie.

"Thank you. Tell him I'll be there."

Feeling much like the defendant who has just been told that the jury has reached a verdict, I walked into the classroom and began establishing order so that instruction could begin. The day's assignment was plant cytology, the function of cells in plants, admittedly not the most attention grabbing of subjects, especially for young males whose blood and hormones are racing around in a thoroughly mammalian, not botanical, manner. The combination of the subject and a mind distracted by concern over an upcoming interview probably produced a pretty indifferent hour of instruction. But the hour ended on a higher note as I handed out grades for the previous day's quiz and Billy Reston got a B minus.

He stopped by my desk as the class was filing out, grinning shyly. "I guess I'm improving a little, Mr. Aspen," he said, waving his test paper.

I rallied my attention to focus on the handsome boy. "Yes, you are, Billy. I'm proud of you. Keep up the good work."

"I'm trying, sir." He turned to leave and then turned back grinning broadly. "I just wanted to tell you, sir, I beat Caxton at squash, two out of three, yesterday afternoon. Drove him crazy with dinks in the corners."

"Great, Billy, that's great. I told you it would work."

Turning from his desk as I rapped on the door jamb, Headmaster Makepeace greeted me ingratiatingly. "Come in, Aspen! Come right in. Sure is a pretty day outside, isn't it?"

Until that moment I had paid no attention to the kind of day it was but then I glanced out the large window and saw brilliant sunshine casting bluish black shadows from the great trees across the glistening snow. "It's a fine day," I said.

"Well, come in and sit you down while you and I have a good talk about this Reston matter. In my view, the whole thing has been blown way out of proportion, and I think you and I can put our heads together and settle this thing in the right way."

"I hope so, Headmaster." I took a chair across from his desk while he perched on his chair in his characteristic way.

"Well, now, my friend, everybody's agreed that the boy's work last semester was not up to standard, and you recognized that."

I nodded.

"And by so doing you demonstrated you had good judgment in assessing a student's achievement level."

Again, I nodded.

Then, after these appeasing words the Headmaster moved briskly to his proposed solution. Just as Roger Altby had predicted, his plan was to change Billy Reston's grade to Incomplete and instruct me to tutor Billy individually. "I'm sure you can bring that lad up to class standard with some personal attention. I have that confidence in you as a teacher. So much so, that I telephoned Trevor Reston first thing this morning and told him that after reviewing the situation the school was changing the first semester grade to Incomplete and counting on the boy's improvement through your personal tutoring to bring the year's work up to a passing grade." When he finished he nodded briskly at me across the desk. "Now I'm sure that having had several days to think the matter over calmly you now agree with me that that's the best solution." After a pause while he searched my face with his beady eyes, he said, "What do you say to that, young man?"

I looked steadily back at the little man perched absurdly on his chair seat. "Well, sir, I would like to say two things. First, I am already tutoring Billy separately. I have been since the term began and Billy is now doing B work."

"What?" he spluttered. "I didn't know that." He shook his head in annoyance. "Wish I had so I could have told Trevor."

"You acted before you discussed your decision privately with me," I said bluntly.

He glared across his desk. "You're danged right I did! When a strong supporter and fine man like Trevor Reston comes to me with a justified complaint I've got to respond and respond fast."

I let a moment of silence gather and then I said, "Yes, sir." I waited a moment longer. "The second thing I want to say is I plan to resign at the end of the school year. As I told you I would."

"That's a foolish decision, Aspen. Very foolish. You could have a fine lifetime career here."

"Under the circumstances, it's a decision I must make." I got up and moved toward the door. "I suggest you have a talk with young Reston. His family situation and its effect on his academic performance might surprise you." I left him staring wordlessly at me.

Walking back to my office I wrestled with conflicting emotions, justified anger that Makepeace had acted before discussing his proposed solution with me and growing chagrin that pride had kept me from telling him earlier how Billy and I had created a solid teacher-student bond. All the same, not even a recognition by the Headmaster of my conscientious concern for Billy would erase the challenge to my judgment as a teacher by his arbitrarily changing the grade I had assigned. But by the time I had reached the steps of Edison Hall the anger that action had ignited was dissolving into a rueful realization that even if I had acted on justified principle, my decision to resign from Sloate School in the spring would have profound personal ramifications. It would mean leaving a situation I had found deeply comfortable and fulfilling. It would mean leaving the countryside and the singular atmosphere of New England which I had come to cherish. And it would mean separating myself from the presence of Meg by a mostly unbridgeable distance. At the moment, at least, that last thought caused me the greatest pang.

Nineteen

The night following my interview with Headmaster Makepeace seemed to last without end. In bed I had read myself into an advanced state of sleepiness with Gibson's *Decline and Fall of the Roman Empire*, which dear old Roscoe Bilder had urged me to read, "especially Chapter Fifteen." But then I could find no position where the pillow supported my head at a comfortable angle or where my arms did not feel awkward, no matter how I arranged them, and I could not remember how I had dealt with the problem before. Then, from time to time I would doze off, sometimes flat on my back, mouth wide open, and wake myself with a loud snort. Trying to relax and woo balky sleep, I steered my mind away from angry thoughts about Headmaster Makepeace's handling of the Billy Reston affair. In this I was mostly successful, but keeping at bay regretful thoughts of leaving Sloate School and New England was distinctly less a success. And so went the night. Morning and the sound of boys waking and moving about in the rooms and corridors above me came as a relief.

After negotiating my obstreperous flock through morning chapel and breakfast, I went back to my apartment and considered how to spend my day. It was to be a light day with no afternoon classes. I had a strong urge to get in my car and just drive someplace, any place. But I also felt I wanted more than a destination. I wanted the company of someone I knew well, someone who had a regard for me. And then the desire to be with Meg became urgent and paramount.

I looked at my watch. Eight forty-five. Too early to telephone Meg at home. Stuart would not have left the house for his office as yet. Better to call later. I put on my fleece jacket and walked over to Edison Hall. I spent an hour and a half fiddling in the laboratory. Then I went back and telephoned. Meg answered, her voice lilting and sunny. After her cry of delight I said, "I thought I might come see you today."

"Stephen, how perfect! Come for lunch."

"The other night you said you wanted us to have some time alone together. Will Stuart be there?"

"No. Stuart has gone to Boston for the day. Gets back on the 5:15 train. Today is perfect. We can have the whole afternoon."

"I'm leaving now."

Driving down Route 16 toward Buryport as the Ford convertible cheerfully consumed the miles, I had the same happy expectation I had when setting out for a date as a Cornell undergraduate. But the occasion was different. This was an unacknowledged date and to a degree clandestine. To suppress the surge of excitement that sprang from that thought I told myself I was just going to see an intimate friend. This worked slightly better with my mind than with my body which was clearly experiencing that predate tension and anticipation of my undergraduate days.

Meg met me at her front door, flushed and radiant, arms open wide. 'Oh, Stephen, you were so wonderful to come on short notice!" She hugged hard and then clung to me, and I slid my hands down her supple back to her waist and held her close. Then she pushed away. "Let's look at you. I haven't dared to drink you in while others were around." She held me by the shoulders at arms length and searched my face with her blue eyes. "Do I detect some little worry lines around your eyes?"

"Not exactly worry." I paused. "There have been some problems at school this past couple of weeks."

She took me by the hand and led me to the couch in the handsome living room. "You must tell me about it."

"I will, Meg. But first, how are you?"

She nodded and smiled at me, her eyes direct and candid. "I'm fine." She patted my knee. "No surprises. It's very comfortable."

"That's great," I said, hoping I had hit the right tone of conviction.

Meg smiled again and then quickly leaned over and put her head on my shoulder with her fine, fragrant hair brushing against my face. "Oh, it's so good being with you again!" She straightened then and said brightly, "Let's have a drink before lunch. Everything's ready there on the bar beside the fireplace. There's sherry and gin and whiskey."

"What will you have, Meg?"

She cocked her head, eyes crinkled in thought. "Mmmm. Sherry, I think."

"I will too." I went to the bar, selected glasses, and poured the sherry. As I did I savored once again the richness of the dark panelled room, decorated and furnished with such quiet, elegant restraint, the epitome of a culture I felt deeply at ease with.

"Now tell me about the problems at school," said Meg, her eyes lovely over the rim of her glass as she sipped her sherry.

"Well, the quick summary is that I think I'm going to leave Sloate at the end of the school year."

"Stephen!"

I described to her the sorry mess that had developed and while I talked she clung hard to my hand and murmured sympathetically. "So that's where things stand. I resign in June."

She shook her head. "Oh, Stephen, I'm so sorry. I thought it was so perfect for you. And you seemed so happy there." She paused and smiled encouragement. "But you know, there are other places where you can teach. Stuart has lots of connections. He'll help you find something."

"I may already have something in hand. My professor at Cornell wrote me last week about a research job there. I'm going out to see him during the Easter break. I may go back to Ithaca in June."

"Oh, no!" She lunged forward and put her head on my chest and her arm around my waist. "No, no! That's too far away. I can't bear your being so out of reach."

I lifted her up so I could put my arms around her, and as I did she put her face up to mine and we kissed. There was no restraint in her kiss and she made low sounds in her throat as she slid her hands up the back of my neck and caressed my head. Slowly we slipped down so that we were lying on the couch, our mouths still locked together, and I pressed my body harder and harder against hers. She surged against me as we clung closer and closer and I began to caress her passionately. Then suddenly like a switch turning off she stopped. She pulled her mouth away from mine, panting slightly, and said, "No, Stephen, no. We mustn't."

In a voice barely operable, I asked, "Mustn't?"

She shook her head and pushed me away. "No, we must not. Things are different now."

I straightened up and tried to subdue the uproar that had erupted within.

Meg sat up, her hands raised to her head to smooth her hair. "Let's go have lunch," she said. "It's all ready."

I followed her through the hallway and out to the pantry and helped carry the plates to the table. She was acting very controlled and coolly efficient. "Sit there, dear," she said, gesturing to the place on her right, "where you can see the creek and the marsh off the end of our dock."

Lunch was lobster bisque followed by crabmeat salad. "I tried to think of things you probably don't get in the Sloate dining hall."

"Delicious."

A strained silence fell between us while we sipped our soup. Meg's abrupt breaking away in the living room seemed to have suspended our usual intimate flow, and I could not think how to restore it.

"Let me tell you about Antigua," she said abruptly. "It's a delicious place. Private, isolated beaches. And the water is so transparently clear that when I was standing in it up to my chin I could still see my feet on the bottom." She went on at length about the charms of Antigua while I, head down and looking only at my plate, continued to sip the lobster bisque. "The sunsets and the sunrises are so beautiful you want to cry. And the silky, caressing air—"

"Meg!" I finally broke in. "I don't want to hear about Antigua just now. I want to talk about you and me." My face felt hot and flushed and I was very tense.

She looked earnestly at me, soup spoon suspended in midair. "Yes?"

"A little while ago when you broke away from me in the living room, you said things now are different."

"Yes-s-s?"

"But I want to say that for me and how I feel about you nothing has changed." I kept my voice low but I was speaking with great intensity. "And as far as I'm concerned nothing has changed *between* us."

She gazed at me, mildly surprised. "But I'm married now, Stephen. That's certainly different."

"Do you feel differently about me?"

"Oh, no!" She shook her head and reached over to touch my hand. "You know I don't. You're still my wonderful Stephen. Still my safe harbor. Without you to turn to now and then I would be all at sea."

I put my other hand atop hers and looked searchingly at her. After a moment, she pulled her hand away and said gently, "Let me get the salad."

When she came back and we were eating the salad, Meg asked, "Was the weather pretty terrible around here while I was away in Antigua?"

I put my fork down sharply. "Meg! Stop fencing. I want to talk seriously about us."

She looked up, blue eyes serious and compliant. "Yes, Stephen. What do you want me to say?"

"I want you to say that what you and I have together has not changed."

She nodded. "Yes, that's true. I have said so. But then—"

I reached for her hand. "I want you to recognize that what we share is strictly between us, separate from anyone else."

She hesitated a moment and looked out the window at the snow-covered lawn and the ice-fringed tidal creek beyond. "If what you mean is that I do not tell anyone else how I feel about you, then yes, I do recognize it."

"I mean that, Meg, and more." I could feel my intensity mounting.

She smiled, shaking her head, and said nervously, "You're being awfully serious."

"Yes, I'm *very* serious." Then, leaning toward her I said, "I sincerely believe that what we share when we are alone together does not affect anyone else. It is ours, only ours."

She looked at me searchingly. At last she said in a low voice, "I do understand what you mean, Stephen. I do understand and"—she hesitated—"I do agree."

I released her hand and we both turned back to our salads. After several minutes of silence while we ate, she said, "If you're finished let me bring some coffee into the living room." I walked into the living room and stood by the window, waiting, surging with anticipation. Meg brought the tray of coffee, and I helped her set it down. Then I took her in my arms and kissed her. When we released I held her head close and whispered in her ear, "Oh, Meg, darling, I want you so much!"

I could feel her head nodding against my shoulder and she faintly murmured, "Yes." Then we kissed again and when our lips gently came apart, Meg turned and led me across the hall and up the long stairway to the door of the guest room. "I'll be with you in a moment."

I opened the door and entered the large high-ceilinged bedroom with its canopied four-posted bed. I stripped down to my boxer shorts, draped my clothes over a chair, and opened up the bed. When I turned back, Meg was coming quietly into the room, wearing a pale blue dressing gown, her face flushed and her eyes glowing. I went to her, took her face gently between my hands and kissed her softly. Then I slipped the dressing gown off her shoulders and gazed lovingly at the symmetry and restraint of her slim, smooth-curved femininity. Her small breasts lifted as she raised her arms and put them around my neck, her head snugged closed against my shoulder. We clung together for a moment, and then I took her to the bed, and we lay side by side, caressing and stroking, and slowly, gently, and lovingly, came together closer, closer, and ever closer.

The afternoon wore quietly on with only the rustles and murmurs of our love-making to mark its passing. When I raised my head to look at the small gold clock on the bedside table it read three fifteen. "You know, my love," I said, "I must begin to think about leaving."

"I know, dearest." Meg was lying on her side. She sighed, a deep, joyous sigh and then looked up at me. "What is so wonderful, Stephen, is that being with you seems so very *right*, so perfectly *right*. Surely, what *seems* so right cannot be wrong. Can it?"

"No. It's right, my love, because it's special to us." I pulled her silken body closer. "Oh, Meg, I love you so much. And I have for so long."

She kissed me on the ear. "I love you too, you fabulous man." Then she sat up suddenly. "You must go, darling, so you can get back before dark."

Later, after showering and dressing, we met at the top of the stairway and went down the steps together. "Do come back again when you can," Meg said as we stood at the doorway.

"It won't be until after I've been out and back from Cornell."

She put her hand quickly to her mouth. "Oh, gosh, I forgot!" With concern in her voice, she said, "Call me as soon as you know anything. And, oh, Stephen, don't, don't move away to Ithaca!"

Driving back, moving swiftly along familiar Highway 16, I marveled over how much the look of the passing landscape had changed since morning. Then the sky hung low and glowering and the snow-mantled fields lay flat and dull. Now, the sky shone a luminous grey and the snowy fields glistened a pristine white. Even the gaunt bare trees now had grace and beauty, starkly black against the glaring white. Musing contentedly to the steady drone of the snug convertible's engine I identified the cause for the change. Despite that black cloud of uncertainty that lowered over my future, the glow of a shared love made all landscapes bright.

Whatever its implications for my future, whether I was to be at a nearby New England school or at distant Cornell, the journey out to Ithaca was a joyous adventure. The day after the boys departed, in many cases for Bermuda or the Bahamas, I packed up and pointed the charcoal grey nose of the Ford toward Worcester and then westward across Massachusetts, through Northampton, over and through the Berkshire Hills to Pittsfield and then, crossing the Hudson River, into Albany. Although, as Shakespeare put it, "the hounds of spring [were] on winter's traces," winter still had a sizeable lead and the passing fields were garbed in shades of brown and tan with traces of russet. The crests of the Berkshires were still laced with old snow along the rock ledges. But now and then, along the stream banks and road-side ditches the upper branches of swamp willows sported a bright cranberry red.

In Albany I picked up Route 20 and pushed on west over the roller coaster hills of the Cherry Valley into Bridgewater and Cazenovia, passing south of Syracuse, and on to Auburn where Route 34 carried me south to Ithaca on the high plain east of Cayuga Lake. Returning to the Finger Lakes revived memories of undergraduate days and the hours spent in my room listening to Burl Ives records, especially the folk song extolling the nearby Erie Canal. Recalling those evocative words, I sang at the top of my voice as Burl Ives had taught me, "Oh, the Ear-eye-ee is a-risin', and the gin is a-gittin' low. And I scarcely think we'll git a drink, till we get to Buffalo-oh-oh, till we git to Buffa-*low*." And my eager little car, always spurring me to drive faster, swept swiftly over hill crests and swooped down into valleys. A convertible has a spirit like no other car and, like a spirited horse or a skirt-tossing, eye-flirting woman, makes a man's heart bound.

I went directly to the Faculty Club where Bill Byer had reserved me a room and settled in. Next morning, a typical pre-spring misty, grey day in Ithaca, I set out for my appointment with Byer at Fuertes Hall, named in honor of Louis Agassiz Fuertes, patron saint of ornithologists. Ahead of me, forthright and distinct in the heavy air stood the emblematic clock tower, symbol of Cornell to Cornellians everywhere. Below the campus the mist shrouded almost completely the deep, glacier-carved furrow which embeds Cayuga Lake. The great central quadrangle of the campus, fronted by grey stone buildings on the west and the beige walls of Goldwin Smith Hall on the east, was thinly populated with passing students.

Bill Byer greeted me in his characteristic laconic style as I walked into his office and found him at his desk reading *The New York Times*. "Have a good trip?"

"Yes. Fine."

"Come by car or train?"

"Car."

"Car!" He raised his eyebrows in mock surprise. "I forgot for a moment you're a plutocrat now, teaching at that rich boys' prep school."

"Rolling in money."

"I'm sure." He measured me with his eyes. "If you'd

like some coffee, paper cups and a jar of instant are there on the table beside the electric kettle."

"Thanks. I just finished breakfast."

"Still the libertine, lying in bed till mid-morning."

"That's right." I smiled warily. The conversation up to this point was in the usual cut-and-thrust style Bill Byer mistook for normal human exchange. It was also his way of letting me know I was back in the mentor-student relationship as far as he was concerned.

He pursed his lips and with his high-bridged nose, big front teeth, and sharply narrow face he momentarily resembled a squirrel about to kiss someone or something. "Sit down and let me tell you about this project we are launching that might involve you." He leaned back in his swivel chair, gazing thoughtfully at the ceiling, then trained his hard, intelligent eyes on me, and began to speak in his clipped style, sounding as though he were biting each word separately out of a precast sentence. "The project is to investigate the dynamics of bird migration, the various means by which birds find their way year after year over long distances. We've received a three year grant to investigate each of the several theories regarding the techniques by which birds navigate from one end of a continent to the other, or even, with European birds, to a third continent." He paused. "I don't know how much you recall about migratory guidance. Perhaps such arcane knowledge has evaporated as you devoted yourself to teaching biology to beginners." He grinned at me sardonically.

"Perhaps it's a bit sketchy. But it's always a pleasure to hear you lecture, Bill." I smiled ironically back at him.

He bowed his head slightly. "All right. We plan to organize the work force into six teams, one focusing on the use of the earth's magnetic flow for guidance; one on the use of stars in night flight, celestial navigation; one on daytime sun angle; one on weather phenomena, barometric pressures and wind directions; one on the use of terrain, natural features like lakes, bays, mountains; and finally, one team to do the synthesis, tying together the work of the five investigative teams."

I nodded my understanding.

"Each team will work separately, devise its own experiments to produce the data and then do an analysis. And in sum that's it, that's the three year project."

I nodded again. "A very comprehensive program." I paused. "Where do you think I might fit in?"

Byer pursed his mouth in that kiss-like gesture. "I doubt you've got enough science for one of the investigative teams. You'd need physics and neurophysiology, for instance. Probably we would use you on the synthesis group."

Half-seriously, I said, "How about the astronomical guidance group? I got a Boy Scout merit badge in astronomy."

Narrow-eyed and unsmiling, Bill said, "Possibility."

We sat gazing at each other for a moment. "What kind of a stipend are we talking about?" I asked.

"We're offering—" and he named a figure just over half my Sloate School salary.

I frowned and shook my head. "Whew!"

"I know, I know. You're getting a fat salary now for babysitting rich, spoiled kids. But this project is *real* science. Something you can get your intellectual teeth into instead of changing mental diapers on brats."

I grinned at him. "I don't think I would describe teaching at a first class school quite like that, but never mind. This *is* a fascinating and challenging project." I looked away, pondering. "I can tell you right now I'd like to be considered, Bill, but I'll need a little time, week or two, to think it over. There are some loose ends for me to tie up."

"Think it over! You ought to jump at a chance like this. This is *real* science. Well-funded projects like this don't come down the pike every day." He paused. "Don't tell me you're happy with your present situation."

I hesitated and then decided not to tell him about my problems at Sloate because I knew he would use it as leverage, and I wanted the freedom to be flexible. "For the most part, yes, I am. I enjoy the teaching. Besides, you know, I'm a campus hero. I coach the squash team, and we beat our great rival, Grantly Hill. First time in years."

Bill shook his head as though in despair. "Compare that tiny triumph with uncovering a mystery that has baffled mankind for centuries!" He scanned my face appraisingly. "All right, then. Take a week or two. But I think you'd make a big career mistake if you passed it up."

"You're probably right."

"Yep." He got up from the desk. "Let me take you around to meet some of the people we've got lined up for the project."

We spent the rest of the morning chatting with Bill's fellow scientists. They were all attractive, articulate, and very bright. In fact, the contrast with the more mundane minds of my fellow teachers at Sloate was sharp, and it highlighted for me the difference between the workaday atmosphere of a school and the charged vitality of a research-oriented university. Among these people, my mental horizons seemed to expand and I began using intellectual muscles that had been lying dormant.

After lunch Bill and I played squash at the Law School, just as we had in my graduate school days. I ran him ragged, and later in the showers he grumbled, "Obvious to me you spend all day with a squash racket in your hand instead of a book."

Then, next morning I was back in the Ford convertible headed for New England. I mused as I left the Finger Lakes country for eastern Massachusetts over the difference between the two regions. New York State has a broad, expansive feel compared with compact, contained New England. I smiled as I reflected that in some ways the regional differences mirrored the contrast between the wider horizons of research and the narrower focus of teaching at a preparatory school.

Twenty

The spring vacation break had three more days to run, so I indulged myself the morning after my return by sleeping late and then having breakfast in my own kitchenette: frozen orange juice, bran flakes, English muffin, and coffee. After that I strolled over to the post office, sniffing in vain the damp pre-spring air for hints of buds and greenness. On the pathway I met Roger Altby, smiling cheerfully. "Top of the morning, fella!" he chortled. "Glad you're back. Good trip?"

"Yes, fine." I gazed at his jovial face, free of its usual solemn reserve. "You seem bouncy this morning."

"I just talked with Eve out in Muncie. She's found what she calls the perfect house, just four blocks from the campus. Nice garden and the crocuses and snowdrops are up. She says Indiana looks like Heaven."

"Wonderful, Roger, just wonderful."

"Sure is. How about joining me for dinner someplace tonight? There's that little Italian place in Adams. Ma Pacino's. Decent food. I'm buying."

"Fine by me. See you tonight." I walked on to the post office and pulled a swatch of pamphlets and other assorted junk mail out of my mailbox. But embedded in the conglomerate I found a tiny envelope with feminine handwriting. I tossed the junk into a nearby waste basket and ripped the envelope open. It was from Molly: "Please call me the minute you get back. I have an urgent matter to discuss with you. I need to see you *as soon as possible.* CALL ME!"

This sounded alarming even coming from volatile Molly, so I hurried back to the apartment and called Brixton. Her voice on the phone did not sound distressed. Instead, it had that typical Molly ring—"Hey, let's have a party!"

"It's Stephen, Molly. I got your note. What's up?"

"Stephen, you old dear! Glad you called. How was your trip?"

"Molly, for God's sake! I get a note from you that sounds like your house is on fire or you're being raped, and you give me the time of day. What's going on?"

"Oh, that. Well, it's not something I want to discuss over the phone. When can you come see me?"

"Today?"

"Fine. Lunch?"

"I'll be there."

I straightened up the kitchenette, put on a fresh turtle-neck, called off my dinner date with Roger and got in the Ford and headed toward Brixton. During the next fifty-eight miles my mind veered back and forth between two questions: what on earth was eating Molly and should I accept Bill Byer's research job? Until Molly's call, I had scarcely stopped weighing the pros and cons of returning to Cornell. Since my earliest student days my goal had been to become a research scientist, especially an ornithological scientist. And now here was the chance. Moreover it was a chance that promised a bright future. And yet, pulling in the opposite direction was the wholehearted satisfaction I had found in teaching in a fine preparatory school. Teaching at Sloate was richly fulfilling despite the necessity for being constantly "up to my ass in boys," as that oaf Brickson Jaeger had put it. And then there was the magnetic pull of New England, that fostered an indefinable but pleasurable resonance in me. The Finger Lakes were ruggedly beautiful, but they did not

set off that happy glow I had found amidst the long traditions of New England. And finally, there was the nearness
of Meg, the dear and essential nearness of Meg.

But then, back to Molly. What could cause that strident
note of urgency and alarm? Nothing in her manner as she
greeted me gave any hint. She looked blithe and brimming
as usual with blood-stirring vitality and she pecked me on
the cheek as I came in the door. "Welcome back, Stephen.
How was Cornell?"

I frowned at her. "We'll get to that later. What's going
on with you, Molly? Whatever it is, it sounded urgent."

She smiled a strange smile, kind of a suppressed secret
smile. "We'll get to that in a minute. How about a nip before
lunch? Sherry, martini, manhattan?"

"Sherry'll be fine." She turned and walked toward the
kitchen, and despite my irritation with her I relished the
image of those elegant hips slipping through the doorway.
"I must say you baffle the hell out of me, Molly," I called.

"Woman of mystery," she said archly as she came back
with the sherry. "Nothing wrong with your being baffled
by me."

"All right. All right."

She motioned to me to sit on the sofa. Her smile was
still mysterious but now it had a strain of knowingness,
almost vengeful knowingness. "Cheers!"

"All right, Molly. Stop playing games. Tell me why you
sent for me."

"No games." She pressed her lips together momentarily
and then said, "I've just found out you and Meg are having
an affair. And I think it's hilarious. Funniest thing I ever
heard."

I was stunned. Stunned and outraged. "It's not an affair!" I said hotly. "Meg and I are *not* having an affair!"

Her smile now became hard-edged. "Would you prefer
the term 'one-night stands'?"

I exploded. "No, goddamit! Neither one. It's not like that
in the slightest."

"What is it like then?"

I hesitated. "It's simply a natural and loving relationship that does not affect you or anyone else."

Her eyes narrowed. "A relationship known everywhere in the world as adultery. Not to mention one that betrays a trusting friend and benefactor."

Now I nearly choked with hot anger. "Listen here, Molly Satterlee! I didn't come here to listen to you talk trash about Meg and me. What in hell gives you the right to speak to me like this?"

"The right of a sister and a friend." She was still smiling that smile of superior knowledge, and it was beginning to irritate the shit out of me. "And I still think the whole idea of you and Meg having an affair is funny as hell."

That remark did nothing to relieve my anger. "Funny? What's so damned funny about it?"

She giggled. "You two. You two just don't have the talent for it. Two nice, simple people like you trying to manage an illicit affair, dealing with the secrecy, the evasions, the hypocrisy—it's hilarious. You two babes in the wood don't have the faintest idea what you're letting yourselves in for."

"This is the voice of experience I'm hearing, as I remember," I said derisively, hoping to be wounding.

"That's right," she said, looking boldly at me and nodding her head. "And let me tell you, compared to Meg I've always been a rogue and an adventurer. I'm better suited for handling one of these behind-the-back deals than she is by a country mile. But eventually I found it was more than even I could manage while still maintaining any peace of mind."

I glared at her while I tried to come up with something devastating to say.

Molly patted me companionably on the knee. "Tell me, Stephen, my good friend—and don't forget I *am* your good friend—what do you think gives you the right to go to bed with the wife of your friend, Stuart Price?" She gave me that saucy, I-dare-you look.

Still smoldering, I said, "I doubt you'd understand if I told you."

"Try me."

I stared down at the floor and then said slowly, "Meg and I have been close to one another for a long time. We were intimate long before Stuart asked her to marry him." I glanced toward Molly. "And, incidentally, I urged her to accept him."

"Yes, I know."

"Well, Meg and I both feel that our long and loving relationship has a life of its own, independent of her marriage. We feel that expressing our love in the normal way does not involve anyone but ourselves. It does not affect or harm anyone else."

Molly shook her head regretfully. "Stephen, Stephen. That's the most juvenile, romantic nonsense I ever heard to come from an intelligent man." She clicked her tongue against the roof of her mouth. "How would you like to try that explanation on Stuart after he had come home unexpectedly and found you and Meg tight together in bed?"

I looked at her silently for a moment while visualizing that scene all too graphically. Then I said grudgingly, "I doubt he would understand it."

"Or accept it." She reached over and took my hand. "You are playing with fire, my dear. If you and Meg go on, sooner or later there will be a slip, and Meg's marriage and your relationship with Stuart will blow wide open. I assume you do value your connection with Stuart and all he has done for you. Stephen, the risk for both of you is far too great." She patted my hand softly. "Besides, even if you are not found out, the strain on Meg will eventually sour her feelings toward you and she will turn against you."

"I doubt that."

"Trust me. I know my sister."

That brought to mind a question. "Incidentally, how did you find out about Meg and me?"

"Simple. I wiggled it out of her. We had lunch and she

was acting both exhilarated and a little anxious. Sisters sense each other's vibrations, and I could almost reach out and touch her secret. A few adroit questions and out it popped."

"You said 'anxious'?"

"Yes. She's not at ease with what you two are doing, and as time goes on her anxiety will grow greater and greater."

"You speak with considerable certainty."

"As I say, I know my sister."

"I think I have some claim to know her too."

"Yes, you do. As a man knows a woman he loves. But you're still a man and she's a woman, and there is an impermeable membrane between the two on some matters. I'm telling you, Stephen, Meg will not be able to sustain your present relationship very long. And it will end up with both of you getting terribly hurt."

We sat silently side by side while I tried to deal with Molly's bluntness. In a moment, she leaned against me and kissed my cheek. "I'll stop beating on you now. You know how I feel. Finish your sherry and let's have lunch."

We sat down at the small, round maple table in the dining room looking out on the back garden. In the summer it was a gathering of lush greens but now a few leafless apple trees lifted their bare black boughs toward the grey sky and a few patches of green spotted the tawny grass. Molly brought in steaming hot fish chowder and toasted cheese sandwiches. "Glass of beer with lunch?"

"No, I'm fine." My mind was in a swirl from Molly's onslaught, and I was finding it hard to be civil.

Molly broke the silence that followed. "We haven't talked about your trip out to Ithaca. How did it go? Did they offer you a job?"

"Yes. Working on a three year research project." I described the project and my possible role in it.

"It sounds great. How do you feel about it? Are you interested?" Molly was doing her best to get us back on an even keel but I was finding it hard to respond.

"Yes and no."

"Oh? Why the 'no'?"

"Several reasons. I like teaching at a school like Sloate. I like the life, and I like living in New England. I find this part of the country stimulating somehow. To me it has a magical feel, almost romantic."

Molly put her spoon down and stared at me as though I had said something outrageous. "New England romantic!" she said. "My God, have you ever been in Bridgeport? Anywhere in Rhode Island, for that matter? *Romantic?*" She shook her head. "Stephen, old chum, you're coming up with some mighty strange ideas today."

"You are a New England native," I said irritatedly, defensively. "You're too close to it. You don't see what's really here."

"Stuff and nonsense. I've been from one end of this country to the other travelling with Charles and the Symphony. I'll admit there's some interesting history here in New England, but for romantic country I think the Pacific coast north of San Francisco is romantic. I think those enormous Great Lakes are romantic. I think the Rocky Mountains are romantic. But moth-eaten, bankrupt, run-down New England—"

"All right, all right," I said hotly. "You asked me why I might not want to go back to Ithaca and I gave you the reasons as I see them. To me, New England has a special appeal."

"Right you are. Sorry. I seem to be attacking you at every turn today, don't I?" She gave me a saucy grin. Then she leaned forward and said seriously, "It's only because I am very fond of you and wish you nothing but the best." She reached over and touched my hand. "And don't ever think otherwise."

We finished the sandwiches and Molly bought in sliced peaches for dessert. "When will you give your answer to Cornell?"

"I asked for two weeks to consider."

She looked thoughtful. "All things considered, Stephen, it might be best if you went to Ithaca."

I looked glumly at her and then out the window at the bare trees. "All things considered, you may be right."

Twenty-One

That night was another one of those when the bed seems inhospitable, no arrangement of legs or arms feels right, and the mind races down one broken thought-trail after another. Looming over my mental chaos was the sense that some essential element of my equilibrium had become unhinged. Molly's stinging words, especially "adultery" and "betrayal," and her sharp questions and blunt assertions, had pierced my armor of assurance and left me exposed to deep self-questioning. Certain words pertaining to morals and ethics acquire an unchanging validity by virtue of their being implanted early in a young mind and repeated often thereafter. Quaint as it may seem in the mid-1990s when I am recording these events, "adultery" and "betrayal" had for me that incorruptible certainty. To be guilty of either I had been told from my earliest days was as wrong as wrong can be.

Molly's attack forced me to look squarely at things and ask whether "adultery" and "betrayal" truly described my relationship with Meg. The answer I found was one I did not like. Up close and face to face our love-making had seemed so irreproachably right. Now, seen through Molly's eyes and described in Molly's words, it had become something quite different. It became "adultery" and "betrayal."

And it became something I knew I was very uncomfortable with.

How had it happened? How had I got so far away from my usual values? Searching within, I slowly came to recognize the truth. Emotionally I had never accepted the established fact of Meg's marriage to Stuart. Certainly I had accepted it intellectually, even to the point of urging her to make the marriage. But emotionally, deep down, I felt she still was mine. I loved her; she loved me; and no relationship with anyone else had greater validity. That notion, as Molly bluntly put it, now seemed juvenile and romantic.

Then, thrashing from one side of the bed to the other, I asked myself, what happens now? To recognize past error does not by itself indicate the right future course. But in my present weary state I was unable to deal with the question. What to do now, I groggily told myself, would have to take its place alongside other uncertainties in my future.

Next morning, bleary and air-headed, I stumbled around making myself a breakfast in my kitchenette and then threw on some clothes and walked out the front door into a dazzling early spring morning complete with a lapis lazuli sky and a soft, southern wind. As I turned from pulling the door closed I saw parked at the front curb the red cart and pretty black pony of Matthew Makepeace.

"Top of the mornin' to you, Aspen!" he called cheerily. "Gertie'n I are just headin' out for a little trot, and we thought we'd come by and ask you to join us."

I hesitated. Company just then I would have been happy to avoid and Matthew Makepeace's company in particular had less appeal than most.

"'Nless you got somethin' else special to do. It's a mighty pretty mornin' for a spin."

"No." Pause. "No, sir, I don't." Then, feeling it would be ill-natured to refuse such an invitation, I walked out and climbed onto the high seat beside the Headmaster, gazing at Gertie's glossy back and smelling her dark horsey fragrance. "Thanks for asking me."

He slapped the reins gently on Gertie's back and clicked his tongue. "Just heard yesterday you were back," he said as the cart moved forward with its steel-shod wheels rattling and grinding on the gravel. "I've been wantin' to talk to you."

I said nothing as we rolled down the winding roadway under the great elms and oaks. There was a pause and then the Headmaster said, "You know, Aspen, one thing I have to keep learnin' again and again, is that no matter how smart I think I am or how right I am about somethin' I can be an awful danged fool at times."

I turned to look at the gnome-like man beside me, groping without success for something to say.

"Now take, for instance, that decision I made to change young Reston's grade. That was a mighty dumb thing to do."

"That's over and done now, sir." I said helpfully and watched as Gertie lifted her tail in a high arch and began dropping reddish brown balls on the road.

"No, it isn't," he said urgently in his chirpy voice. "It was a bad mistake and it's gotta be fixed."

"I wouldn't know how, sir."

"Well, my friend, I'm about to tell you how. But first, let me tell you that I had a long talk two mornin's ago on the long distance with Trevor Reston. He told me that when his son, Billy, came home from school he told his father you are the finest man and the best teacher he has ever known. He says—that's Trevor says—you've turned the boy's whole attitude about school completely around."

"Billy's a good boy. He just needed a little personal attention."

"That's right." He slapped the reins again on Gertie's back. "Git along there, Gertie. You've had your mornin' constitutional and now you can git down to business." He turned toward me. "But Trevor also says that givin' Billy that F is what woke him up because he knew his father would be mighty upset. And then, your followin' up with personal instruction in both biology and squash—that was the perfect thing to do. Especially takin' him down and playin' squash with him."

"As I say, Billy's a good boy. He's also a pretty good squash player. I wouldn't be surprised if he made the squash team next year."

"Which I hope you'll be coachin'."

"Well, sir, I don't know about that. You remember I told you I would resign at the end of the term and I've had a fine offer of a research job at Cornell I'm considering."

The Headmaster turned and put his hand on my knee. "I can't let you leave, Aspen. You're too valuable to the school."

By this time we had reached the front gate at the county road, and Makepeace made a wide swing around to head back. "Steady, now Gertie. Steady, girl." The turn around completed, he turned to me again. "Goldang it, Aspen, I just wish I had known what you were doing with Billy before I made that fool decision."

"I guess that was partly my fault, sir. I got my back up when Brickson Jaeger popped off during the meeting, and I was too proud to defend myself."

"No, son. No fault of yours. Just the ill-considered act of an impulsive old fool." He plopped the reins on Gertie's back again. "Look awake there, girl! Keep your mind on your business." Gertie quickened her pace for a few yards and the Headmaster turned to me again. "You said a while back you didn't know what could be done now about the Reston matter, but I'll tell you what Trevor Reston wants me to do. He wants me to give you a sizeable increase in stipend and some kind of a permanent position. Like dean of scholastic standards or some such."

"That's very flattering, Headmaster."

"Flatterin', *hell*—pardon my French—it's just fair recognition. You're a real asset to Sloate School, no question about it, and we need to reward you accordingly."

We were both silent for a while as the pony and cart

trundled up the gravel driveway in the brilliant New England morning. Finally, I said, "I don't quite know what to say, Headmaster. I've got this Cornell offer to think about and some personal considerations as well."

"I guess that's understandable. But just let me tell you, if you do decide to leave I'm gonna be in an awful mess with the school's best fund raiser and next chairman of the board of trustees." Once again he put his small bony hand on my knee. "Aside from that, son, I just hope you'll stay for the school's sake—and for mine."

"I'll have an answer by the end of the week."

When I got down off the red cart in front of Sudbury Hall I stood watching the eccentric little Headmaster drive away, Gertie's small hoofs clop-clopping on the gravel driveway. Hesitant, I stood for a moment and then decided to go for a walk. The conversation with Matthew Makepeace had, I felt, changed the should-I-go-or-stay equation entirely. His acceptance that failing Billy had actually been beneficial, combined with his regret that he had acted without hearing me out, seemed to me to cancel the justification I had for resigning at the end of the term. And that left me with essentially a free choice between going with Bill Byer and doing research and staying at Sloate School and teaching. The thought of sitting in my silent, empty room while weighing those alternatives was highly disagreeable, and I decided a long walk through the awakening fields and woods was much preferable.

I walked down across the campus to the field house, and then beyond on a path which led along the Nashua River and into a woods beyond. As I walked and pondered I posed myself the question: would doing research with Bill Byer bring greater satisfaction (and, incidentally, a lot less money) than teaching well-to-do boys amidst handsome surroundings (with, fortunately, a lot more money)?

After an hour or so of walking and weighing, with no

firm decision emerging, I was nearly run down by a man on a bicycle coming silently around a bend. It was Gilman Brooks riding a bottle green Raleigh, and he swerved and stopped quickly. "Oh, sorry," he said in his softly husky voice. "Nearly smacked you."

"No harm done."

We stood smiling at each other for a moment. "I'm riding over to South Harting and back before lunch. It's one of my favorite short rides, lovely hills and woods."

"I used to bicycle a great deal as a teenager in southern Michigan."

"You ought to get a bike and take it up again. This is superb countryside for bicycling, lots of small, quiet roads." He smiled again in his charming way. "We could take trips together. Lot more fun with two."

"It's an idea."

Again we stood smiling inconsequentially at each other, and I was struck again by his graceful boyishness. "Look," he said, "I'll be back in an hour. How about coming by my place at Elledge Hall for sherry before lunch? We'll talk some more about bicycling."

Weary of balancing and weighing I said, "Fine. I'll be there."

Gilman Brooks's quarters were like the man, quietly tasteful and charming. One wall was covered with rich fabric hangings and another was centered with a Braque still life. An ebony figurine of a prancing antelope stood on a small side table. The easy chairs and sofa were covered with a coarse fabric in large black and white squares. "Come in, come in," he said, his greeting ending with a sort of self-deprecatory chuckle. It struck me as I shook his smooth, firm hand that much of his appeal derived from his non-aggressive, nonthreatening manner, rather like, as I say, that of a colt. "I was about to play some music. Do you like music?"

"A friend educated me to like Mozart. I guess the next step is Beethoven."

He shook his head smiling. "No offense, but I don't much care for Beethoven. All that hubbub and blunderbussing. It always seems to me that Beethoven is hacking his way through a symphony."

"Did I read somewhere that someone called the Beethoven Seventh Symphony the apotheosis of the dance?"

He chuckled gently. "A dance of elephants to my taste."

"My friend who loved Mozart had a grudge against Brahms."

"Oh, I think Brahms is either turgid or sickly sweet. No, I don't much like Brahms either. I prefer music this side of the heavy Germans. I like Debussy and Ravel. In fact, almost anything after Vincent D'Indy. Do you know his 'Symphony on a French Mountain Air'?"

"No. In fact I don't know his name at all." I remembered then my musical session with Molly. "How about Sibelius?"

"Oh, he's fascinating. But a tad bleak for me. I have to be feeling strong and upbeat before I listen to his music." He turned to his phonograph at the end of the room. "Let me play the D'Indy. You may like it."

The music began while Brooks poured sherry from a heavy, crystal decanter. French horns led off and it did seem the music had a sort of airy, mountain quality but to me it seemed light, loose, and almost frivolous compared to Mozart. I missed the structured symmetry and the dancing complexity of Wolfgang Amadeus. My thoughts slid away from the music, and when I looked up from my sherry I found Gilman looking at me.

"Forgive me for asking, but did you have a talk with Matthew Makepeace this morning?"

Surprised, I stammered, "Why, ye-s-s."

"Cordelia Makepeace told me last night he was going to try to persuade you to stay on."

"So it was her idea?"

"No, no. He was agonizing over it and was uncertain how to approach you so she suggested the morning pony cart ride. How did it go?" he asked blandly. "Did he persuade you to stay?"

"Not entirely." I hesitated. "Let's say he moved me a little in that direction." I paused again. "I've got some related personal problems to resolve."

He looked at me with a steady, friendly gaze. "You really ought to stay. You could become Headmaster of this place in a couple of years."

"Headmaster! That's ridiculous. I'm not only an outsider but I'm much too young."

"Both beside the point," he said gently. "You've caught the eye of the next chairman of the board of trustees who thinks you can walk on water." He chuckled softly. "And old Matthew is 66 and Cordelia is nagging him to retire soon and move back to New Haven where they can resume that madcap highlife she remembers so fondly."

"You astonish me."

"Think about it, my friend, and think twice before you turn down a fine opportunity."

I shook my head wondering and sat silently sipping my sherry and staring with unfocused eyes across the handsome room.

Gilman Brooks broke the silence after the D'Indy symphony came to a close. "Whether you decide to stay or not, why don't you get yourself a bicycle and join me in some trips around the countryside? These hills are gorgeous in the spring, and it's marvelous exercise."

I turned my attention to the figure lounging in an elegant posture across the room. "You know, I might do that, Gilman."

"Gil."

"Gil."

"Anytime you say I'll take you down to the Raleigh shop where I got my bike. The owner's a friend of mine, and he'll give you a good deal."

That afternoon in my room I finished weighing the staying or leaving question. When I got really serious I realized there was no uncertainty. The keen pleasures I got from dealing day after day with the bright, verging toward brilliant, minds of boys like Jefferson, Wiener, and Ross, engaging them hand-to-hand so to speak in the challenge of molding their minds to the modes of scientific discipline and objectivity—these pleasures I knew could not be matched, even in the high octane intellectual environment of Cornell, by the arduous daily work of research, the slow grubbing out of data bit by bit and the fashioning of problematic hypotheses. Besides, there was the even greater pleasure of rescuing a boy like Billy Reston, drowning in neglect and inattention, and breathing into him renewed self-respect and a desire for achievement. In addition, there was the physical delight I took in my surroundings at Sloate, the quiet abundance of the campus itself, and the endearing beauty of the New England countryside.

The choice was clear. With or without Gilman Brooks's fanciful suggestion I might someday become Headmaster of Sloate School, I ought for my personal satisfaction and best interests stay on as the school's biology master.

That left me with just one unresolved question. I went to the telephone and called Brixton. Molly's bright-as-the-morning-sun voice chirped, "Hello, and good day to you, whoever you are."

"Molly, it's Stephen. May I come see you tomorrow morning?"

"Come now. Spend the night! Stay a week!"

"Tomorrow morning, you temptress. Tomorrow morning."

"Morning it shall be, dear man. And stay for lunch."

"I'll be there mid-morning."

Twenty-Two

A fter knocking on Molly's front door with no response I tried the doorknob, found it unlocked, and walked in while calling "Molly!" No answer. Then through the dining room window I could see her out in the back garden. She was wearing faded blue jeans and a white blouse and she was bending over with her back toward me. I went to the back door and called, "Molly."

She straightened quickly. "Oh, hi. You caught me trying to put these blasted stones in place around my flower garden."

I walked out across the still dewy grass. "Let me give you a hand."

"Those grey granite blocks over there against the garden shed," she said, pointing. "Daddy got them years ago for some project or other, and I decided they would make a nice border for my flower bed. They're heavy as sin." She smiled warmly at me, her face rosy with exertion and a tiny row of sweat beads glistening across her forehead. "By the way, good morning, and how are you?"

"Fine, Molly. You look a bit warm. Let's move those blocks."

Molly was right. They *were* heavy as sin or perhaps heavy as all the Seven Deadlies lumped together. After twenty

minutes of grunting and waddling from shed to garden plot
with blocks held only inches off the ground I was dripping
with sweat. But we had them set in place to form a solid
border around Molly's flower bed.

"Come inside, old dear," she said, "and let me pour you
a cold beer."

Sitting around the dining table, mopping our damp brows,
and gulping our beer, we grinned amiably at one another.
"Thanks heaps for your help," Molly said. "I was getting
pooped." She patted my hand. "I haven't had time until now
to ask what brings you here."

I took another gulp of the cold beer. "I've just about
decided what I want to do about the Cornell research job,
and I wanted to talk with you before making it final."

"Check with me, bubble-headed Molly? I'm flattered
speechless."

"I'll ignore that, Bubble Head. You remember, the last
time I was here you said it might be best for me to go to
Cornell. In other words, leave this area."

"Did I? Don't remember." She shook her head. "But I
must have been out of my mind. Why would I want you to
leave this area?"

"Because of Meg, of course. Meg and me."

Her mouth opened into a wide red O. "Stephen, you
silly goose! You took that offhand remark seriously?"

"Well, yes," I said defensively. "I was half inclined to
agree with it."

"But you dummy, that's not the issue at all. No one
expects you to abandon your close friendship with Meg.
What's at stake is whether or not you are going to keep on
jumping into the sack with her. I strongly recommend you
not. That's all."

"And you think that's what Meg wants?"

"Absolutely. She hasn't formed the idea completely in
her mind yet, but if you were to take the initiative she would
be happy. Relieved and happy. But she certainly doesn't want
you to go away. That's the last thing she'd want."

I chugged another gulp of cold beer.

Molly cocked her head with that saucy grin. "I gather from the trend of this conversation you've decided to stay at Sloate."

"Yes, but I've told no one else yet."

"Good decision. It's the right place for you. You'll end up as Headmaster there one day."

I jerked my head toward her. "What on earth makes you say that?"

She smiled mysteriously. "Oh, woman's intuition. That plus your seriousness, your dedication, your intelligence." She cocked her head saucily again. "That intelligence part applies, of course, only to your profession. Not to your dealings with females."

"Hmmph." I sat silently for a moment. Beside me Molly put her hands to her head, fluffing and arranging her hair. I sat trying to envision a conversation with Meg about the future of our relationship and found it a painful prospect. "Molly, I don't know how I would go about talking to Meg now. What I ought to say."

"Ah, Stephen, Stephen. You won't have to say more than two words. She'll understand before you get to the end of your first sentence."

"Sounds easy. Easy and painless."

"It will be." She reached over and put her hand on my arm. "But, tell you what. Let's have a quick lunch and then both go up to Buryport. I'll lend moral support and offer interpretation if needed."

An hour later in Buryport, Meg opened her door, surprised but pleased by our unannounced arrival. "Why, you old darlings! I'm just finishing lunch. Come in and join me with a cup of tea."

I was nervously silent as we all three sat at Meg's dining table but Molly quickly filled in the gap. "Stephen has been telling me he has decided to stay on at Sloate next year."

Meg turned to me, radiant with joy. "Stephen, how

perfectly marvelous! Now you won't be miles away and we can all go on seeing one another."

Molly seemed suddenly to be seized with the sniffles. She sneezed and then left the table saying, "I'll go find a kleenex."

"In the powder room, Moll," called Meg. Then she reached across and put her hand on mine. "I'm so happy, darling. You know what your company means to me."

Thinking this was going to be even harder than I had thought, I said, "Meg, dear, Molly has been talking to me about us."

"About—?"

"Us. Our relationship."

"Yes?"

I hesitated and then plunged. "After talking with Molly and hearing about the conversations she has had with you I've about decided we ought to stop—well, seeing each other alone."

Her eyes widened in alarm. "Not see each other alone? But, Stephen, I *need* to see you, talk with you. You're my anchor, my stabilizer."

"I don't mean just talking, Meg. What I really mean is going to bed together. From what Molly tells me, I think maybe that's been asking too much of you."

Her blue eyes narrowed in a frown. After hesitating a moment, she said, "Yes, Stephen. I'm afraid that may be true." She looked away from me out the window. "I'm fine until Stuart comes home and then there's a sort of transparent barrier between him and me. I am able to break through it in time but it bothers me that it is there at all."

"Then you agree."

She looked intently into my eyes. "Yes," she said softly. Then she clutched my hand hard. "Oh, Stephen darling, I don't want to hurt you. And I don't want to lose our close, wonderful friendship. But—"

Just then the kitchen door leading to the garage opened and Stuart Price's strong voice called, "Hello, hello! I see we've got company." He walked into the dining room and at the same time Molly entered from the other side. "Oh ho!" said Stuart. "The whole family is here. What's up?"

I was tongue-tied by the situation but Molly as usual rose to the occasion. "I telephoned Stephen this morning, Stuart, and asked him to come down and help me move some heavy blocks in my garden, and afterwards he brought me here on his way back to Sloate."

Stuart turned to me. "Going back this afternoon, Stephen? No, no, old chap," he said heartily. "You and I can go downriver this afternoon in the skiff, look the place over, and then come back and have supper here before you drive back. We'll make it a party, a family party."

I looked at Meg who was smiling noncommittally. "I don't know, Stuart. I ought to get back."

"Nonsense, Stephen. School doesn't resume until day after tomorrow. Please stay. Urge him to stay, darling," he said to Meg.

"I wish you'd stay, Stephen," she said sweetly.

"There, settled," he said, pulling up a chair and sitting down. "By the way, I saw Headmaster Makepeace at a board meeting last week, and he said you were giving him a hard time. Threatening to leave."

"I've just decided to stay, Stuart."

"Great. Good man. You're on your way to a great career at Sloate. You'll end up Headmaster there one day."

Startled, I asked, "What makes you say that?"

"Just a hunch. Based in part on some things Trevor Reston told me. He thinks you're the greatest teacher since Socrates."

The afternoon sailing downriver in the lap-straked skiff with Stuart and the "family" supper of our four passed quietly. In the skiff my camaraderie with Stuart remained as warm and solid as ever. If anything, my feeling I was helping Meg regain peace of mind made me feel even more comfortable and at ease with him. The evening came to a close and I got ready to leave. But not before I caught Molly in a corner and said, "That was a lovely, timely lie you told Stuart when he came in. Saved the situation. My tongue was stuck to the roof of my mouth."

"Proves my point," she said with dancing eyes and that sassy tilt of her head. "You have no talent for intrigue, no head for deviousness."

I looked at her, half annoyed and half admiringly. "I'm not certain I'm glad that *you* have that talent or not."

"I use it only on rare occasions to assist my dearest friends." And she reached up and kissed me quickly on the lips.

Immediately after breakfast the next morning I went to my desk and wrote a letter to Bill Byer telling him of my decision. "*Dear Bill,*" I wrote,

> *I have made a decision which I suspect you will not understand so I will try my best now to explain how I see it. I have decided to stay on as a biology teacher here at Sloate. I was flattered and strongly tempted by your offer to join your research team on the migratory guidance project. The research work itself attracted me greatly and the opportunity to work side by side once again with you was to me even more compelling. In the last analysis, however, it was your influence that caused me to remain as a teacher here at Sloate. That sounds paradoxical but it is a fact. You are a great teacher. You not only taught me how to teach by both precept and example, but you caused me to revere teaching as a profession. So, in the end I decided that I could offer no greater tribute to your influence than to make teaching my lifetime occupation. I hope you will accept that and understand.*
>
> *With great respect and admiration, your disciple,*
> *Stephen Aspen.*

After reading the letter several times over for grammar and spelling—Byer was a bear on such things—I addressed the envelope and walked to the post office. On the way I encountered Gilman Brooks. "How about going down to Worcester this afternoon to look at bicycles with me?"

"Sure, I'd love to," he said with a soft smile.

From the post office I went to Headmaster Makepeace's office and was immediately received. He gazed at me intently with his beady eyes. "Well, Aspen, do you bring me good news or bad?"

"I have decided to stay on, Headmaster."

He let out a loud, high whoop. "Son, that's the best news I've had since Gertie won a blue ribbon at the county fair! That's absolutely gut-splitting wonderful!" He reached over and pumped my hand up and down. "Goldang, Aspen, you've made this my happy day. And I'll tell you this, we're goin' to do some things for you that'll make certain you won't regret your decision." He practically hopped back and forth behind his desk. "We gotta celebrate this somehow. You come by tonight after supper and we'll have some friends in and break out a bottle or two of bubbly. Now, you do that, son. You hear?"

"I'll be there, sir."

After lunch, Gil and I drove to Worcester and went directly to the bicycle shop. After very little deliberation I selected a gleaming black Raleigh with gold striping and Sturmey Archer three-speed gears—a truly handsome, beautifully crafted machine. "Get saddle bags to fit on the rack over the rear wheel," said Gil. "Keeps the weight low and they're wonderful for carrying your gear on overnight trips."

"He's right," said the salesman.

The transaction completed, I then undertook to put the bike in the car and immediately learned what every bike owner knows: cars and bicycles do not like each other. They resist in every possible way your efforts to put them together. After four or five tries we finally got most of the bicycle inside the trunk, and then tied the lid down with twine.

"You made a good buy," Gil told me as we drove back. "We'll have a lot of fun exploring the countryside. And maybe, after you get your saddle muscles hardened, we can take a 40 or 50 mile trip and stay at an inn or motel overnight."

As we approached Sudbury Hall I saw standing in front a chartered bus unloading returning school boys who had arrived in Worcester by train or Greyhound and had been gathered together by the bus for the rest of the journey. I stood by the walk and greeted them as they trooped by carrying their suitcases or duffle bags. Blaisdell, Cook, Gallagher, Pontius, Fox, Greene, Wolfe, Seiler, Reston—ah, Billy Reston. Billy stopped, a wide grin on his handsome face. "I've brought a present for you, sir. It's in my suitcase. I'll bring it down after I unpack it in my room."

"Okay, Billy. And welcome back."

When the line of boys had passed I extricated my new Raleigh from the trunk—not much easier than stowing it in the first place—and rolled it into my hallway. In a few minutes Billy knocked at the door. He came in, still grinning broadly, and handed me a beautifully wrapped oblong package.

"It's from my father," he announced.

I unwrapped the long white box, opened it, and found inside a large, butter-soft, calfskin wallet. "It's very handsome, Billy. It's beautiful. You must give me your father's address so I can write and thank him."

"There's more inside, sir," said Billy.

Almost apprehensively I opened the wallet and found inside two first class, open-dated tickets for passage from New York to Southampton and return on the *S.S. United States*, the new super-luxury liner. Clipped to the tickets was Trevor Reston's card with the inscription, "Please accept this token of my extreme gratitude. T.R."

I barely held back a gasp. I stared at Billy trying to find something to say.

"My father says you probably have a friend or a relative you'd like to take with you to England during summer vacation."

"I guess I'll have to think of someone, Billy. Maybe I'll take you."

"Oh, no, sir. I've got to keep working on my squash game this summer."

"Well, all right." I reached out and shook the hand of the compact, good-looking boy. "If you talk to your father before he gets my letter tell him I'm overwhelmed by his generosity."

"Sure will, sir." He grinned and shuffled his feet. "Well, I've got to finish my unpacking," he said and left.

As I watched the door close behind Billy I asked myself who *would* I invite to sail with me across the Atlantic to England and back aboard the *United States*? My list of eligible friends was remarkably short. In fact, at the moment it was so short as to be nonexistent. But before I faced that matter, I would have to ask the Headmaster whether it would be right even to accept so lavish a gift.

His answer that evening as he stood holding a glass of New York State champagne was vehement. "Hell, yes!—pardon my French. Trevor would regard it as an insult, a slap in the face if you turned him down. Take 'em and use 'em. You'll have a great time."

I left him soon and joined Roger and Eve, standing together near the fireplace. "I understand we're celebrating your decision to stay," said Roger. "Eve and I think it's great."

"I wish you two were staying too," I said. "You're my best friends here."

"As I remember," said Roger in his solemn way, "you are the guy who urged us to leave."

"Yes," said Eve. "Bless you."

I signed. "You're right. And I'm happy you took that advice. Friends don't usually take my advice."

Later, chatting with Gil Brooks, he looked around and then said softly, "If you don't mind being toasted in indifferent champagne, here's to the next Headmaster!"

"I'll ignore that. But it *is* indifferent stuff, isn't it? It's too sweet."

"Yes, it's labelled 'extra dry' which for reasons known only to the champagne world is sweeter than brut."

Cordelia Makepeace approached, her bright red hair seemingly frizzier than ever. "Two of my favorite men," she said. "We must see a lot of each other in the weeks ahead."

Gil and I exchanged sly, knowing glances, and it occurred to me that I was finding his company so agreeable he might be the person to take with me on the *United States.*

Twenty-Three

We stopped at the top of the long hill, my thighs as limp as warm rubber. "How are you making it with that new bike?" asked Gil Brooks.

"Fine," I said, my mouth dry almost to desiccation. "That low gear makes a big difference." Around us on a Saturday morning in late April small birds fluttered and chirped in the roadside hedgerows, and the sky was a blue sea with white cloud ships slowly voyaging on an easterly course.

"South Harting is at the bottom of this long hill ahead, and it's a tremendous ride," said Gil. "You'll go like a bat so keep your bike under control and don't make any sudden swerves." He smiled his soft, charming smile. "Ready?"

"Wait a sec until I get my legs back." I stood with legs astride the crossbar watching a white throat sparrow flitting back and forth through the tiny-leafed branches and then piping that clear-noted, faltering song. "Let's go," I said after a few moments.

"We're off," he said and pushed away on his trim green Raleigh. I followed about twenty feet behind. The strong, solid bicycle rolled smoothly over the crest of the hill and then gathered speed as the slope increased. The wind, at first a faint whisper around my ears, grew stronger and stronger and rose to a roar passing my ears.

In a very short time I was moving very fast down the long, steep hill. Surprisingly I felt no sense of danger. At speeds of 35 or 40 miles an hour a bicycle acquires a wonderful stability. Whether it is the gyroscopic effect of the spinning wheels or something else I do not know, but I got the feeling that the bike was so rigidly stable I could if I wished get up and walk around on it. But I did not. I kept a firm grasp on the handle bar grips and crouched low over the crossbar to gain maximum speed.

Whether the ride down the hill lasted five minutes or ten I do not know. I was having too much fun to keep track of time. Brooks braked to a stop in front of South Harting's general store. I pulled up beside him wearing a face-wide grin. 'Wow!'' I said. ''Wow!''

''Isn't that a tremendous ride?'' he asked in his softly husky voice. ''Worth all the effort of climbing the other side, wouldn't you say?''

''Absolutely.'' I looked around. ''Can we get a bottle of coke here? My throat is a desert.''

''Sure.'' Inside the shabby store with a worn wooden floor we found a red metal bin and standing in ice water within were bottles of soda and coke. At the counter, beside an antique brass National Cash Register machine were sandwiches wrapped in wax paper. The square-faced woman behind the counter took our money and made change without comment.

''Tell me,'' said Gil to the woman in his gentle way, ''where does this road go?'' He pointed to the crossroad that ran beside the general store.

There was a long pause while the woman with her head down busied herself arranging things on the counter without speaking. Gil and I exchanged wondering glances and were just turning away when the woman said solemnly, ''It goes both ways.''

We managed to get ourselves outside the door without exploding in laughter but once outside we laughed and

laughed. "Goes both ways!" Gil said and we chortled together again.

And so the day passed in pleasant companionship. We
ate our lunch of wax-paper-wrapped sandwiches and coke
beside an effervescent stream, and we gazed admiringly at
long vistas of greening fields and red barns and burgeoning
woods. After nearly twenty-five miles up hill and down dale
in the richly varied countryside we got back to the Sloate
campus about four in the afternoon, and as I threw my left
leg over the crossbar and walked the bicycle into my hallway I became quite aware that what Gil had referred to as
my "saddle muscles" were very, very sore. At the same time,
it struck me once again that a man whose company was as
delightful as Gil Brooks's might be the right person to join
me on my voyage to England.

Next morning as I was strolling back from Sunday chapel
in the spring sunshine with Roger Altby, he glanced sideways at my somewhat stiff gait and asked, "You're walking
as though you've hurt your back or something."

"No, not that. I've got a mighty sore tail from bicycling
twenty-five miles with Gil Brooks yesterday."

Roger looked surprised. "Gil Brooks? I didn't know
you'd been spending time with him."

"Gil got me to buy a bicycle and he and I have been
making short trips around the countryside."

"Hmmm," said Roger as we walked along. Then he said,
"I don't know whether I ought to mention this or not, but
Jason Dunlap told me some time ago he saw Brooks in a
bar in Worcester with a group of limp-wristed, swishy guys."

"Did you ask Jason what he himself was doing in that
bar?"

"No. No, I didn't," said Roger in his deliberate way. He
walked along looking down at the walkway. "I just thought
I'd mention it."

"Well, okay, Roger." I too walked with my eyes on the
stone block walk while I mulled over what Roger had told

me. "You know," I said, "Gil is an artistic fellow, teaches art. Probably those other guys Jason saw with him were also art teachers or maybe artists. I suspect there may be some correlation between artistic types and limp wrists."

"Yes, I would guess so."

I thought some more. "But I would not put Gil in that category. All his attitudes and mannerisms seem perfectly masculine to me. Gentle but masculine."

"Yes-s-s. I think I would agree with that." By this time we had arrived at Roger's entry and we parted with the customary injunctions to "Take care" and "Be good."

Over the course of a spectacular New England spring Gil Brooks and I covered most of the easily reachable nearby hamlets and villages. By then I had come to the conclusion that the bicycle is the ideal vehicle for enjoying a landscape. Walking is fine but slow; automobiles move too fast; but a bicycle moving at speeds from five to fifteen miles per hour gives you ample time to savor each new view as it opens before you. At the same time, the views succeed one another at a pace that provides a new one before you weary of the old.

And as I say, the show that New England put on the Spring of 1954 was remarkable. I had never before appreciated that New England's spring colors are as varied, though muted, as those of its brilliant autumns. Patches of warm rose glowed in the woods amidst vibrant sea-greens and tender young yellow-greens. Tall, reluctant oaks still clung to their leaves of last year, now tattered brown rags, and their somber hue made a counterpoint to the lively tints burgeoning in the fields and woods. In the roadside ditches large-headed dandelions blazoned their flamboyant, butter-yellow blooms while here and there pale, whitish flowers clung to the banks near the standing ditch water. Out of curiosity, Gil and I picked several of those plants and found immediately that our hands were stained by a reddish juice from the stems.

We took our specimens for examination by the solemn

woman behind the counter at the South Harting general store, the woman who had advised us that the road running beside the store ran "both ways." "Them's bludrut," she pronounced authoritatively.

"Bloodroot," Gil whispered in my ear as we went out the door, and we both chuckled softly.

Gil had been suggesting for some time that we spread our wings wider and make a long, overnight trip. "We've pretty well covered the immediate area," he said. "I'd like to bicycle over to Greenfield. There's a nice inn there and an elegant French restaurant called 'The Hermitage.' On the way we'd go through some gorgeous country around the Quabbin Reservoir."

"Sounds good to me."

"Okay. I've got county road maps and I'll lay out a route that avoids main roads."

"Great."

During the week before our planned trip I packed my saddle bags with "the necessaries": rubber poncho, changes of shorts, socks, shirts, an extra pair of pants, and a pair of pajamas. But the night before we were to leave Gil showed up at my door. "Sorry, Stephen. Something has come up and I won't be able to go tomorrow."

"Oh?" I looked at him expectantly, waiting for an indication of what the "something" was, but no explanation came. "We'll try again in a week or two," he said and left. Somewhat hurriedly, it seemed to me.

But I was all packed and primed for a long trip. Somewhere, anywhere. It occurred to me I could bicycle down to Brixton—that would be sufficiently long—and look in on Molly. Then I could get one of Clint Avery's skiffs and go downriver and spend the night in my shed on the shore of Beach Plum Sound. I got out the county road maps and a pencil and ruler and drew a straight line from Sloate to Brixton. Then I listed all the back roads that ran anywhere close to that line. And then, finally, after some thought I rang up Molly and told her my plans.

First she said, "Wonderful!" Then she said, "You know, Stephen, you've got to stop pursuing me mercilessly like this."

"No need to worry. I'm too slow to catch you."

"Haven't you noticed? I'm slowing down. Next I'll be running backwards."

"I'll see you tomorrow."

"What time?"

"Oh, mid-afternoon or so. It's a long way."

"All right, dear. Be careful and don't get your pants cuff caught in the sprocket."

"My bike's got a metal guard over the—"

"See you tomorrow, Stevie," she said and hung up.

I banged the telephone down a bit hard thinking that no one in the world, not even my mother, had ever called me "Stevie."

The trip to Brixton had essentially one quality: it was long. A lot of it was also drab as I skirted middle-sized towns and crossed main highways. But at last I wheeled up in front of the Satterlee house and threw a weary left leg over the crossbar.

Molly met me at the door. "Come in, come in. There's a cold beer waiting for the dusty throat." And she reached up and kissed my cheek. "Ummm. Sweaty."

"Yes. I need a shower."

"Fine. I'll scrub your back." She was wearing that Molly look, provocative sass.

"Never mind. I'll manage. Let's have the beer."

"Coming, sir. And I have news for you," she said as she turned toward the kitchen. "I talked to Meg this morning and when Stuart heard you were coming down he invited you and me to come up and join them in a 'family' supper."

I flopped down on the maple dining table chair. "Tell me, why in the world does Stuart keep calling these occasions 'family' suppers?"

Molly brought a foaming glass of beer and set it before me. "Only one reason I can think of," she said, easing into a chair beside me.

I chugged a long draught of beer and could feel the grateful liquid trickling down among the cracks in my parched throat. "What's that?"

Again came that quintessential Molly look. "He expects you to marry me so you'll become a brother-in-law and we'll all be family." She pursed her lips provocatively. "You do plan to, don't you?"

Tired enough to approach grumpiness, I asked, "Plan what?"

"Marry me, as Stuart expects."

I took another long draught of the wonderful beer. "Haven't given it any thought."

She pressed her lips together in a kiss-like way. "Just wait until that love potion I put in your beer hits bottom."

I was weighing whether to quip "Where?" or "Whose?" but decided for neither. "I'm going to take a shower."

"The towels are in the shelves beside the tub, dear," she said.

When I came down fifteen minutes later, refreshed and dry clothed, Molly and I wrestled the bicycle into the family Oldsmobile she had inherited from Meg. Again, it was a partial but adequately successful operation with more of the bike inside the trunk than was outside. While I drove us up to Buryport Molly chattered cheerfully about her growing record collection at the library. I said little but I was wondering whether there would be awkward tension between Meg and me after our last meeting.

I need not have been concerned. Meg was serenely at ease, fully in command of herself and the social situation. When I became aware of that my own tension slackened, and I found I could look at Meg and talk with her without experiencing that possessive hunger I had previously felt. As for the rest of us, Stuart was hearty and warm; Molly was impish and bouncy; and I became quietly content while sipping Stuart's full-bodied bourbon. It was indeed easy to think of the four of us as family, a family mutually happy in one another's company. Especially as we sat amiably chatting in Stuart's splendid living room with drinks of the finest quality in our hands.

"Well, this *is* first rate," said Stuart. "All of us being together like this. The only thing I can think of that might be better would be for us all to be sipping our evening drinks in the cockpit of a cabin sloop anchored off an island in Casco Bay."

"Do you plan to go cruising this summer?" I asked.

"Thinking about it. How about you? Would you like to join us?"

"Not this summer. I'm sailing to England on the *S.S. United States.*"

"*What?*" they all cried, nearly in unison.

"It's true. The father of one of my students, Trevor Reston, made me a present of two round trip tickets to England on the *United States.*"

"Well, I'm damned," said Stuart. "Is this the upshot of that affair involving the failing grade you gave his son?"

"Yes. Mr. Reston has decided I did the right thing after all."

"I should say he has. He thinks you're a pedagogical genius. If Mat Makepeace retired tomorrow he'd make you Headmaster the day after tomorrow."

There was a brief lull and then Molly asked with what sounded to me like mock innocence, "Who's going with you?"

I turned to her and saw the impishness behind her question. "I don't know. I haven't asked anyone yet. I'm thinking of asking Gilman Brooks. The fellow I've been taking bicycle trips with."

"Art teacher, I believe," said Stuart. "Great favorite of the Makepeaces."

"Cordelia Makepeace, especially."

Molly spoke up. "I think you ought to take someone who knows a thing or two about England. I spent a week there once with the Symphony. I could show you the Horse Guards Parade, the Tower of London, Trafalgar Square, the National Gallery, St. Martins in the Field, and on and on."

"Now, Molly," said Meg gently. "Maybe this Mr. Brooks has spent time there too."

"I doubt it," said Molly boldly. And we looked at each other and grinned broadly.

As the evening drew to a close Molly said she wanted to drive back to Brixton that night—"Got a meeting bust of dawn tomorrow"—and Meg and Stuart insisted I stay in their guest room and leave in the morning. I walked Molly out to her car and as I opened the car door she turned and kissed me good night. Not with the kind of sisterly kiss she had been giving me for the past year or two but one of the volcanic variety such as I had experienced that first time at my building site down by the shore. When we released I held her by the shoulders and I could see in the semidarkness that devilish look and her dancing eyes. "Good night, you sweet old thing," she said.

"Good night, Molly." Dealing as best I could with the physiological tumult she had ignited, I closed the car door behind her and walked back into Stuart and Meg's house all the while marveling over Molly's piquant mixture of sassy little girl, intelligent woman, and sultry lover.

Gil stopped at the top of a small rise looking down at a village ahead. "That's Montague," he said. "It's only about five miles farther to Deerfield."

"Thank God!" I said. "I want to get out of these wet clothes and into a hot shower."

Rain had begun to fall when we were about ten miles out of Sloate and it had fallen all day, sometimes in heavy, plopping drops and sometimes in a misty drizzle but always steadily. My pants over my thighs were sodden and water had run down my neck between my shoulder blades and into the small of my back.

It was after five when we pulled up before the Deerfield Inn. I waited under the portico keeping an eye on the bikes while Gil went inside to make arrangements. "They were out of double rooms," he said when he came back, "but I got a suite, two bedrooms, bath and hallway in between."

"Fine. How about the bikes?"

"The man is coming to put them in the ballroom for the night."

Hot water from a stinging shower never felt so good as it did that time. In a half hour we were both bathed and ready to go out to dinner. "It's less than a half block to The Hermitage."

"Let's go." The Hermitage proved to be a fine French restaurant, as Gil had said. The interior had two connecting rooms, the main one panelled in warm brown wood with a high vaulted ceiling, the other one low ceilinged with a tiny dance floor and an upright piano. For me, the first order of business was to knock back two or three bourbons on the rocks and then address myself to some food. I was ravenous and the whiskey increased my hunger. From a menu almost two feet long and eighteen inches wide I selected lobster bisque, prawns, and *coq au vin*. Gil insisted on having wine with the dinner and chose a very expensive Graves.

Replete and glowing with whiskey and wine we strolled back to the smaller room where a plump middle-aged woman was playing the piano with only moderate success. As we watched and listened to her botching "Tea for Two" and then finishing with a missed chord, she got up from the bench and said, "I give up. Somebody else try."

"Go ahead, Gil," I said.

He needed no coaxing and in a moment was playing a lovely, rippling version of Noel Coward's "Ziguener." A crowd formed behind the piano and one couple in their thirties began dancing. When he finished that song someone requested Gershwin's "Rosalie" which Gil played, again beautifully and without hesitation. And so it went for the next hour, one request after another. Once or twice he said, "I forget how it goes. Sing a bit of the melody." Then he would pick it up and play the tune perfectly.

I was getting leg weary standing by the piano, and at

last Gil said, "I've got to quit." He got up despite protests from the bystanders and we left the restaurant and walked back to the Inn. The rain had stopped and black clouds were scudding across the sky toward the east.

"You were terrific, Gil," I said. "How can you remember all those tunes?"

He put his arm around my waist. "I play by ear. I don't know where it comes from. It just seems to flow." I responded by putting my arm around his shoulders as we walked the short distance in the dark night. At the door of our suite we said goodnight, and I very quickly undressed and got in bed.

I was about to lay down my book, a collection of Thomas Henry Huxley's lectures on evolution, and turn out the light when my door opened gently and Gil, smiling softly said, "Not asleep? Good."

He came and sat on the edge of my bed. "I was wondering," he said in his softly husky voice, now almost caressing in tone, "whether you are feeling affectionate?"

Wonderingly I asked, "Affectionate, Gil?"

"Yes." He smiled warmly at me. "After that fine dinner and an enjoyable evening I am feeling very affectionate, and I was hoping I might share it with you."

"I'm not quite certain what you mean," I said, feeling at the same time I was more certain of what he meant than I wanted to be.

He leaned forward and put his hand gently on my leg. "You wouldn't have to do anything. I would just caress you. Giving you pleasure would give me great pleasure."

I leaned forward and pushed his hand away. "Gil, I don't know how to say this except to tell you I'm not remotely interested."

He smiled gently, forgivingly. "Maybe you are too tired tonight, Stephen. I understand."

I shook my head. "It's not that I'm tired. I'm simply not interested. Not in the slightest."

He looked at me intently. "Have I made a mistake about

you? You are a bachelor and I've never heard you once mention women. I thought perhaps—"

"I'm afraid you thought wrong. I guess I'm reticent about some things but the fact is I'm totally addicted to women."

He sat up straight, his face proud. "In that case, I'm sorry. Very sorry. And, Stephen, I hope to God I haven't destroyed our friendship."

I looked thoughtfully at him, still charming and boyish despite the rebuff. "I don't know, Gil. At the moment I'm confused. Confused and very tired. Give me some time to think about it."

He got to his feet. "All right, my friend. Sleep well and I'll see you in the morning."

After he left I picked up Huxley again but soon put it down. I was just reaching for the light when Gil appeared at the door again. "Sorry, Stephen, but I need to say this. I hope you won't turn me in at the school."

"I don't—"

"I have always drawn," he interrupted, "a hard and fast line against undertaking anything like this with anyone connected with the school, either students or staff. "You're the first one I've ever approached, and that was because of our fine friendship and my misreading you. I want you to understand that that kind of activity need never concern the school."

"So far as I can see at the moment, Gil, so long as you maintain that hard and fast line I would have no reason to divulge your secret."

"Even after you become Headmaster?"

I smiled. "You're safe from that unlikely occurrence. But yes, probably even then."

"Thank you, my good friend. And again, good night."

This time I did turn off the light, and my last thought before I sank into deep sleep was to thank my guardian angel for somehow keeping me from having invited Gilman Brooks to join me on the voyage to England.

Twenty-Four

The 1954 spring term at Sloate School wheeled along smoothly while Spring itself, that fickle skittish princess, having displayed her winsome charms and subtle beauties now chose to exhibit her witchiness with blustery winds and icy rains. Tender, timid buds of cherries and apples got blasted off their boughs and tossed onto the coarse green grass below while more prudent leaf and bud bearers waited for the nasty mood to pass.

Meanwhile, in the classroom it seemed to me my teaching skills were at their best. Comparisons and analogies came readily to hand, new and unhackneyed, when I was explaining a biological process and the rapport between the boys and me was comradely and good-humored. My constellation of first magnitude stars—Jefferson, Wiener, and Ross—shone at their brightest while little Billy Reston had settled into a solid B+ performance level. My teaching life had never before been so much fun or so rewarding.

One late April afternoon, when the rain had moderated to nasty mist, Julie North, Headmaster Makepeace's girl Friday, met me at the entrance of Edison Hall. "HE wants to see you. Now, if possible."

I walked, head down against the intrusive mist, over to

the Headmaster's office. He was seated at his desk reading a paper before him.

"Oh, there you are, Aspen," he said in response to my knock. "Come in," he said genially, "and sit you down." He gazed at me for a moment. "Nasty weather, eh?"

"Just now it is. But we've had some lovely days."

"That's it, my lad. Be an optimist. Look on the bright side." He smiled warmly and then stood up and perched in his birdlike fashion on the chair seat, squatting on his heels. "Reason I called you in is to tell you I'm going ahead and making you Dean of Scholastic Standards. A slight raise in stipend of $2500 goes along with the post."

"Thank you very much, Headmaster," I said. I stared at him thoughtfully. "I guess I would be more enthusiastic about the job if I had some clear idea of its duties. What does a dean of scholastic standards do?"

The small, narrow-faced man turned his head and gazed out the window. "Well, son, I don't 'xactly know myself. I created the job because Trevor Reston said you deserved special recognition for maintaining scholastic standards. Quite right, too." We sat for a moment or two while the Seth Thomas clock overhead dutifully reported the passing seconds. "Mebbe the first thing you ought to do is write a sort of charter for a Dean of Scholastic Standards. A list of responsibilities and duties, you know."

For a while we went back to looking thoughtfully at one another once again. Then I said, "Suppose I begin by putting together a credo of scholastic standards for Sloate School."

"That's it, Aspen!" he exclaimed, jumping down from his chair. "Capital! You've got it!" He nodded vigorously. "Now get right to work on it and we'll distribute it to the faculty when it's finished."

After thanking the Headmaster once again, I left the office, carrying with me a mandate with more name than substance. Over the next several days I spent a couple of hours wrestling with the problem, never getting much beyond: "Grades are to be awarded in strict accordance with achievement."

Then I got another summons to the Headmaster's office. This time he greeted me wearing a worried expression, and he paced up and down with agitated steps. "Sit down, son. I've got a delicate matter I want you to investigate. Kind of connects in an indirect way with your new post as Dean."

"Yes, sir." I sat in a chair facing his desk while he kept on pacing in a quick, nervous gait.

"Here's the situation. Sleepy Handley was down in Springfield last weekend, recruitin' for the football team, and he took one of the coaches—fella he was doin' business with—to dinner at a fancy restaurant. And there, at one of the nearby tables, he saw Gilman Brooks, *our* Gilman Brooks, having dinner with a young fella. And the young fella was wearing *lipstick* and actin' real feminine like. You know the way they do. And Sleepy says when Gil looked around and saw him he got up suddenly and left. Now, you know, Aspen, that sort of funny stuff goin' on in your faculty can kill a school. Kill it dead. You just can't have it."

He took a deep breath and shook his head, clearly feeling keen discomfort. "So that's what I want you to do. Investigate the truth or not of Sleepy's story and give me the basis for firing Brooks if that's what the situation calls for." He looked at me forlornly.

"This doesn't strike me as exactly the sort of thing a dean of scholastic standards does."

He turned to me fiercely. "Don't you think I know that?" he snapped. "But goldang it, I've got to have an outside investigation of some sort before I act. You know how much Cor—Mrs. Makepeace—thinks of Gil. I need good solid support before I do anythin' drastic."

I tried again. "Of course, you know, don't you, sir, that Gil and I are friends?"

"Sure, I know that." He stared at me like a fierce sparrow. "But you're a scientist, aren't you? Trained to be objective." He nodded his head rapidly at me. "Just give me an objective report. That's what I need."

I sat thinking for a moment. "If I do the investigation I'd like to have someone to work with me."

He looked suspiciously at me. "Well, now, that depends. Who do you have in mind?"

"Roger Altby."

"Oh, Roger. Good solid fella. Pity he's leavin' us. Sure, Roger'll do fine."

When I talked to Roger about it, he was a little appalled. We were sitting in the faculty lounge having coffee. "I don't like to get involved in things like that, Stephen."

"Neither do I. But the Headmaster laid it on me and I need your help."

He shook his head. "Well, all right, if that's the case. God knows I owe it to you."

Our first step was to call Sleepy Handley to my office to hear his story. Sleepy, a thick-necked, heavy shouldered former fullback at Middlebury, told us there was no doubt about what he saw. "The Brooks fella was sitting about three tables away, and it was him all right. And with him was this swish, you know, wearing bright red lipstick and swishing around. Boy, it was real disgusting. But, I'll tell you the truth, fellas, I'm not the least bit surprised. These arty guys are almost always that way, you know."

"Did Gilman Brooks seem to be acting the same way? You know, what you call 'swishy'?"

Handley thought a moment. "No, I can't honestly say I saw him acting like that. But, you know, he looked around and saw me and got up and left real quick."

"So you watched the two of them sitting together and the other guy was behaving in an exaggeratedly feminine way but so far as you could see Gilman Brooks was not."

"That's about it. But like I say, the instant Brooks saw me he vamoosed."

I turned to Roger. "Any more questions?"

"Not now."

I said to Handley, "We may need to ask you more questions later, Coach."

"Happy to oblige. We need to stamp that sort of thing out. Fast and hard."

The next day Roger and I met with Gil Brooks. He was extremely surprised and very resentful. "Gil," I said, "I want you to understand I'm doing this—actually under protest—at the Headmaster's insistence. What I've been asked to do is to get an accurate account of something that has been reported to have happened involving you and another man in a restaurant in Springfield last week."

After I said that, Gil quickly regained his usual debonair composure and in his softly husky voice described the incident at the restaurant. "I met this guy, Mason Green, at an art teacher's workshop last fall. He seemed to be an intelligent, serious guy, so when he asked me to come to Springfield and give a talk on the French Impressionists to his high school art class I agreed. He asked me to stay in his apartment with him but I stayed in the local Holiday Inn instead."

"Did you entertain him there?" I asked.

"No. After my talk he suggested we meet at the Colonial Restaurant for dinner. We had a few drinks before dinner and the entire time talked nothing but shop, teaching problems and so on. After dinner we had coffee and I treated us to cognac."

"How was he dressed when you met at the restaurant?" asked Roger.

"Normally. Blazer and flannel trousers. Like any other young academic. He looked like a perfectly straight guy."

"Go on," I said.

"Well, after the cognac he excused himself to go to the men's room. When he came back his mouth was plastered with lipstick and he started acting like a slut. You know, waggle-headed and swishy gestures."

"What did you do then?"

"Well, I was absolutely appalled. I detest that kind of

behavior. I hate sluts of either sex. Absolutely hate them. I looked around at nearby tables and saw people were staring and giggling, so I got up and left. I went back to the Holiday Inn and came back here next morning."

"When you looked around, did you recognize anybody at a nearby table?" I asked.

"In Springfield? No, I don't know anybody in Springfield." He looked at me curiously. "Oh, I see. Your informant, someone from here. No, I didn't recognize anybody I knew."

After Gil left I said to Roger, "We've got to talk to Sleepy again."

"Right. And clear up that question of recognition."

Handley arrived, cheerful and voluble. "Got the goods on the pansy yet?"

"Not entirely. But tell me, Coach," I said, "how long did you see Gilman Brooks and the other man sitting together while the other one was putting on his act?"

"Oh, only a minute or two. We'd knocked back a few drinks at my guy's house first, and we'd just arrived. But I recognized Brooks the minute I sat down."

"You said Brooks looked around and recognized you. Did he give any sign, any kind of reaction, that showed he recognized you?"

The bull-necked coach grew thoughtful. "You know, I can't honestly say he did. But he must have recognized me. We were only three or four tables away."

"But he didn't nod or look surprised or anything when he looked around in your direction?"

"No-o-o. No, I can't say he did."

After he left, I turned to my colleague. "Well, Roger, whom do you believe?"

Roger, ever solemn and conservative, assumed a judicious air. "On the evidence we've heard, Stephen, I'll have to accept Brooks's account. It seemed to have been simply an unfortunate incident and Handley just happened to be there to observe it."

"And misinterpret it."

"That's right."

"Then you and I concur. Let's go tell 'Mattie,' as Cordelia calls him. He'll be relieved."

"Now, that's not to say," Roger went on in his slow, staid way, "that there may not have been other incidents like this that were valid. You remember what Jason Dunlap said he saw."

"Whoa, Roger, whoa! We investigate one incident at a time. And we don't credit hearsay." Even as I spoke I was wondering why I was being so protective of Gil, knowing what I did know about him. But fair is fair and I had assured him I would not expose him so long as he observed that hard and fast line he had described. I also felt that my assurance extended to denying innuendo.

Headmaster Makepeace was jubilant about our report. "That's simply wonderful, gentlemen! I can't tell you how relieved I am. You know, there have been one or two rumors like this about Brooks in the past—that old gossip, Dunlap, came up with one a while back—but I think your investigation puts those doubts about Brooks to rest, once and for all."

This seemed to me to be pressing our finding a bit hard, and I said, "Let me point out, Headmaster, that we were asked to investigate an incident, not a lifestyle."

He squinted at me for an instant. "Far's I'm concerned, that's a distinction without a difference."

I smiled and said nothing.

Gil Brooks was as jubilant as Matthew Makepeace. "You're a prince, Stephen! I knew I was safe in your honest hands. Let me thank you most sincerely."

"Roger and I decided that your account was the correct one."

"Of course. It was just a damned silly episode." He looked pensively at me. "By the way, who was the spy, your informant?"

"You don't want to know that, Gil. I think it was an

honest mistake. He arrived about the time your companion came back from the men's room and when you looked around at the other tables he thought you recognized him and left hurriedly. I think the mistake was honest," I concluded, perhaps giving Sleepy Handley more credit than he strictly deserved.

Gil shook his head. "Public places," he said. "Never put yourself in a compromising situation in a public place."

"Excellent advice, Gil," I said. "And speaking of public places, watch yourself in that bar in Worcester."

He jerked his head up in surprise. "Ah, yes, my friend. Ah, yes. Thank you."

I gazed at him with mixed feelings. I still found him almost irresistibly charming but somehow I could no longer view him as I viewed other men. Say, as I did Roger Altby, for instance. That episode at the Deerfield Inn had placed him in my mind in an alien category. There was a difference in him now, an irreconcilable difference, and although I could view him charitably I could not ever again view him as a close male friend. Still, as we parted I said, "Let's have another go soon at that tremendous ride down the hill into South Harting, Gil."

"Great idea, Stephen. Maybe next week."

By this time Shakespeare's hounds of spring had caught up with winter and tossed it aside, and the term at Sloate School was approaching its finale. In the hallways of Sudbury Hall I overheard scraps of the boys' conversations concerning summer plans in which the names Martha's Vineyard, Nantucket, the Cape, Blue Hill, and Casco Bay figured. My own plans were still on hold because I still had not come up with anyone to take with me to England.

But more immediately at hand was the Graduation Ball. I had thought I would skip it but Eve Altby insisted I attend. "It's our last social event at Sloate," she said plaintively, "and I don't know when Roger and I will see you again. Maybe never. You've *got* to come. Roger and I are chaperones."

"But I don't know who to ask, Eve. None of the girls here on the staff seem likely to me. Besides, most are married."

"You *must* know someone. Don't you have friends down by the shore? Buryport or wherever you go? Ask one of them and she can stay with us in our little guest room."

With that suggestion, Molly, of course, was the one I invited. "A graduation ball?" she asked. "What kind of dancing do they do up there—quadrilles? Or have they advanced as far as the waltz?"

"Whatever it is, it won't be anything you can't handle, Twinkletoes."

"Oh, ho! Well, if you're going to flatter me like that, how can I resist? I would love to come, Stephen."

And come she did, wearing a white, red-sashed, off-the-shoulder gown that dipped across the upper slopes of her breasts and was cinched tight at the waist. She wowed the Altbys immediately, and when I danced with Eve she said, "She's absolutely lovely, Stephen, and so sweet and friendly. I felt at ease with her right away. She's not stiff like these Yankees around here."

I was about to divulge to Eve that Molly Satterlee was a fifteenth generation Yankee but decided not to puncture her innocent notion. But Eve was not finished with the subject. "You know what I think, Stephen? I think she's the perfect girl for you." She patted my shoulder maternally. "You ought to marry her and settle down. Roger says you're going to be Headmaster here some day, and she'd make a wonderful Headmaster's wife. She's so easy with people, so forthcoming."

Imagining pixieish Molly as a Headmaster's wife, or even as the wife of just a preparatory school master, was a far stretch for me, but I said, "Oh, Eve, I'm too young and giddy to settle down yet."

"Oh, Stephen," she said and poked me with a finger.

As for Molly, she was having a ball at the Ball. After watching her swinging around in the arms of a half dozen colleagues I gathered her for myself. "You seem to be enjoying yourself up here in the wilds of central Massachusetts dancing with a bunch of dusty pedagogues."

"Oh, they're great people, Stephen. Bright and lots of fun. And the ones I've met all seem to have a good sense of humor, *my* kind of humor. You know, wacky." The orchestra finished playing "Tenderly" and we stood waiting for the music to begin again.

"These people here remind me in some ways of symphony musicians. Bright and friendly. Except musicians have such weird senses of humor. You know, a musician thinks it is the funniest thing in the world when a cello player, for instance, breaks a string in the middle of a solo passage and has to improvise on the spot with his remaining strings. Or when the conductor lets go a loud fart while he's cavorting around on the podium. Telling about it to one another, they'd whoop and holler like little kids. That always amazed me about musicians—so sensitive, really, but childishly coarse in their humor."

Just then Gil Brooks came up to us with a stunningly pretty girl on his arm. Black hair, black eyes, and the slender figure of a ballet dancer. Gil was smiling his soft smile and he gave me an almost imperceptible wink. We introduced the ladies to one another. His stunner was named Rita Martin, and she said little. But then there was no need when she was lighting the place up as she was with her glittering beauty. Gil was ladling out boyish charm by the bucketful, and I could see Molly was nearly bowled over by the onslaught.

When the music started and they danced away, Molly asked almost breathlessly, "Who was that?"

"Gilman Brooks. Teaches art. He's the fellow I've been bicycling with."

"Wow! He could charm the birds from the trees."

"Cole Porter. One of Gil's favorites."

"What? What do you mean, 'Cole Porter'?"

"That line you quoted, 'birds from the trees.' That's from a Cole Porter song. 'Get Out of Town,' I believe."

"Oh, heavens, Stephen! You're so knowledgeable and sophisticated."

"Just your average man of the world."

And so the evening passed in banter and dancing. Molly was an excellent dancer, but for me just having her luxurious femininity in my arms was pleasure enough without the music and the dance steps. At last midnight came and Molly and I walked with the Altbys back to their entry. "Come in, friends," said Roger, "and I'll pour us a nightcap."

The May night was chilly and Eve suggested a fire would be nice. "I'll make it while you get the drinks, Roger," I said.

"Stephen is a good fire builder," Eve confided to Molly in her ingenuous way.

"I know," said Molly innocently. "I've seen him start several hot fires."

"As a matter of fact," said Eve, missing Molly's jibe but proceeding in her self-appointed role of matchmaker, "he's a wonderful guy in every way. I happen to know."

Molly smiled and leaned confidentially toward Eve. "I like him a lot too," she said.

We four sat sipping our drinks before the snapping fire for about a quarter of an hour, and then the Altbys excused themselves to go to bed, and Molly and I had the fire and the sofa and the quiet to ourselves. With a situation so romantically perfect and a desirable woman by my side there was only one appropriate move. I leaned toward her, cupped her chin in my hand and kissed her. It was a prolonged, thoroughgoing kiss, and at last Molly put her hand on my chest and pushed me away. "That will do for now," she said coolly. "For tonight, at least, and on after that until we get some things sorted out."

"Things? What things?"

"Oh, for instance, I would like to know whether you are still irretrievably in love with Meg?"

"Irretrievably? Strange word for it. Strange but probably correct. But no. I think the answer is no." I paused, wanting to say it right. "I still love her, Molly. But not like I did. Not so intensely, not so single-mindedly. I'm not fixated on her, so to speak, as I was." It was true. After our final conversation in her dining room, I had disciplined myself toward thinking differently about Meg. I needed to remove her from her place as the centerpiece of my life. And I could honestly say that the intensity of yearning I once had was gone. I could now think of Meg as a woman I had once loved intimately but now loved as one loves a cherished friend or former lover. "Does that answer your question?" I asked Molly.

"Yes. That will do just fine."

I gazed at her face, rosy and lovely in the reflection of the fire before us. "What else would you like to sort out before I am permitted to kiss you again?"

She turned to me with that inimitable Molly look. "Since you ask, my man, I will tell you very frankly, brazen hussy that I am. I have been a widow now for over a year and a half. You may not have noticed, but I am not a nun-in-the-cloister type. I need the company of a man, a good man, and I am ready for a real relationship, not just fooling around. I mean a good, honest relationship with a man I can love to my heart's content."

I started to answer with a quip but it was clear that Molly was very serious. I decided it was time for me to be serious too. "Molly," I said, "we have been warm, good friends for a long time, and I am very, very fond of you. In fact, I like everything about you. And we do have wonderful fun together. Tell me, could I be a suitable candidate for that relationship you are looking for?"

She leaned forward and pecked me on the lips. "The only one on my list."

"I'm glad." Then I turned away and sat looking deeply

and thoughtfully into the flickering, dancing fire for some time, a long enough time to reach a solemn, vital decision. "Then, Molly," I said at last, "I want to ask you a very serious question."

"Yes?"

"Do you get seasick on ocean voyages?"

"Seasick? What do you mean, seasick? What are you talking about?" Then she said, "Oh!" as comprehension dawned. "You're referring to your trip to England this summer on the *United States*, aren't you?" Then she pursed her lips together hard. "All right, Stephen Aspen, tell me this. Is this simply an old-fashioned proposition to get me into your bed for several nights on an ocean liner or is it your cockeyed idea of a proposal for marriage?"

I slid off the sofa onto my knees and took her hand in mine. "Molly, dear, you lovable imp and bewitching woman, will you marry me and be my wife and join me in my bed not only on ocean liners but in drab motels and princely palaces and villas by the sea?"

She leaned forward and kissed me sweetly. "Stephen, you adorable man. I want to marry you more than anything else in life. Yes. Yes, I will."

I got back on the sofa. "Now about that kiss," I said. "Just one." Pause. "For now." Pause. "Tonight."

The clock on the side table read 8:45, mid-Atlantic Ocean time. Lying beside Molly who was breathing softly and moistly toward my ear, I raised my head and looked around the large cabin. The heavy beige drapes over the portholes were engaged in a slow dance, swinging slowly away from the wall a foot or more at the bottom and then slowly swinging back tight against the portholes. I slid out of the queen-sized bed and went to the porthole and pulled the drape aside to investigate. The sea beside the ship was grey and glassy but molded into long, smooth heaving slopes and broad shallow valleys. It was a so-called "dead sea," the remains of some distant storm that had left the sea still grumbling in its way about the heavy blasting winds that had rumpled and tossed its green surface.

I turned back and saw that Molly had raised her head, hair tousled and her eyes bleary. "Why did you get up?" she asked.

"I wanted to see what the day was like outside. It's grey and there's a slow swell running."

"Good day to stay in bed," she said and let her head plop back onto the pillow.

"Have you given thought to breakfast?"

"Have the steward bring it here. Orange juice, toast and coffee for me. I recommend three eggs for you."

"Eggs. That's an old wives' tale," I said.

Eyes still closed, she said, "Well, those old wives knew a thing or two."

I telephoned for room service and then went into the bathroom. When I came out, Molly was propped up in bed with a pen in her hand and was writing in a small, green book. "What are you doing, Moll?" I asked.

"Starting a diary of our trip. First entry: August 2, 1954. Became Mrs. Stephen Aspen in wedding at Brixton Congregational Church, Meg as bridesmaid and Stuart as best man. Train to New York. Boarded S.S. *United States* and took Cabin 312 on Promenade Deck. Sailed at noon, passed Manhattan skyscrapers and Statue of Liberty. That night experienced marital bliss three—"

"Whoa!" I said. "Your children may be reading that diary some day."

"I'm coming to the question of children later," she said imperturbably. "Let's see, second entry: August 3, 1954. Lovely, lazy day at sea. Sipping champagne and eating fruit from enormous bon voyage basket from a certain Trevor Reston. Parens, thinks Stephen can walk on water, close parens. Experienced more marital bliss—" She paused and looked up at me with assumed innocence. "Would you prefer I did not record the number of times?"

I reached over and snatched the book from her hands. "Let me see that!" I looked at the first page and saw that she had written only "August 2, 1954." "Well, I guess so long as you keep on writing with that invisible ink it's okay."

She reached her hand out toward me. "Come and sit close beside me, my darling husband."

I sat on the edge of the bed and leaned over and kissed her forehead. "I want to discuss the matter of children," she said. "How many do you think we should have?"

"Twelve."

"No, silly. I'm trying to decide between two and four. Not three. I think uneven numbers are not good."

"Since they come one at a time, isn't this discussion premature?"

"Not necessarily. A man of your—ah, strength—might set me up for four, five, or six at any time."

"Well, then, two. I'll try to hold back."

There was a gentle knock on the door and slick-haired, smooth-faced Armand came in with the breakfast trays. He set them down and then looked with concern at Molly. "May I ask, is madam being made queasy by the roll the ship is having? Because, if she is, no liquids or—"

Molly beamed him with a 1000-watt smile. "No, Armand. Madam is feeling just great. If Madam felt any better it would be criminal."

Armand smiled uncertainly. "Very good. Thank you, madam." He left, closing the door softly behind him.

I took her breakfast tray to Molly and then slid into bed beside her with mine. We were silent for a time and then Molly leaned her head over on my shoulder. "Oh, Stephen, this is pure heaven. How long does this voyage, this state of bliss, last?"

"The voyage lasts only a little over three days. This is the fastest ship on the Atlantic."

"Darn," she said. "You mean I have to get out of this lovely bed sometime tomorrow?"

"Afraid so. But then straight into a lovely bed at Brown's

Hotel in London where the state of bliss can be resumed. In fact, I understand that with proper management it can be made to last a lifetime."

"It will," she said and pushed her tray aside to lean closer and put her arm around my waist.

We clung awkwardly together for a moment with the trays getting in the way. Then I said, "You know, I'm starting to think those old wives may have had something after all. Those two eggs I had seem to be having an effect."

"Oh, my goodness," said Molly, "I see what you mean. Let's get rid of these damned trays."

We slid the trays off the bed onto the floor and I turned and took my lovely, ardent wife in my arms. When we broke away briefly from a kiss Molly murmured, "Diary. August 4, 1954. Experienced more marital bliss."

Twenty-Five

N ews item from *The Boston Globe*, 6 June 1994:

NOTED EDUCATOR RETIRES AT SLOATE

Alumni and dignitaries joined today in ceremonies at Sloate Preparatory School marking the retirement of Dr. Stephen Aspen after 38 years as Headmaster. Dr. Aspen succeeded the late Matthew Makepeace in 1956.

During Dr. Aspen's tenure the reputation of the 300-year old school for high scholastic standards steadily grew. He holds academic degrees from Cornell and honorary degrees from Yale and Princeton.

In retirement Dr. Aspen plans to spend more time with his family, his wife, the former Mary Satterlee, a son, Adam Aspen, a daughter, Mrs. Mark Hall, and four grandchildren.

Postlude: Autumn 1994

"You know, Molly," I began—At the moment the final swallow of my second scotch rested amidst the rocks at the bottom of my glass, and I had reached that stage of philosophical reflection where truth and understanding lay broadly before me, bright and refulgent and immediately accessible to my exalted perception. It was the last night of our long summer in Maine, and we were sitting on the deck of our summer house overlooking rocky Widgeon Island in Casco Bay. In the last rays of the western sun we were bundled up in parkas against the early October chill. The car parked by the back door was packed and ready for our departure for Brixton next morning.

"You know, Molly," I said, "I have been thinking about the way things have gone for me over the past forty years, and I would defy any biographer or novelist to find any coherence or make any sense of the events in my life."

Molly, white-haired now but as handsome and, to me, as appetizing as ever, asked calmly, "Are any likely to try?"

"Come on, Moll, I'm being serious." At the sound of my voice, Cynthia, our English setter, thumped the floor with her tail, then got to her feet and laid her noble head against my knee. "What I mean, is, there doesn't seem to have been any purpose or direction in it. It's been rather like one of those mazes we ran white rats in at the bio lab. I entered at one point expecting to exit at another and lo! and behold I ended up at still a third hole."

261

"Yes, dear. Oh, look!" she said suddenly, "there's a seal just off the dock."

"Yep, I see it." I went back to examining the philosophical truth and understanding which scotch whiskey had revealed to me. "No," I said, "that's too regular a concept, the maze metaphor. What I need is something more random." I pondered the question. "Oh, I think I've got it, a whirligig. My life has been lived aboard a whirligig. I got on at Point A, expecting to disembark at Point B and instead I ended up at Point 64."

Molly had put her drink down and was busy knitting something with heavy grey wool. "Don't you mean a merry-go-round, a carousel?"

"No, that's too regular for what I mean." I fondled Cynthia's smooth, furry head in response to her demanding nudges. "I'm thinking of a whirligig more like a child's toy, spinning this way and that, and the passenger, me, like an ant that inadvertently got on between whirls."

"Ummhuh," said Molly absently, being accustomed to these evening philosophical excursions following my second drink. "I'm about to start cooking the string beans. Can I fix you a lagniappe on the way back?"

"That would be lovely, my love. But I've got more wisdom to impart to you."

"Save it. I'll be right back."

I handed her my glass and gazed at her appreciatively, still splendidly made and warmly loving. As she moved away I thought to myself that the one absolutely 1000% right thing I had done in my life, done deliberately and not through inadvertence or force of circumstance, was to marry Molly. Suddenly, in the water beyond the dock there was a flutter as a flock of goldeneye ducks came splashing in to a landing, making me momentarily nostalgic for those early days in the salt marsh.

"Here you are, sweet man," said Molly, handing me my lagniappe, a half drink.

"You know, I've been thinking, Moll—"

"Yes, love."

"—that the three most important people in my life have been Bill Byer, Roscoe Bilder, and you."

"That's order of importance?"

"Chronological. In importance you'd be the only one on the list."

"Thank you, sir," she said, curtsying daintily.

"I'm ignoring flippancy in this serious discussion." I frowned, thinking, as I gazed out at the sea. "Those three people have been pivotal in my life, each contributing tremendously but each influencing me in a separate direction. That's what I mean, no coherence."

"Don't forget to drink your drink. Dinner will be ready soon."

I took an obedient sip. "And beyond those three, I've encountered the most remarkable, unlikely set of human beings on the face of the earth. Again, no coherence."

"I supply the coherence, darling."

"Yes, and a great deal more. But until you forced me to marry you—"

She jabbed me hard in the ribs, almost causing me to spill my drink, and Cynthia got to her feet, wagging her tail and looking at us both anxiously. "It's all right, girl," I said, patting her head, "just a little normal husband abuse." I leaned toward Molly and gave her a kiss.

She patted my face gently. "But you know, Molly, when I look back at the 40s and 50s, our years, that really was a wonderful time. Compared with the disruptive 60s, the turbulent 70s, and the degraded 80s and 90s, the 50s were a golden time. I'll bet social historians will someday refer to the 50s as the golden age in America."

"We've been down this road before, Stephen. But you've never explained to me what happened to make those succeeding decades so bad."

"I'm very glad you asked, Miss Satterlee, because I've got the answer right at hand."

"I'll take notes."

"First, in the 60s you had a collapse of authority, ethical and societal. A by-product was the so-called sexual liberation including open homosexuality. That brought forth genital herpes, AIDS, and related social diseases. I've always thought that if you did not believe in a just God the advent of AIDS among the sexually promiscuous and drug users would make you think twice."

"Good point, Socrates. Push on."

"Then in the 70s and 80s unparalleled affluence came to this country. Almost everyone had money to spend on pleasure. Such things as boom boxes, audio tapes, records, VCRs, and so on. With a huge number of consumers who were possessed of the lowest possible level of taste, free from ethical restraints, the pleasure providers gave this enormous market what it craved. And thus we have this perverted popular culture—rock, rap, and gangsta, sexually explicit and violent TV shows and movies. All this swamps the entertainment world of this country and leaves little room for culture with traditional values and standards. In the 50s we had sex and other delights but it was wholesome, not wholesale, and private, not exhibitionist."

"Great stuff," said Molly. "You ought to write a book. Meanwhile, I'm certain the beans are done and dinner is ready."

I finished my drink and got up and followed her to the dining room, enjoying as ever the view from behind as she walked before me. I held Molly's chair for her and bent and kissed her before going to my chair and we addressed ourselves to the dinner.

"It's hard to believe summer is over," said Molly. "Tomorrow night we'll be back home in Brixton."

"That's right. With a long, cold winter ahead of us."

Molly took a sip of white wine and said, "What do you plan to do with your time now that you are fully retired?"

"Oh, several things. As you know, Sloate has made me a member of the board of trustees and I still have the nature sanctuary to keep on eye on."

"But none of that's full time. You'll still have lots of time on your hands."

I looked up at her, straight-faced. I thought I might spend it chasing you around the house."

"Not much time involved there. For you I'm too easy to catch."

Molly looked up from her plate and gazed at me intently. "I was half serious a moment ago when I suggested you might write a book. Why don't you?"

I chewed thoughtfully on a piece of cold roast beef. "I guess I might do that at that."

"Write on the subject you were discussing on the deck, the decline of American culture."

"No. That's been done by more thoughtful people than I. Allen Bloom, for instance."

"All right, then something about biology or teaching."

"No, that doesn't interest me much." I corralled a helping of beans on my fork. "What does interest me is what I was talking about earlier. The extraordinary mixed bag of personalities I've encountered and the lack of connection or coherence among them. I might write a sort of semi-autobiographical piece about those people and some incidents connected with them."

"That's a fun idea, Stephen. That's your 'whirligig' notion. I like that." Molly looked up from her plate, greenish eyes narrowed. "Besides, that would mean you would have to include me in it somewhere."

I extricated a small piece of beef gristle from between my teeth. "You, my dear, would be the sunrise at dawn, the star of evening, and the brass ring at the end."